WHERE
THE Sun
RISES

WHERE THE Sun RISES

A NOVEL

FRANK RICHARDSON

Bonneville Books
Springville, Utah

The views expressed within this work are the sole responsibility of the author and do not necessarily reflect the position of Cedar Fort, Inc., or any other entity.

This is a work of fiction. The characters, names, incidents, places, and dialogue are products of the author's imagination, and are not to be construed as real.

ISBN 13: 978-1-59955-315-3

Published by Bonneville Books, an imprint of Cedar Fort, Inc., 2373 W. 700 S., Springville, UT 84663
Distributed by Cedar Fort, Inc., www.cedarfort.com

LIBRARY OF CONGRESS CATALOGING-IN-PUBLICATION DATA

Richardson, Frank, 1943-
  Where the sun rises / Frank Richardson.
    p. cm.
  ISBN 978-1-59955-315-3
  1. Alcoholics--Rehabilitation--Fiction. 2. Seattle (Wash.)--Fiction. 3.
American fiction--21st century. I. Title.
  PS3618.I3446W48 2009
  813'.6--dc22
                                    2009032037

Cover design by Jen Boss
Cover design © 2009 by Lyle Mortimer
Edited and typeset by Melissa J. Caldwell

Printed in Canada

10 9 8 7 6 5 4 3 2 1

Printed on acid-free paper

To those courageous souls who mend their lives,
To the Good Samaritans who help them do it,
To the families who wait in anguish for good news, and
To the Kind Providence who arranges the miracles that make it possible.

prologue

Seven hundred miles southeast of Seattle, in a remote community barely large enough to appear on a map, a pretty young brunette—far too thin for her age and build—faced the back door of a seedy-looking auto parts store. She had endured an endless night of emotional battle with realities she could not change. By the time dawn arrived, she had made peace with the universe. She faced the day assured that her plea had been granted and everything she cared about would be safe. The torch she carried had finally passed to another—someone unseen by her, unknown to her, but chosen by the benevolent fate she trusted in to wield the life-giving gift that had been hers since birth and her mother's before her.

Her hand shook so noticeably that she steadied it with the other as she guided the key toward the tarnished lock. With a slight shrug and a weary smile, she pressed the key home and turned it until the dead bolt clicked open. She then leaned her weight against the weathered door. A new workday had begun, and she was glad of it.

one

T HE FIRST WORKDAY AFTER A LABOR DAY weekend was just getting underway downtown when an errant ray of sunlight pierced Seattle's thinning fog and struck the corner of an eye. The eye belonged to a drunk lying mostly concealed from the view of passing traffic by a sports car parked at the curb. The drunk had apparently lurched to this point from the site of his last drink, had steadied himself against a parking meter post, and then had slumped to the concrete in an alcoholic stupor.

How long he lay there, no one knew, least of all the drunk.

The ray of sunlight played about the drunk's eye for a moment or two, until a fractional turn of the drunk's head revealed a plump teardrop formed perfectly at the inside corner of the eye. Refracted by the liquid orb, the ray slipped at last between the slightly parted lids and burst into a spectacular prismatic array of brilliant color. This instantaneous light show elicited more than a passive reaction from the drunk lying there in blatant defiance of Seattle's vagrancy ordinance.

At the precise instant the piercing ray burst into color, the drunk's entire body contorted as though struck by a mighty jolt that could be expected at the moment of electrocution. Having accomplished its fateful mission, the ray vanished, cut off somewhere in the swirling fog above.

The tear remained momentarily. Then the surface tension disintegrated, and the orb burst, spilling its liquid content across the horizontal plane of the nose. It trickled down onto the lip where it mixed with a silvery stream of saliva issuing from the corner of the drunk's mouth and stretched toward the sidewalk below.

Following this unparalleled arousal, the drunk did not stir further. He lay there, gathering the disdainful glances of business-suited men and women hurrying to be first into the office. A stray homeless dog— one of the mangy cur varieties—padded down the sidewalk as if relishing the freedom of wandering about during the hour that belonged to early risers and delivery workers. He casually lifted a leg to pee on the back tire of the sports car and then sniffed the drunk at a distance as he passed, continuing his rounds.

two

HATCHER ALVIN STEPHENS III AWAKENED GRADUALLY. His head was pounding. But what made him really uncomfortable were the crick in his neck and the hard concrete against the side of his face. It took him a long time to piece together some picture of reality that he could identify. This was not the first time he had awakened in unfamiliar surroundings. Before he opened his eyes, he heard the sounds of the city, the passing traffic, the shuffling of shoes passing near his head, and the ground-shaking rhythm of an auto boom box passing slowly on the street.

Before he dared to look, he knew he was lying in a public place. He knew that passersby were looking at him. He could imagine their disdainful glances. He had seen them before. Even though he felt lousy and totally hammered, the horror of knowing he lay exposed to public view was excruciatingly painful. On other occasions, at the end of similar nightmares, he had awakened to find that he'd wet himself. The urine after a binge was especially acrid. The dark stain on his pants and the puddle under and around him were inexpressibly humiliating.

He knew it was silly to continue lying there, acting like he was still unconscious. But playacting separated him a little from the terrible reality he had awakened to. Like an ostrich with its head in the sand, at an instinctual level he felt that if he couldn't see them, they wouldn't see him.

At length, he opened the bottom eye just enough to orient himself.

Gratefully, he found himself facing the curb, his back to the storefronts. Eighteen inches away was a car tire. The only other object he could see was the base of a steel post rising out of the concrete. The post had been painted repeatedly; its chocolate outer layer was pitted and uneven. The post had likely been there longer than Hatcher had been alive. How many drunks, he wondered, had awakened over the years at the foot of this post?

Fighting a headache and dizziness, he gradually opened both eyes. He was lying beside his own car, his BMW Z4 3.0 roadster. The car was his first—and these days, his only—love, one of the few vestiges of his vanishing world.

His task at the moment was to get into the car and out of this place, while attracting as little attention as possible. With that end in mind, he moved both of his feet forward from the fetal position, hooked them over the edge of the curb for leverage, and tried to push up into a sitting position with the arm he had been lying on.

No way! After a second of exertion, the arm failed him. He toppled back to the hard surface. He knew that each effort to move would attract more attention. That was the very sort of thing people scorned in the behavior of drunks. Loss of control. Slurred speech. Public display of bodily functions. Hatcher reflected momentarily on the irony of the bystander reaction to a downed drunk—some sped their pace to avoid any chance of personal contact; others slowed their pace to get a better look, satisfying their morbid curiosity.

With considerable effort, he rolled forward enough to bring his other arm across him and awkwardly lifted himself to a sitting position, feet in the gutter, head down, arms hanging at his sides, and eyes closed again until the world stopped spinning. He gradually opened them enough to look down at his crotch to see if he was wet. His fear was confirmed. The light-colored Dockers were stained unmistakably.

He sat for several more minutes trying to look nonchalant, to be inconspicuous—if possible, to be invisible. He reasoned that each passing minute would allow his pants to dry out more.

Hatcher knew he couldn't stand yet, and he would need two hands to get himself into the car. As he waited for his sleeping arm to revive, he tried to remember the night now past. Fragments of the early evening spent at a bar on Water Street were still retrievable. Some light drinking as a warm up, mixed thoughtlessly with a steady string of meaningless conversations with other people in various stages of intoxication, always carried on over the too-loud music against a backdrop of silent television coverage of a Mariner's game.

He knew there was no way to reconstruct the night. Past efforts to do the same had only proven that nothing good ever came from a binge. On the contrary, anything really memorable was likely to have been bad. Still, he found himself lingering in the memory game longer than usual. Somewhere barely below the threshold of consciousness was the feeling that something important had happened to him while he was out.

He didn't dare to think about this directly. At the moment, any mental effort was painful. But something had happened. What was it? Awareness of it was lurking somewhere in the periphery of his thoughts. For whatever reason, as he turned his attention to this matter, he sensed arising in him a feeling of urgency to coax it, whatever it was, out into the open.

What was that feeling? Why was it flirting with him now? He was not in a philosophical mood. At the same time, he sensed a twinge of panic, the fear that if he let this thing go, it would vanish along with everything else connected with a wasted night.

Just as he was turning his thoughts back to his arm, the meter post, his pants, the curb, and getting into his car, his memory bank coughed up an impression. It crossed his mind with the speed of light. It was, indeed, a light—a flash of light. He had seen a brilliant flash of light. He couldn't see it now, not even in his mind's eye. But he was sure of it, a dazzling, blinding, consuming, electrical bolt.

He began to worry anew. A flash of light could be the result of a fall or a blow to the head. He wondered briefly if a flashing sensation accompanied a stroke or an injury to the optic nerve.

The more he thought about this, the more it concerned and intrigued him. He had the fleeting impression that the source of the light was outside him and that it had come from up the street, from the east. Perhaps it was an electric sign or a bright reflection off a window. He instinctively glanced over his left shoulder up the hill and into the eastern sky above, where the morning sun was trapped behind swirling mist and partial cloud cover.

At length, he felt he was recovering enough to stand. He pulled himself up the parking meter pole. His left arm was still mostly numb, and the pins and needles in the hand were severe enough to be very uncomfortable. Nevertheless, he managed to get to his feet. It was to be his only success for the day.

Three

HATCHER'S EMOTIONS WERE SO NUMBED AND HIS head hurt so badly that he hardly reacted to the realization that he had become separated from his car keys sometime during the preceding night. Amazingly, despite a night on the street, his wallet was still in his back pocket. His watch was still on his wrist. His class ring was on his right ring finger. The ring missing from the left ring finger was the work of the biggest thief of all—alcohol.

The keys were not in the ignition. He thought that he might have put them under the floor mat for safekeeping and then locked the doors. No stupid stunt like that would surprise him after all the stupid stunts he had pulled while under the influence.

He would return for the car after getting himself cleaned up. He made a mental note that the car was in front of Cooper's Bar. But he also knew that a mental note in his condition was like writing in the air or scribbling on the surface of water. He just hoped he'd be able to remember.

Not sure how he was going to get back to the apartment, Hatcher turned up the street toward the bus stops along Fifth Avenue. As he walked slowly along with his eyes averted, trying to avoid contact with any living creatures, he found himself looking from one light source to another as if needing light to recharge something inside him. The sensation was not unlike the relentless thirst for alcohol. He realized that the new sensation was somehow connected with the flash of light he had seen. At some elemental level, he was thirsty for light.

There was a bus stop at the corner of Fifth and Yesler. Hatcher had caught the bus there many times while employed at Austin, Stephens, and Park. He continued toward it, walking next to the buildings so he could reach out to steady himself from time to time.

As he turned to check for a coming bus, he found himself looking into the face of Grace Cunningham. Grace had been his junior associate for nearly three years. She had been walking behind him, possibly unaware that he was there. Both were startled.

Grace looked undecided as to whether she should stop and speak or keep walking. Hatcher could sense the awkwardness she was feeling. *After all*, he thought, *attorneys are lousy at covering their feelings.*

"Hi, Grace," he said without emotion and lacking any of the old charisma he had sported in his glory days.

"Hatcher!" Grace replied. "Oh my gosh! I didn't even recognize you."

Grace instantly flushed as though realizing she had said just the wrong thing.

Before he could think about what he was doing, Hatcher involuntarily looked down to see if his front had dried. Hurrying his gaze back up, he caught Grace looking at the same place. This all transpired in an instant, and of course, it wasn't her fault. She was merely following his eyes, as people are apt to do during a conversation.

But Grace was not a novice. She was a professional. She knew how to turn momentary embarrassment to her advantage, and she did so now.

"Sorry, Hatcher. You have a spot on your pants. It's great to see you. I hope all is well. Got to rush. Bye!"

She strode off with a look of complete composure.

Hatcher was dumbfounded.

You've completely lost it, he thought to himself for the nth time. The encounter was followed by recrimination and acid self-talk that lasted for at least twenty minutes until the bus pulled into view. How he hated Grace and her kind. And worst of all, he was her kind. Only, she was still polished, shining, and sitting atop her pedestal. He had not only fallen from the pedestal, but the pedestal had fallen on him and crushed him to powder.

A new hybrid-fuels bus headed to the University district slowed to a stop. His bus. The voice inside his head telling him what to do said,

Get on. This is you. Your past, your future, everything you know lies at the end of this bus ride. You have no choice. This is who you are.

But his body would not move.

The driver inside the bus glanced through the open door at Hatcher and then up into the rearview mirror. He looked back at Hatcher and gave him an open-handed shrug as if to ask, *Well, buddy? What's it going to be?*

Hatcher could not move. With a whir, the bus merged back into traffic.

Hatcher Stephens was no longer acting on reason. He had used up his capacity for reason and found himself stranded. Though it made no sense, he wanted to walk. He wanted to walk to where the sun rises each morning. He needed to find the fountain from which light spills and washes over the earth. He needed to drink the light in. He was thirsty—with thirst that even alcohol could not satisfy.

four

HATCHER ALVIN STEPHENS III HAD BEEN WALKING steadily, but not quickly, for what seemed several lifetimes. At about noon, he passed through Yesler Terrace and started down toward Lake Washington. He crossed the I-90 Bridge using a utility walkway, something he could never have imagined himself doing. He crossed Mercer Island and was now walking along the residential streets of Bellevue. He carried his sport coat hooked on a finger over his shoulder.

The late afternoon had warmed. The temperature was still cool but generally pleasant. He thought long about what he was doing. If he were driving his Z4, he would turn around and head back. If a bus stop were convenient here, he was sure that this time he'd board.

He considered calling someone to come get him but couldn't bring himself to do it. For the time being he just wanted to keep walking, though there was no sense in which he could say that he was enjoying himself.

His feet were sore. He had blisters on both heels and on the outside of both little toes. He wasn't hungry because he was sick to his stomach. His head still hurt badly. His throat was parched.

When the sun slipped near to the western horizon, Hatcher knew he had come to a decision point. He needed someplace to be during the night. It wasn't safe on the streets. He'd also been without a drink for maybe eighteen hours and was now hurting all over. He needed a drink. He'd been here before. Not here, as in *on the street*, but here as in *the first stages of drying out*. He knew that the miserable way he was feeling right then gave rise to the quip among alcoholics, *If this is how sobriety feels, I don't want any part of it.*

He walked on into the deepening darkness of the evening, wondering what this was all about. He had no plan. He kept walking because it was something he could do. He couldn't go home. He couldn't think his way through the mess his life had become. He'd tried that too many times before, always arriving at the same result—confusion. He couldn't decide to be different. That didn't work. He couldn't look for help. No one could solve this problem for him. He could run away, but there wasn't a place in the universe that a man could get to where alcohol wasn't available. Hatcher was a man in a trap. His walk had no purpose and no destination. He walked because there wasn't anything else he could do.

Still, he definitely felt drawn eastward. As he walked he had been imagining the sun as a fountain. Around the fountain stood the sun drinkers, imaginary beings awash in light, drenched with light, and light spilling out of them. To the west lay the darkness like a drain to which the leftover rays flushed, washing before them the filth and refuse of the universe. Around the drain stood the darkness drinkers, imbibing in the filth, awash in filth, and drenched with filth. Hatcher had already been to the drain. He'd had his fill. Now it was time to go to the fountain.

"This is nuts," he said aloud as he paused to decide which direction to walk at a street corner. Still he walked on.

He was becoming increasingly uncomfortable. Partly, this was the result of his anxiety about being deprived of alcohol. He knew more than a little about the dangers of trying to quit drinking cold turkey. Sudden withdrawal from heavy and prolonged drinking can bring the shakes, tachycardia, possible hallucinations, seizures, and in extreme cases, delirium tremens or DTs. Unattended withdrawal could open the way to various forms of head trauma from injuries sustained during seizures, pneumonia, and suicidal impulses. Hatcher was too miserable to try thinking his way through this. He felt so lousy that even though it was less than twenty-four hours since he'd had a drink, he thought he might be experiencing all these symptoms at once.

Looking for a place to rest and maybe spend the night, he passed a church. The building was not one of the older gothic structures, but a modern, single-story, built of glass and stone. The large parking lot behind the building was empty. The neighborhood looked respectable. He felt this might be as good a place to spend the night as any he would find.

Of course, he didn't want to be outside. It was too cold to be out. Trying to find some warmth, he settled against a wall in a rear doorway, away from any breeze. He turned the collar of his sport coat up next to his neck, pulled his knees up to his chest, and rested his forehead on his knees. He was hungry, thirsty, sick, and exhausted. As he sat there, the muscles in his legs trembled uncontrollably. He pressed them together, his arms clasped around them and his fingers interlaced in front. He could not stop the shaking.

How long he remained there trying to rest, he couldn't tell. There was no way he could sleep. He also could not think about his situation. All he could do was hunker down and survive the night.

Eventually, he felt he could sit no longer. When he tried to rise, however, his joints had become so stiff from the exertion and cold that he rose with great difficulty and had to lean against the cold wall for support. He was trembling all over, so he sat again. He didn't think he could stand the discomfort any longer, but there was no relief.

There followed a black, despairing agony that Hatcher could only equate with the pains of hell. He knew that a few drinks would cure his misery, if only temporarily. He cursed himself for getting into this hopeless situation, which seemed to last forever. He kept wishing he would pass out but was repeatedly awakened by his own groaning. In his partially wakened state, he noticed a light at some distance. He couldn't see it distinctly at first, but eventually recognized it as an automobile approaching the entry gate to the parking lot off to his right. The sudden fear of being discovered began to crowd out his agony in some measure. He saw the driver pull up to the gate and step out. Hatcher staggered to his feet and steadied himself against the wall. He couldn't leave, and he couldn't hide. He gladly would have settled for dying.

The parking lot was only partially fenced, but each entryway had a locked swinging gate to prevent unauthorized traffic. Hatcher could see that the driver was a large man in uniform, likely a security guard of some sort. The man stood directly in front of the headlights, shook the gate to make sure it was secure, and then turned on his big flashlight and began a visual inspection of the back of the building.

five

TREVOR MARTIN WAS JUST FINISHING THE AFTERNOON shift, working from two to ten o'clock on residential patrol for United Security Service's Seattle branch. United had grown during the later 1990s to be one of the leading national security providers, with more than fifty locations. The company paid Trevor well. While the work was mostly mindless, Trevor needed the job to give structure to his life. The hourly wage, added to his military retirement, made life more than comfortable.

Residential patrol was a cakewalk in a community like Bellevue. The shift had been eventless. Trevor had only a few more stops to make and was looking forward to a pizza and a couple of Cokes at Martelli's.

He pulled the car up to the gate on the south side of St. Mark's Presbyterian and stepped out to check the lock and sweep the back of the building. In three years on this shift he had never had a reportable incident at this account location, but that was security work: follow the same routine, every shift, no matter how many times things turned up the same. In this business, no news was the best of all possible news.

The gate was securely padlocked, as always. Trevor shifted the big MagLite to his right hand and switched it on, sweeping the back of the building from left to right. He had done this so many times that he moved right across the doorway on the northeast side of the building and switched the big LED lamp off before he mentally registered the scene before him.

"What?" he grunted.

Switching the light back on and throwing the beam into the doorway, he now saw the figure of a man leaning against the wall, steadying himself with one hand and using the other to shield his eyes from the light.

"Hold it right there!" Trevor called out.

Keeping the light trained on the intruder in the doorway, Trevor stepped around the gate, shifted the light to his left hand, and unsnapped the strap on his hip holster with his right hand.

"Put your hands up on the wall," he ordered as he approached. "You are trespassing on posted private property."

Trevor's right hand rested on his weapon, still in the holster. He stopped six feet from the intruder, directing his light into the man's face.

The door behind the intruder was closed, the glass window apparently unbroken. Trevor saw no signs of burglary but did not move his hand from the weapon.

"Sir, I am a licensed security officer. This property belongs to our client, and you are in violation of a city trespassing ordinance. Step away from the building and tell me what your purpose is here."

Intruder did not move but leaned forward and retched. His hands went to his knees, and he retched repeatedly.

Trevor backed away several steps but maintained contact with the light and kept his hand on his weapon. He said nothing more, recognizing Intruder as a drunk. He watched, leery of the man's plight, but not disgusted. He had been in the same predicament more times than he wanted to remember.

After retching five or six times, Intruder got his gag reflex under control. He was gasping for breath, his chest and shoulders heaving. His legs and arms were shaking so violently that Trevor feared he would collapse. Trevor's natural compassion inclined him to reach a hand to help steady Intruder. But many years of military police and security training warned him against concluding too quickly that Intruder was incapable of aggression. He held his distance and stance.

"Sir, you'd better go to the ground before you fall."

Without looking up, Intruder tried to speak. The voice was barely audible. "I'm sick."

"I can see that, sir," Trevor replied, not harshly, "but I can't help you until I am sure that you are not armed."

He moved the powerful beam of his light off the shaking intruder to the side so that the man could look up if he needed to.

"Can you reach your hands to the sidewalk and get on your hands and knees?"

"I don't have a gun," Intruder said, his head still down, hands still on his shaking knees.

Trevor waited. He wanted to get through this without doing anything foolish and without subjecting this probably harmless intruder to any further discomfort.

"I believe you," he said in a less confrontational tone. "I'll do what I can to help, but first you have got to put your hands on the ground."

Intruder moved one hand from his knee toward the ground as if to comply. As he did so, his knees collapsed together, and he fell forward onto his shoulder, his face striking the cold, unforgiving pavement.

Intruder groaned with the force of the impact.

Trevor cursed. He was now at Intruder's side, holding him against the pavement with one hand while searching his sides and pockets for a weapon, the light on the ground within reach. Before he released the pressure pinning Intruder's shoulder to the ground, he said deliberately, "I'm going to help you turn over. Keep your hands on your head."

He grasped Intruder under the armpit and stepped backward, rolling the sick and injured man toward him. Intruder had one hand on his face. The other flailed above him.

"Listen," Trevor spoke before doing anything further. "You are not armed. You don't look like a criminal. I haven't called for police backup, but I will if I need to."

After another pause, he said, "Do you want me to call an ambulance?"

Intruder said nothing. He lay on his back, trembling pathetically.

Trevor finally spoke again. "Look, you have two choices. If you can get up and walk off this property, you are free to go. If you can't, I have to either call the police or an ambulance. What's it going to be?"

Intruder shook his head slightly. "I'll walk," he croaked and made an effort to roll to his side.

Trevor reached for his radio, then shrugged, picked up the light, and knelt down beside the prostrate figure.

"Look," he said, knowing he was stepping over the line of company policy that protected his professional actions, "I'm going to try to help. I'm going to take your hand and help you sit up."

Still, all those years of training would not let Trevor abandon caution completely. He stepped to the side, clear of Intruder's legs, and reached forward with his left hand, the right hand again on his weapon.

"Give me your left hand."

Intruder's left hand was shaking so badly that Trevor had difficulty grasping it. Trevor then braced himself against any sudden jerking motion and applied upward pressure on Intruder's arm and shoulder. The sick man was large. He looked like he might weigh 250–260 pounds. He cooperated with Trevor's effort, and together they pulled him into a sitting position.

Trevor knelt beside him again and put a hand on Intruder's shoulder.

"Why are you sick?"

"Drunk," answered Intruder slowly.

"Thought so," returned Trevor. Now that he was close to the man, he could smell the sour stench of urine. "What are we going to do with you?"

No answer.

"You're well-dressed. You don't look like a street drunk. I'm guessing that a night in the slammer probably wouldn't do your career any good."

Intruder shook his head.

"Didn't think so," continued Trevor. "We need to get you home so you can sleep this off."

"Can't sleep this one off," Intruder said barely above a whisper.

Intruder's violent shaking now worried Trevor. "Are you withdrawing?" he probed.

Intruder nodded slightly.

"Great," grunted Trevor, looking toward his car. "A drunk in withdrawal and probably suffering from hypothermia. I'm going to have a corpse on my hands."

He glanced toward the still-idling security vehicle and made a decision. "Look, it's against company policy and will probably cost me my job, but I'm going to take you home. I don't want to watch you die, especially on my account's property."

six

HATCHER STEPHENS AWOKE FROM AN ENDLESS NIGHTMARE so many times that he was not sure whether he was awake or asleep. He was lying on something soft, but whatever it was, it was sticking to him. He was warm and wet all over. He could smell himself and that was not pleasant. It had been so long since he brushed his teeth that he could feel the fuzz growing on them. His mouth tasted like he had been feeding off a river bottom. Everything on his body ached except the tip of his nose. That was numb.

For the first time in eternity he opened his eyes. That did him little good because there was no light. He was clearly in a bed. The bedding on top and beneath him was soaked through.

The room was very cool. Cooler than a typical early fall night in Seattle. There was actually a bite in the air.

Hatcher had no idea where he was. He did know that, other than for a consuming hunger, he felt far better than he had before he fell asleep. At least, he assumed he had fallen asleep. He speculated that it must be close to morning, because he could vaguely remember walking through a Bellevue neighborhood just after dark the previous evening. Waiting for daylight, he lay uncomfortably, tossing in the wet sheets until he fell asleep once more.

Finally he awoke to the sound of a door across the room moving on squeaky hinges. As the door opened, light poured into the room. Hatcher flinched involuntarily as he opened his eyes to find a huge man standing over him.

"Didn't mean to startle you," the giant announced. He was so tall that he stooped somewhat to avoid hitting his head on the ceiling of the room. "Welcome back to the land of the living."

Hatcher was still sick and miserable, but not so miserable that he wasn't a little alarmed by this encounter. "Where are we? Who are you?" he asked more forcefully than he intended.

"Take it easy, Hatcher," the big man replied, showing his open palms in a sign of peace. "You're with friends."

"How do you know my name?" Hatcher asked.

"Got it off your ID when you checked in."

Hatcher lifted himself onto an elbow so he could look around the room. From this more elevated perspective, he could see that the room was very narrow and the ceiling low. The wall sloped up from his right side to intersect with a ceiling that couldn't have been more than six feet from the floor. He now realized that his host was not a giant, though he looked to be well over six feet tall.

The only furniture in the room were the single bed Hatcher lay on, a small nightstand near his head with a lamp on it, and a coat rack on which his own clothes hung in disarray.

Assuming from the host's comment that he must have rented a room, though he could remember nothing about it, Hatcher asked, "What kind of place do you run here?"

The big man chuckled. "Nothing like that. This is the spare bedroom of my home."

He extended his hand. "I'm Trevor Martin. And you're Hatcher Stephens III. Fancy name you've got there."

Hatcher felt like putting off the pleasantries until he could get more comfortable. "I guess I've wet my bedding pretty badly," he offered apologetically. "I must have had a pretty rough night."

"You did have a rough night," returned Trevor. "Actually a string of them."

"How long have I been here?"

"You came to stay on Tuesday evening. Today's Saturday."

"No way!" Hatcher was stunned by this revelation.

"Sure 'nough."

"Where are we?"

"I'll answer your questions, but what do you say we get you up and into the shower. The city is threatening to condemn the place as a source of hazardous pollution. If you can get into the shower, I'll burn this bedding. Think you can get up?"

Hatcher looked at this stranger, who now stood patiently waiting for a response. He was indeed a big man, probably six feet five inches tall, probably in his early- to mid-fifties, much thinner than Hatcher, with excellent muscle definition. He was dressed in baggy casual pants, running shoes, and a tight-fitting T-shirt that showed off his massive pecs and biceps. His hair was jet black, wiry, and had a bit of frosting at the temples. He was square-jawed and handsome, with an ebony complexion.

Hatcher scratched the back of his head, feeling somewhat embarrassed in thinking about his own slovenly and overweight appearance. His hair was soaked.

Getting out of bed was not at all easy. He felt extremely weak. Getting his feet clear of the covers and onto the floor, he dragged himself upright and sat on the edge of the bed. He was acutely aware of his copious stomach hanging over the elastic in his boxer shorts. He was also shocked by his own offensive odor.

"Sorry about that," he apologized again.

"The latrine is down the stairs on your left. I put a clean towel on the counter by the sink. Leave those disgusting shorts on the floor outside the door, and I'll get 'em into the trash."

Trevor hoisted a paper shopping bag onto the bed beside Hatcher. "I took the liberty of doing a little shopping with your funds. I bought you some basic things that should fit. We can return what you don't need."

He turned to leave the room and then added with a backward glance, "By the way, you should know that most of your credit cards are maxed out. In fact, you're going to owe me a little. But we can iron out the expenses later."

Trevor was gone. Hatcher sat for some time trying to piece things together. He was still alive but not well. Of course, the first thing that came to mind was getting cleaned up so he could go out and get something to eat. He also had a powerful thirst.

It was a new day. The diffused morning light glowed through the windows as he descended the stairs. He found himself wondering vacantly if he had found the place where the sun comes up. With that thought, bits and pieces of memory began to return. Deep inside,

Hatcher Alvin Stephens III sensed that the rules of the game had changed. The world he had built—that had been built for him—had passed away.

seven

EN ROUTE TO THE BATHROOM FROM TREVOR'S spare bedroom,
Hatcher realized that the bed he occupied was in a room under
the eave of a home with a hip roof. The room was more an attic than
a guest room. Hatcher was badly out of his element. He could see that
Trevor's house was comfortable—simply finished and furnished. It was
small for a man of Trevor's size. Almost from the moment he awoke,
Hatcher began to feel increasingly claustrophobic. He had never spent
any significant time in a cracker box like this. The general condition of things discomforted him even further. The house didn't show
overt signs of dirt or clutter. However, Hatcher had grown to maturity
and beyond with the unspoken but indisputable conviction that old
things, especially cheap old things, were meant for a different class
of human beings. Trevor's house, though tidy, was worn—carpets,
drapes, furniture, fixtures, appliances, and everything in sight—all
were dated and needed replacement. The paint on wooden doorjambs
and window frames showed underlayers of different colors in spots. Of
course, Hatcher felt guilty about snobbishly assaying the possessions of
a man whose charity had lifted him from peril. But he also rationalized
that he could not help who he was or his instinctive reaction to things
around him. Right or wrong, he took refuge in the hope that once
showered and dressed, he could escape to some location more suitable
for him. He worried slightly that something had happened to him,
something had changed; some cosmic alignment of the stars or fates
had catapulted him into a parallel dimension. In short, he feared for

whatever reason that he had fallen from grace. What if things would never again be as they were in his glory days? What if he had squandered his birthright and all good things were now beyond his reach? Though not new to Hatcher, these thoughts aroused an uneasy anxiety that he hoped to wash away in the shower.

Hatcher could discern the layout of the home almost at a glance. The main floor featured a relatively spacious parlor with a small attached dining room, a narrow vinyl-floored kitchen, the bathroom, and an additional room that had probably served as a bedroom in previous generations. Trevor had equipped this room on the lower floor as a gym, probably because the weights needed a solid, load-bearing floor.

Hatcher's shower could have been delicious in another setting. In this case, the shower stall was a precast plastic insert shoehorned into a tiny and generously dingy bathroom. Though Hatcher needed the shower badly, he was anxious about getting athlete's foot or a variety of other communicable diseases in someone else's shower. He hurried through the shower ritual and did not enjoy it as he hoped.

The clothes Trevor bought for Hatcher fit well enough, but Hatcher was uncomfortable in them from the moment he dressed. In all his life, Hatcher's mother had never bought clothing for him at K-Mart, Walmart, Penny's, Macy's, or any place of the sort. Nor had Hatcher and Patty ever bought cheap clothing for their kids. Even in the past year when his financial world hit the skids, Hatcher continued to dress in the way he was accustomed. As he looked at his new outfit in the bathroom mirror, he wondered, *If clothes make the man, how would I have been different if I had worn clothes like these all my life?*

Hatcher found Trevor at a kitchen table reading a morning paper and sipping a cup of black coffee. While he marveled that a man could take a total stranger into his home and provide life-sustaining support, Hatcher's cynical side demanded to know what would be expected in return. Was Hatcher a guest or a prisoner? What would his stay in this inn by the wayside cost him?

An awkward pause ensued. Trevor looked up at Hatcher over the rim of his cup but said nothing. Hatcher was still struggling with his own uneasy feelings. He was self-aware enough to know that he held a few prejudices that barred him from getting comfortable with people and situations that differed dramatically from his accustomed life. Of course, his accustomed life had undergone a dramatic downgrading as his disease progressed. The divorce, the loss of his position at the firm, frequenting public bars, associating with less savory elements while gambling—all of these factors gradually introduced him to people and lifestyles inferior to the standards that had defined Hatcher Stephens.

The man in front of him was no exception. Hatch could imagine the man as a client, he could envision him behind the bar, he could tolerate him across a poker table, but he could not bring himself to address the man as a peer, much less as a benefactor to whom he now owed a debt of gratitude for rescuing him from the demons inside him.

Trevor apparently didn't speak by choice. Hatcher didn't speak because he couldn't. Nor could he move. Hatcher Stephens was imprisoned, not by his host, but by a lifetime of judgments, a pattern that rendered him incapable of free and easy discourse with any person of inferior social status who deserved to be thanked.

Clearly the next move belonged to Hatcher. The frank expression on Trevor's face suggested that he could guess what was going on inside Hatcher. Yielding the higher moral ground to someone of inferior social standing angered Hatcher and, at the same time, embarrassed him. Like a man outside himself watching his own behavior, Hatcher condemned his own snobbery. At the same time, he didn't believe it was completely unjustified.

Hatcher knew he couldn't slay this emotional dragon directly while being put on the spot. He had to ease his way into a conversation that allowed him a little time to adjust. He stepped past Trevor and sat in a wooden chair at the other side of the table.

"Shower felt great," he lied. Hatcher let his eyes scan the kitchen as he spoke.

Trevor said nothing.

"I hope I smell better." He still did not look at Trevor. A longer silence ensued. From the corner of his eye he could see that Trevor was looking directly at him, still sipping his coffee.

"Nice house." Big lie. Hatcher was feeling alarm rising within him. As an attorney, he knew the value of silence as an offensive weapon. The combatant who could afford to remain silent clearly had the upper hand. At this moment, Trevor had the upper hand. Hatcher found himself wondering if the man had been trained in litigation or negotiation tactics.

By instinct and training, Hatcher knew that the time had come for him to either feint or fold if he was to get a conversation going. The only other option was to rise and walk out the door. Something in Hatcher wanted to do that, but he admitted to himself that doing so would require a level of strength and courage he did not presently possess. Hatcher folded.

"Are you going to talk?" He finally looked at Trevor.

Again, Trevor did not speak for a long moment. Then, like a warrior who knows when he has subdued his opponent, he set the coffee cup on the table in front of him, leaned back in his chair with his slippered feet outstretched, and nodded. "Well, I wasn't quite sure if you were talking *to* me. Seemed like you were talking *at* me."

Trevor's meaning was instantly clear to Hatcher because he knew that is what he had been doing. Trevor's insight startled him enough that the attorney involuntarily looked at Trevor. It was the gaze of one who suddenly recognizes an unexpected strength in an opponent and wants to get a closer look to see what other strengths might be present but have been overlooked. *If you underestimate them once, you can recover,* his father had coached him. *Underestimate them a second time, and you are beaten.*

Hatcher had underestimated. He now had a choice. He could either level with Trevor, or he could try to deceive him. Trevor had called the first shot correctly. Either he had some skills at the bargaining table, or he was lucky. Luck seemed unlikely. Skills argued for candor. Hatcher decided on candor.

"You're right," Hatcher countered. "I'm at a bit of a disadvantage here. I don't know you or anything about you. I'm not sure where to go with this."

Trevor smiled but not softly. "You're free to go anywhere and anytime you want. In fact, our first order of business is to get you headed toward home, if you've got one."

Hatcher looked down at the loaner clothes Trevor had provided for him. "Do I look homeless?" he asked.

"No," began Trevor in a calculated tone, "you don't look homeless. But that's where you are headed. Most homeless people are better off than you because they know where they are going. You don't know where you are going. And most of the homeless know how to survive on the street. You don't know how to survive on the street."

Hatcher let his gaze fall to the table. It was made of wood, possibly a softer wood like pine. The surface was dinged and scarred. He had underestimated Trevor twice. He weighed his next move, but Trevor spoke first.

"Homelessness is all about survival. Seems to me that you are still about saving face. You maybe should move on to survival sooner than later."

"What do you know about me?" Hatcher's tone began to reflect the hostility he was feeling.

"That's better," said Trevor, smiling and signaling his satisfaction at getting an authentic reaction from his visitor.

"You've been napping for three days. While you were sleeping I took the liberty of finding your home so we'd know where to deliver you when you had slept it off. Your name and residence show on your state driver's license.

"I checked with the manager of your apartment building to see when they expected you back. She told me you were not expected back. In fact, they have initiated eviction proceedings against you. Your lease has expired, and you are behind on your month-to-month. I'm sure you know all of this."

Trevor's rundown was painful for Hatcher. He wanted to explain it away or blame it on his unreasonable landlady. But Trevor's earlier charge of "saving face" had stuck in his mind. He didn't want to provide more evidence that the accusation was well founded.

"Furthermore," Trevor continued, "you should know that others are looking for you. The apartment manager told me two men had been by. They frightened her. One of them told her that he was your brother-in-law and said they were worried about you."

Hatcher mumbled, "I don't have a brother-in-law."

"I thought as much." Trevor sipped again from his cup and then stood to freshen it from an electric coffee pot on the kitchen counter. "Her description didn't register *police*. That's good. It did register *bill collectors*. That's not good."

Trevor looked matter-of-factly at Hatcher. "Do you owe any big sums? To anyone who might come collecting?"

"I owe lots of people right now. I'm clearing up the bills."

"I doubt that."

Hatcher looked at Trevor carefully. The black man was clean cut and healthy, his eyes clear, his posture erect, and his expression incisive.

Hatcher asked, "Who are you?"

"I think I told you earlier. Name's Trevor Martin."

"What do you do?"

"I earn an honest living."

Hatcher was fighting desperately to gain the offensive in his exchange with Trevor. "You know something about interviewing or interrogation."

"Hatcher, what I know is that you have just awakened from the depths of withdrawal. You feel lousy and the gains you have made are temporary unless you can follow up with some concrete, positive steps.

"You've got some people looking for you. Whoever they are, they are not your family. They are not your employer. I checked with SPD. No one reported you missing even though you've been gone for three days. No place to live. No job. No one cares. This is not a good picture.

"So, Hatch, unless you want to have a bite to eat and walk away, I'd suggest we put together a little plan for you."

Hatcher blinked. He had never allowed anyone to call him Hatch, even in school. "The name is Hatcher," he replied in a surly tone.

"As things stand, I don't think you can afford a name like that." Trevor's even stare dissuaded Hatch from arguing.

eight

TREVOR MARTIN KNEW WHEN HE HELPED THE fainting drunk into his car behind the St. Mark's Presbyterian Church in Bellevue, Washington, that he was subjecting himself to the Good Samaritan dilemma. He learned the biblical parable of the Good Samaritan when he was a Sunday school child in Mississippi. But he learned the Good Samaritan's dilemma the first time he tried to walk in the Samaritan's sandals. He now knew from a series of similar experiences why the priest and the Levite of the parable gave the half-dead traveler wide berth. They feared the moral obligation that compassionate assistance imposes on the doer of good, an obligation that may not be easy to discharge.

Like the Good Samaritan, Trevor knew that by helping Hatch he tacitly assumed a burden for the drunk's well-being until he would be able to care for himself—a fearsome burden.

In the parable, the Samaritan gave the needed immediate aid. He bound up Traveler's wounds, pouring in wine and oil. He transported Traveler to the safety of an inn where he arranged for continued care. There was the dilemma and the cause for fear.

Trevor was no stranger to the dilemma. He had once been Traveler. He revered his own Samaritan. He had tried his hand at Samaritan's work on several occasions. He knew of the impending obligation. He felt the burden of fear in the moment when he decided to care for Hatch instead of making a 911 call.

Trevor knew that since the dawn of time the *what ifs* had frightened many a priest and Levite away from giving vital, compassionate assistance. What if Traveler needed prolonged and expensive care? What if Traveler was a dependent personality and more than happy to be cared for—indefinitely? What if Traveler was deranged, or dangerous, or domineering, or dogged by past sins and debts? The Samaritan's work was not for the weak. It was the domain of moral Titans.

Trevor felt he was up to the challenge. He now looked across the table at Traveler, partially dried out and bathed. He sensed a man who had gone to flab in body and character, a man who had never yet found himself, a man too focused on pleasing the world. But for all that, a man who might become a man.

Trevor nodded and moved toward the fridge. "Can I interest you in a glass of orange juice?"

nine

HATCH STEPPED INTO THE COOL MONDAY MORNING air. Night rain left the foliage and walkway wet. He shivered and put his hands into the pockets of his pants as he looked at the outside of Trevor's house for the first time. When he came to the house nearly a week earlier, Hatch was somewhere beyond consciousness. He hadn't ventured outside since.

Trevor had turned in early on Sunday evening. Before saying good night, the pair had discussed Hatch's plans—or rather lack of plans—for the future. Trevor had generously invited Hatch to stay with him in North Bend until Hatch gained a sense of direction and could earn enough money to finance his next step, whatever that might be.

"I have a friend who runs a little shop in the Historic District. Last time we talked, she told me she was trying to find some help for the shop. Doesn't want to hire any high school kids. You might want to check with her.

"If you can get a job to pay me a little rent and split the food costs, you can stay on for a few weeks, a month or two. That way you can move from a position of strength."

Pride could have kept Hatch from accepting Trevor's offer and almost fatherly advice. But the recognition that he hadn't succeeded too wonderfully in past pursuits and the compelling urge to travel eastward caused Hatch to rise, shower, and head toward historic downtown North Bend, intending to arrive at the shop well before it opened.

The walk was a short one. Hatch was looking for "Sylvia's," a boutique and gift shop with predominantly Native American atmosphere and inventory.

He easily found the general vicinity of the shop from directions Trevor had provided. As he neared the sign hanging from a totem pole at the shop's entrance, Hatch felt a lump rise in his throat. He stopped, looked up and down the row of shops, and took a deep breath. In his thirty-six years he had never asked anyone for a job. His father, Hatcher A. Stephens II, had always smoothed the way for him. All he had to do was show up, make the right impression, and start doing the work.

Hatch was not a beggar. He had no idea what to say. He turned and walked back down the street in the direction he had come, gazing briefly into the store windows, trying to get a grip on his sudden, irrational fear. It helped to know that he couldn't go back to Seattle now. No one there was going to offer him any help. He couldn't call in any additional favors. He was deep in debt and had no way to pay.

When he reached the end of the block, he stopped again. His chin fell to his chest. Why was it so hard for him to ask for help? No doubt it was partly the humiliation of admitting surrender to someone less capable and less favored than he. Then Trevor came to mind. Was he not discovering Trevor to be a man of superior intellect and abilities? Had he not begun listening to Trevor and seeking his advice? Was it possible that he could find a simple shopkeeper to be his superior in some other unexpected way? Hatch had no difficulty looking to those of superior abilities for assistance. Could he assume in advance that this shopkeeper would be someone from whom he could learn life-rescuing skills? If so, why be afraid to ask for a job?

Once more he turned. This time he walked with purpose toward the shop. Still, he felt his pace slowing, and he swallowed hard as he reached for the brass handle on the door. The door didn't yield to his gentle pressure. He pushed harder. Locked. Almost relieved, he let go the handle and thought of walking away.

What Hatch needed was a drink to help clear his head. But he had no money. He had kept an eye open for any spirits in Trevor's house. He saw none. Trevor seemed to be a teetotaler. Hatch was in a bind. He could not turn to the right or the left and could not go back.

Leaning slightly forward to try the door again, Hatch caught a glimpse of a person on the far side of the shop. He rapped lightly on the door and waited. Seconds later he could hear the click of heels on a stone floor as the person approached the shop door from within. Fingers tugged the blinds, prying the *Shop Closed* sign aside just enough for the insider to see that Hatch stood without, and then rattled the lock.

The door opened briskly, framing a striking, self-assured woman, perhaps a year or two older than Hatch. His first glance met her dark eyes. She had pulled her deep brunette hair back away from her face into an eye-catching chignon. A flawless, burnished complexion shaded her prominent cheekbones and slender aquiline nose. Provocative smile lines finished and softened her inquiring expression. She was not gorgeous, but naturally glamorous and immediately and decidedly sensuous.

This was one of those moments—and one of those women—that silently warned men to restrain their wandering eyes, but Hatch could see that she dressed in a mid-calf, light-weight wool skirt and fitted top, a silver chain belt accentuating her tiny waist. The jewelry on her ears and wrists added a Native American flair.

Hatch was attracted. She returned his gaze expectantly, and he thought he detected a similar spark in her.

"Hi." Her voice was low and melodic, adding to Hatch's instant appraisal. "Not open yet." She pointed to the sign. "We open at nine." There was no hint of "go away" in her voice.

Suddenly Hatcher Stephens was on familiar ground. If there was anything he knew how to read, it was a woman's reaction to him. If any aspect of his self-confidence had survived five devastating years of personal decline, it was his confidence in meeting and charming the opposite sex. If any interpersonal dynamic had remained constant since his earliest memories, it was the realization that women found him nearly irresistible—until they got to know him. Even in his dilapidated state, he knew he had not lost all of his appeal.

"Hi," Hatch replied, the verve in his voice matching hers. "Sorry to trouble you. A friend suggested I stop by. He thought you might be looking for some help in the shop."

Despite the coolness of the morning, Hatch began to see a sheen of moisture on the woman's forehead and cheeks.

This is going to work out okay, he assured himself.

"And who might that friend be?" She still held the door with one hand. The other hand moved to her hip.

"Trevor Martin," Hatch said simply.

The shopkeeper gave a bit of a start. "Really?" she asked.

"Why does that surprise you?"

"I'm not surprised. Just curious." She stepped to the side and opened the door wider. "Please come in. Let's visit."

The mention of Trevor's name had opened the door, but it also altered the shopkeeper's demeanor. She seemed to adopt a more business-like air. "I'm Sylvia Rencher," she said, gesturing Hatch toward a small office behind the shop's counter. "And you are?"

ten

"HATCH STEPHENS." HATCH EXTENDED A HAND. HE struggled to comply with Trevor's insistence on calling himself Hatch. In the presence of an attractive female, he was mightily tempted to revert to Hatcher for its added impression value.

Sylvia did not respond to his extended hand. "Nice to meet you, Hatch. Do you have any retail experience?"

"Not exactly," he replied. "I've done my share of retail buying but not much selling. It looks like you have some pretty nice stuff. With a few pointers, I think I can help sell it."

Hatch's confidence had begun to slip precipitously. He wasn't sure what had happened with the mention of Trevor's name.

Sylvia stiffened noticeably. "Hatch, we don't sell any *stuff* in this store." She was smiling, but her voice had a distinct edge.

"Sorry," Hatch backpedaled. "You sell inventory, right? Not stuff. Inventory."

"Or offerings," Sylvia supplied.

"Right. No offense intended."

"None taken." She seemed to relax slightly. "I am seeking some competent help for the shop. I'm sure you realize that this position doesn't pay a professional salary or even a living wage. It's nine dollars an hour. No benefits. Regular eight-hour shifts include Saturday and Sunday with no overtime.

"What did you have in mind?" she asked as an afterthought.

"Something like that," he replied. "But I'll level with you. I'm not seeking a long-term position."

"How long?" Sylvia asked.

"A couple of months, maybe three."

"Won't work for me," she replied. "I need someone I can rely on at least through the Christmas holidays."

Hatch tried to that far ahead. The urgency he felt to travel eastward pressed on him. Could he settle in for four months? He had fantasized being in Denver before the weather got really cold. He imagined himself on the East Coast by spring. Still, Trevor's words from the evening before rang in his ears, *You have to move from a position of strength.*

"Works for me," he echoed Sylvia's words, conceding agreement.

"It all depends on your success at selling retail *stuff.*" She smiled as she emphasized the word.

"I hear you." Hatch acknowledged the irony in her statement.

Hatch was used to things happening quickly. In the glory days, he could cope with the best of them. But in those days, every game was played on his home court. Now he was clearly on someone else's home court. Every play seemed new. He wasn't really sure he knew what game they were playing.

eleven

B Y THE END OF HATCH'S FIRST WEEK at Sylvia's, neither Hatch nor Trevor had learned much about the other. Hatch asked but could get almost no information from Trevor, and Trevor knew all he needed to know about Hatch. The question of what to do with Hatch had been settled temporarily by Hatch's commitment to stay at Sylvia's through the approaching holiday season.

Hatch was feeling somewhat better. He still suffered severe headaches. Of course, he had a terrible thirst that could not be satisfied with any amount of water or orange juice. Hatch had never been a coffee drinker. He thought constantly about going out for a drink, but there was no cash left in his wallet. He accepted Trevor's report that all of his credit cards were maxed out. Pride would not allow him beg or borrow money from either Trevor or Sylvia to get himself a drink.

Noticeably, Hatch had calmed regarding his temporary surroundings. The house that seemed so claustrophobic a week before now seemed more tolerable. Hatch discovered that though the house was worn, it was clean. He noticed that Trevor was constantly cleaning the home in bits and pieces. If he saw a dusty surface, Trevor would dust it. If something were carelessly laid aside, Trevor would pick it up and put it away. When hand washing a few dishes, Trevor also washed down the countertops and tabletop. This was behavior Hatch knew from birth, and he was careful to comply.

That is not to say that Hatch had grown comfortable. His physical condition admitted no feeling of relief. Knowing that he needed to move on and leave Trevor to his home also kept him in a constant state of agitation.

One evening, Hatch flipped restlessly through the pages of *Time* magazine. He still wore the bargain store clothes Trevor had bought for him. Trevor's head rested on the high back of the upholstered rocking chair in the spacious parlor. He had finished his shift at four in the afternoon and was still wearing his security uniform.

When Hatch saw Trevor's eyes open momentarily, he spoke. "I've been thinking about my next step."

Trevor turned his head slightly to look directly at Hatch but said nothing.

"I'll keep going east. I've never lived anywhere except Seattle, but there is really nothing there for me to go back to." More than explaining his thoughts to Trevor, he was really thinking out loud.

"I can work. I am still a member of the bar, so I could practice law. But that would raise some unpleasant questions. I don't think I'm ready for those yet."

Hatch fell silent.

"Sounds like the beginning of a plan." Trevor's tone was more matter-of-fact than Hatch's, betraying no judgment.

When Hatch said nothing further, Trevor asked, "Any actual destination in mind?"

Hatch's voice was low, barely audible. "I know it sounds crazy," he replied, "but since I began this walk I've been feeling driven to find out where the sun comes up. That's somewhere east of here."

Trevor studied him for a few seconds. "Good luck with that. This is sounding like some kind of mystical odyssey. Forgive my intrusion, but it seems to me that a man could get real hungry trying to find out where the sun comes up."

"Sure," answered Hatch. "You're right. I can't explain it. I only know that I left everything behind me in shambles. Every time the sun comes up, it's like a new start. I guess I'm looking for the land of new starts."

"Like I said," Trevor said, sitting forward and reaching his arms into the air as if stretching his back muscles, "a man could get real hungry looking for the land of new starts. Any plan for feeding yourself?"

"Work," answered Hatch.

"Where?"

"I don't know."

Silence.

"Any suggestions?" Hatch was beginning to enjoy his visits with Trevor. He found the older man resistant to any discussion about the past and seemingly not much interested in the present. But he became more animated as they tried to peer into the future.

"You could start walking, but in about a day you'd be out of fuel and out of reach of any known resources. When you left Seattle you may not have been thinking about the realities of the road. There are lots of realities, but foremost among them is that you have to eat to keep walking."

Trevor's willingness to talk surprised Hatch. He could see a sudden intensity in the man's eyes, like a veteran coaching a first-timer. "Have you been on the road before?" Hatch asked.

"Oh yeah, I've been on the road."

"Tell me about it." Hatch was forgetting his misery for the moment. He wanted to know more about Trevor.

"Nope. The problem here isn't mine—it's yours. And it doesn't lie in my past. It lies in your future. I'm just suggesting that you always start with an answer to the question, 'Where do I get my next meal?' I'll tell you now that there are a lot of beggars on the road. That is nasty work. You don't want to beg—for more reasons than you could remember even if I was to list them all."

Trevor was now up. He walked to the front window, parted the heavy curtains with his hand, and looked out to the house across the street as if viewing the past he refused to talk about.

"The alternative to begging is work. Hard work. As I said before, when you move, you have to move from a position of strength. Never run from your problems. Running only helps until its time for the next meal."

This was said with an intensity that made Hatch catch his breath. It sounded like a dire warning from an old soldier.

Trevor turned back to face Hatch, a self-conscious smile on his face. "Sorry, you caught me in an off moment." He walked toward the kitchen. "I must have food on my mind. Let's see if we can find a bite to eat."

Hatch rose slowly to follow the big man. *Who are you?* he asked silently. Where did this big, powerful security guard come by his obvious intelligence and refinement? Hatch suddenly found himself wanting to know what Trevor knew. *Who are you?*

twelve

A MONTH PASSED SWIFTLY. THE WEATHER COOLED AND dried out. The days were gorgeous. Hatch had fallen in love with his walks to work and back. He became intimately acquainted with the five blocks along his route. He even made a few visual acquaintances. It felt good to wave and smile at familiar faces.

Trevor's two-story coastal-style home was on Third Street. Hatch walked south on Bellerat Avenue for three blocks to North Bend Way. Most of the homes near the town center appeared to be of the same vintage as Trevor's. Like every community on the west side of the Washington's Cascade Range, North Bend was overwhelmingly green. The yards and public spaces seemed well tended, suggesting a healthy respect for tourism. Located just north of I-90 at a bend in the South Fork of the Snoqualmie River, North Bend was principally a tourist stop. Because the town lay thirty miles east of Seattle on the approaches to the Cascades, it provided a logical water hole and pit stop for summer hikers and winter skiers.

The town's commercial district was only five or six blocks along North Bend Way. The colorfully painted shops and storefronts offered tourist fare.

Each morning as Hatch rounded the corner onto North Bend Way, he gazed up the street to the east knowing that the crests of the Cascade Mountains were only fifteen miles distant. His compulsion to travel eastward toward the rising sun had not diminished. Daily he endured a private battle to keep his commitment to Sylvia, remaining in the shop through the year's end. He occasionally dreamed of walking through sagebrush flats and finally arriving in Denver. He had never seen such country, except while passing through at freeway speeds. But he felt a distinctive draw, and he was roughly counting the days to his next departure.

His daily obeisance to the rising sun was becoming ritual. He reflected daily on the new pattern of his life. Hatch was a cerebral being. He was introspective. He analyzed, as he always had, his own thinking and behavior. He had discovered many years earlier that alcoholism is not just a lifestyle; it is the product of a highly patterned existence. Alcoholics tend to follow a daily routine that focuses increasingly on drinking until drinking crowds everything else out and becomes their life. When the alcoholic discovers a watering hole or a comfortable social setting that includes alcohol, he will return again and again until the day can't be complete and life can't go on without living inside that pattern. Everything reinforces the pattern—sights, sounds, and especially smells. Music, lighting levels, the texture of furniture, the smell of a freshly-oiled dance floor, and, of course, the familiar presence of other drinkers all lead to a drink that leads to another, and so on.

Hatch now realized that in one fateful day, he had stepped completely outside the pattern of his former life. He was in a new world. It wasn't that alcohol wasn't present everywhere around him, but that he had not yet begun to create any alcohol-related patterns. The leap was not intentional on his part. He hadn't chosen to run away or to try drying out. He had simply walked toward the light and suddenly found himself in a place where he could create new patterns without any drinking in them.

He still thought about drinking—all the time. But the physical misery of drying out had lessened significantly and for some hard-to-explain reason, his emotional addiction was in a state of uneasy abeyance. He did not dare disturb it, so he held desperately to his new daily routines and tried to avoid any patterns or people that might bring him into direct contact with a drink.

As Hatch thought about these patterns, Trevor often came to mind. Trevor lived a highly patterned life. Hatch realized that waking up in Trevor's home was a stroke of immensely good fortune for him. Trevor had transported him from one world to another.

With these insights, Hatch continued his walk to the shop, deferring his Denver plans to another day.

Hatch received two paychecks during his first month of work for Sylvia. He realized that Sylvia was taking a few legal shortcuts with his employment. When she said the job had no benefits, she had evidently meant that it was below the radar. She paid him with a company check marked *contract services*. The checks didn't include any federal or state withholding.

Claiming his employment as contract service was not altogether legal. More accurately, it was altogether illegal. Hatch knew he should and would eventually have to pay taxes on the earnings, but for now, he reasoned that he was already tens of thousands of dollars in the rear on his obligations. He wasn't trying to hide from his creditors, but he was happy to stay out of sight until he was in a position to start meeting creditor demands.

Things at the shop were going well. Hatch was succeeding in his work as sales help. In reality, he was more than sales help. He was also clerical and custodial help. He unloaded deliveries. He walked mailers to the post office and deposits to the bank. But clearly, his superior good looks and polished manner were helping to increase return visits by local women, many of whom made periodic social calls. Hatch became familiar enough with the inventory to run the shop alone and close about half as many sales as Sylvia. That spoke well for him, since Sylvia was very good at what she did.

Despite his attraction to her, and what he supposed was her attraction to him, their relationship remained decidedly business-like. Clearly, that was better for both of them. Still, something about her relationship to Trevor tempered her personal behavior toward Hatch. Hatch didn't understand why. He asked only once what Sylvia knew about Trevor. Her cryptic response told him little.

"Trevor is well-known in North Bend. That's not to say he is known well. But he is regarded with a certain reverence."

She would say no more.

Hatch regarded Trevor with his own type of reverence. He didn't know much about Trevor but felt he knew him in the sense that he could predict Trevor's reactions and often his words. The man was a machine. He arose before sunrise, left the house for a short jog regardless of the weather, and returned to a prolonged workout in his personal gym. Trevor retired to bed early every evening except those on which he worked a late shift. On those evenings, he went directly to bed. His schedule never varied beyond that. He seemed to have no vices. He sought no comforts other than those already offered by his modest existence. He took no recreation. He went off to church on Sunday morning if he wasn't working. He attended the city council meetings on Tuesday evenings if his shifts allowed.

During the last week of the month, Hatch barely saw Trevor. He waited in the living room until Trevor returned from his shift and handed him the agree-upon rent for the month now past. He hardly understood his own feeling of personal satisfaction as he handed Trevor the cash. Hatch was working for a mere fraction of the income he previously enjoyed. The rent was a pittance. Yet Hatch had earned every penny in honest labor. The payment was a matter of personal honor. Trevor acknowledged the payment with a nod and threw the money onto the top of the secretaire desk where he wrote out his bills and carried on correspondence.

"Sorry to pass up the party this evening, but I'm bushed. Off to bed. Good night." Trevor was gone.

After the movement in Trevor's upstairs bedroom ceased and the house fell quiet, Hatch walked to the secretaire and looked at the cash. He realized how little money had meant to him in his past. Money was never in short supply. It came to him almost effortlessly. His parents were always wealthy. He and Patty had as much as they wanted. Even after the divorce and loss of his position with the firm, he had regarded money as an inexhaustible resource. No doubt that accounted for his sizable debt. Under the old rules he could easily repay what he now owed. Under the new rules, clearing the debts could take a lifetime.

That money on the secretaire was more than a symbol of organized exchange. It was Hatch's sweat, his blood, his time, his effort, and his life. It was a part of him. As he looked at the money, he was tempted for the first time to take it back. Take it and leave. But he still had too little to finance the next leg of his journey. Surely there was too little to begin meeting his past obligations.

Hatch walked away from the money, but for the first time he felt a hunger to earn his own way and to have his productive efforts rewarded.

Thirteen

WHILE CONVERSATIONS ABOUT PERSONAL MATTERS WERE RARE at home with Trevor, they became more common in the shop. These were not discussions of the past, since Hatch was not eager to reveal his past to anyone at the moment. Sylvia seemed to feel the same way. But they did talk about the present and, in a more limited way, about future hopes.

Customers, mostly women, strolled through the shop getting familiar with the inventory. Hatch came to understand that women shop with their eyes and their hands. If possible they want to see the items they may purchase with themselves in a picture. Consequently, Sylvia generously used mirrors in the shop's décor. No matter where customers stood in the shop, they were within a step or two of the closest mirror. When women shop, they also touch nearly everything they look at. They pat. They heft. They stroke. They hold items to their chins, their cheeks, and their chests. Hatch soon learned to pick up items of interest and hand them to the customers.

The shop had two large fitting rooms. Fitting is the ultimate touching experience. Women who tried items on were not only touching the merchandise but being touched by it—touched all over. Hatch now knew that fitting is at least as much about the feel of apparel as it is about the look. The first step in making a successful sale was to let the woman touch the item. The second was to let her try it on to see how she felt wearing it. The third was to help the woman overcome any obstacles to the purchase. The fourth was to help the woman make a buying decision, called the close. When customers left the shop, all merchandise that was not purchased had to be returned to display locations.

Just before noon on one glorious October mid-week morning, two women came into the shop. They wore travel clothes and light jackets. They appeared to be a mother-daughter team. Their financier, a heavy-set gentleman of retirement age, lumbered behind. The women swept through the shop touching everything in sight and leaving a trail of returns behind.

These women were world-class browsers. Hatch smiled his best sales help approval. He happened to look up from this touch-and-ogle fest to find Sylvia smiling at him. He rolled his eyes in mock frustration. Then he noticed the gentleman escort looking at him. Hatch shrugged. The escort nodded his agreement.

The pair lingered by the jewelry showcase, so Hatch served up a variety of Native American bracelets in sterling, inlaid with onyx. These were among the priciest items in the shop. Slipping a bracelet onto each wrist, Hatch simply said, "Very classy." The women bought. The escort paid. Sylvia smiled.

After they left, the shop was empty. Sylvia and Hatch replaced the items the pair had browsed.

"Smooth," said Sylvia. "You're becoming a pro."

"How long have you been doing this?" Hatch asked her.

"A while."

"You're very good. I suppose you know I've been studying your . . . technique."

Sylvia arched her eyebrows. "Stay on your side of the line," she said.

Hatch smiled.

"You're a good student," Sylvia continued. "Are you planning to make retail your career?"

"Hum. Good question." Hatch became reflective.

"I didn't mean to pry," Sylvia apologized.

"No problem." Hatch shrugged. "I need a career. The last one was not a rousing success."

The door was open to Sylvia to ask follow-up questions. Hatch knew that she must be curious. He had told her nothing about himself. She couldn't have learned much from Trevor, assuming that she knew Trevor personally. She had taken Hatch in on Trevor's referral alone—at least initially. But Sylvia didn't pursue Hatch's past.

"Some people make a very good living in retail sales. Imagine yourself selling women's apparel at Nordstrom's. Or," she continued playfully, "at Sylvia's."

"I don't know," Hatch shot back with a grin. "I'd have to work a thousand hours a week at nine dollars an hour just to break into a six-figure salary."

Sylvia's tone became more serious. "I should be paying you more. You are producing."

"Nah, I'm just sparring with you. I appreciate the job, really." It felt good to Hatch to actually be talking. He was okay with talking about nothing in particular. In fact, he preferred it. Small talk is a good refuge for people hiding from the world.

"Seriously." Sylvia held a wool blanket that she intended to stuff back into a stack at her elbow. "At the start of the next pay period, we'll raise your wage to twelve dollars." Then she added with a hint of embarrassment in her voice, "I want you to know that I appreciate your investment here. I guess I thought when you started that this was sort of a charity gig. You know, just helping you out a little while you were between jobs. You are earning your pay. You're good. Thanks."

Now it was Hatch's turn to be embarrassed. The sincerity of her comment touched an emotional chord somewhere within him. He noticed her dark eyes, her erect posture, and the pearly quality of the skin on her face, neck, and bare arms. For a moment he savored her charm and wanted to hold her. This was not anywhere akin to the less noble impulse he had often felt to put the moves on a willing or vulnerable woman. Rather, it was a moment of cherishing a person of quality. Sylvia was bright, competent, and spontaneous. She could be willful and demanding. She was in control of herself and still respectful of others. Sylvia was a quality person with a generous streak. And she had just paid Hatch a superlative compliment.

Hatch knew this feeling. It's how he felt about Patty. Right now Sylvia reminded him of Patty. Same woman, different body. Patty in five or six years. The deed was done. The dam broke. With the first thought of Patty, Hatch felt that gigantic rush of guilt. His chest fell.

He felt the weight of his countless failures crushing down upon him. So, he turned away as tears welled up in his eyes.

"I've got to catch my breath," he said faintly. "Be right back." Hatch strode out the shop door onto the street.

fourteen

THE SAME MELANCHOLY THAT HATCH FELT FOLLOWING his encounter with Sylvia earlier in the day continued as he walked toward Trevor's house after closing the shop. Sylvia had been very distant through the remainder of the day and had left early. Hatch was sure that his unexpected reaction to her compliment had left her confused and uncertain.

Great way to reward a kindness, Hatch thought as he approached the house. Trevor's sedan was parked on the street in front. Trevor was already away when Hatch arose that morning. Having no idea what Trevor's work schedule was, Hatch did his best to adapt each day.

He found Trevor in casual clothes, rocking in the living room. He had a cup of coffee in hand and seemed to be absorbed in a copy of *Car and Driver* magazine.

Hatch hung his jacket on the back of the door as he entered. He drew a glass of water from the tap and crossed to the divan. "Evening. How was your day?" he asked as he sat.

Trevor looked up from his magazine a bit surprised.

"Well." A smile crept up his face and took seat in his eyes. "You're not usually one for small talk."

"I've been pretty sour, haven't I?" Hatch knew it was true.

"You've been through the wringer. Not surprising you haven't been at the top of your game."

"That's generous of you," Hatch said sincerely.

"This is a red letter day." Trevor's smile grew. "You're also not

49

usually one for handing out thank-you notes."

Trevor's quip touched the same emotional chord in Hatch that he'd felt with Sylvia. Trevor was right. Hatch seldom said thanks. He admitted to himself that he had forgotten how powerful the words *thank you* could be until Sylvia had said them earlier in the day.

He felt the guilty rush coming on. This time he resisted. He had business to do and didn't have time for one of his private pity parties.

Hatch noticed again how handsome Trevor was. He didn't have classic features. But he was clean, healthy, strong. Like Sylvia, Trevor was in control of his own life. Trevor was another quality person. Hatch found himself wondering how he could have been lifted out of a life where he seemed drawn to people who were troubled and lost and placed into a world with a man and a woman who were the opposite.

"Did I ever say thanks to you for saving my life?" The question itself startled Hatch. Hearing it come from his own lips was shocking.

"Don't recall that you ever did." Trevor's direct gaze was more than Hatch could bear. He looked away.

"This is hard for me," he began haltingly. "I don't know why it's so hard."

Trevor relaxed in his chair as if willing to wait out Hatch's awkward feelings.

"I was in trouble. You really stuck your neck out. There were all kinds of reasons you shouldn't have. All kinds of possible liabilities. And you've followed up. I couldn't have done that in a million years—wouldn't have done it. You did." Hatch fell silent.

Trevor nodded. He waited

"So . . ." Hatch turned the palms of his hands up, shrugging his shoulders.

"What are you trying to say?" Trevor asked.

"Thanks. Thank you. Thank you for what you did—what you're doing. Thank you."

Trevor's smile warmed. "Hatch, you're worth it."

Then Trevor stood up and signaled for Hatch to do the same. "Give me a hug like a man," he ordered. The two men embraced.

Trevor was four or five inches taller than Hatch. He backed away and put his hands on Hatch's shoulders. "We got to do something about your waist. I can hardly reach around you."

Hatch laughed. "You're right. I haven't always been this way. That alcohol is mean stuff. It doesn't bring out the best in a guy."

Trevor returned to his seat shaking his head. "Don't I know that? I know that. I know that."

Hatch wanted to ask Trevor how he knew it but reasoned that he really didn't have to. Questions could only satisfy his idle curiosity. He already knew that the details might vary, but alcoholism treats everybody the same.

Instead, he had a different question for Trevor.

"Today, at the shop, Sylvia thanked me for my work. For some reason it made me think of my wife and kids. I was married to a splendid woman. More than a guy can hope for. We have two great kids. The kind of family a man should work for and sacrifice everything for. I threw them away."

Trevor rocked. His eyes were closed, but Hatch knew he was listening. He said nothing.

"I had to be doing something wrong long before the wheels came off. Any ideas?"

Trevor rocked on. Without opening his eyes, he asked, "How often do you think about them?"

"Not much these days. Thinking about them is too painful. Too much guilt."

"How often did you think about them before the wheels came off?"

Hatch thought about that. "All the time. I mean, I lived with them. They were always there."

"How often did you think about them when you were away from them? At work? Traveling? During social events? Making your plans? Doing the things *you* were excited about?"

After a pause, Hatch replied, "Probably not too much. If you are asking whether I took them for granted, the answer is yes. I've always focused mostly on me."

"You're not too different from the rest of us," the big man said, nodding. "We have a tough time making a case for loving someone that we never think about. We leave them out of our thoughts because we're pursuing our self-centered goals. We lose them. Then we leave them out of our thoughts because we feel guilty about losing them."

Hatch knew this pattern too well. "What's the solution?"

"Doesn't it all come down to being self-centered versus being other-centered?"

"What do we do about the pain, besides getting drunk?"

Trevor rose and walked to his secretaire. He took a small, framed photo out of the upper drawer and studied it. His back was turned so that Hatch could see nothing of the photo. Hatch sat quietly.

"We can think of them through the pain. If I think about her, picture her, listen to her voice, list her strengths, remember her kindnesses—it has nothing to do with me or my mistakes. *She* is the focus. If I start indulging myself in guilt, then the focus shifts to me, and she leaves. Then I have really lost her, and all I have is me. Not always very good company."

Hatch wondered yet again where this security guard came by his abilities and insights. That evening Hatch thought about Patty, Jenna, and Ryan for the first time in many months. Hatcher A. Stephens III, the failure, the drunk, the spoiled and self-centered ingrate kept trying to steal the stage. But Hatch Stephens, renter of Trevor's cubbyhole and retail sales helper, kept wrestling Hatcher off the stage, so he could spend time with Patty, Jenna, and Ryan until he fell into an exhausted sleep.

fifteen

O N HALLOWEEN DAY, HATCH'S SECOND RENT PAYMENT was due. At the end of two month's work, he had stuffed almost fifteen hundred dollars into one of his extra socks. He didn't regret that the payment was due. In fact, he looked forward to it.

The day in the shop began well. Sylvia had suggested that they both dress up for Halloween, one of her favorite holidays, but when Hatch balked at the idea, she withdrew.

Hatch was rehanging a supposedly authentic native fishing spear when two men came into the shop. Sylvia was in the office working on month-end paperwork.

The pair were not at all typical shoppers. Both appeared to be in their mid- to late-twenties. They were bulked out, wearing casual dress pants and golf shirts. Both had chin beards and close-cropped hair, spiked stylishly. They wore dark glasses. The larger of the two men sported a sleeve, a heavily tattooed right arm.

Hatch approached them. "Can I help you fellas?"

"Yeah, we're looking for Hatcher Stephens. Know where we can find him?"

An alarm sounded in Hatch's mind. He considered telling them he had never heard of Hatcher Stephens but knew that would not work with this pair.

"I'm Hatcher," he replied somewhat quietly.

"Let's step outside for a sec. We have a message for you from James Quan." Tattoo gestured toward the front door.

Hatch had borrowed a few thousand dollars from Quan to finance a short gambling spree but had paid him back. He had no idea what kind of message Quan would send via a pair like this.

"Let me tell the owner I'll be away." Hatch moved as if to step toward the office.

"Whoa, Bubba." Tattoo grasped the triceps on the back of Hatch's upper arm in a vice-like grip. "Don't disturb her. Looks like she's busy." In the same gesture, he began propelling Hatch toward the door.

Once outside, the two men walked Hatch to the back door of a black Cadillac Escalade. Tattoo's assistant opened the door and then climbed in after Hatch. Tattoo rounded the car and climbed into the driver's seat. Without saying anything further, he pulled away from the curb and headed out of town to the south.

"What's this about?" Hatch leaned forward, addressing his question to Tattoo. Instantly, Assistant's iron arm flashed across Hatch's chest and pinned him against the seat.

They drove to the outskirts of town and then pulled off the street onto an unpaved turnaround. When the vehicle came to a halt, Tattoo turned in the seat to look at Hatch. Hatch felt a sense of relief. Surely he was in little danger in so public a place.

"We work for a collection agency. Mr. Quan is a client. He asked us to contact you and bring back the money you owe him."

Hatch shook his head. "I don't owe James any money. I borrowed a little, but I paid him back."

Tattoo smiled. Hatch couldn't see his eyes behind the glasses, but the bare teeth clearly signaled that the smile was not friendly.

Tattoo waved off Hatch's explanation. "Not what we want to hear," Tattoo said, laughing. "Our client says you owe him ten thousand dollars. We have come to collect."

"But I paid him." Hatch's voice began to betray his alarm. "Besides, it wasn't anywhere close to ten thousand. It was sixty-two hundred. And that included the interest."

Tattoo was no longer smiling. There was no laughter in his voice. "The ten thousand includes penalties and collection fees. Give us the money now, and you walk. Don't give us the money, and you may never walk again."

Hatch groaned. "But I paid him."

"You gave Mr. Quan a bogus credit card number. It didn't pay. He's impatient. He needs the money now. Where do we go to get it?"

"Geez." Hatch reached his hands toward his temples in distress. Assistant slapped them down and shook his head as if to say, "Don't move your hands."

"I don't have ten thousand dollars. I don't have two thousand."

"Listen, Hatcher Stephens." Tattoo's voice rose. "We don't want talk. We want money. The meter is running."

"I'll call James and work out a payment plan." Hatch was stalling for time, desperately trying to think of a way out of this pinch.

Suddenly, Tattoo reached his arm across the seat. In his hand was a pistol pointed directly at Hatch's forehead. "We don't have time for this. Tell me now where we are going to get our money."

Hatch pressed his head back as far as the headrest would allow. His eyes were wide open. At this distance, the pistol looked huge—and deadly.

"Okay," he gasped. "I don't have any money, but I'll get it. Give me a few days."

"No, no, no! We are not stupid. And you are not a good risk. We know you'll run again." Tattoo was laughing again. Hatch was not comforted.

"I'm going to ask you once more. Where do we go to get the money?" Tattoo pressed the muzzle of the pistol into Hatch's forehead until it hurt Hatch badly.

"I'll ask the owner of the shop if I can borrow it from her." Hatch didn't know what else to say.

"That's better." Tattoo let up on the pressure and finally removed the pistol altogether. He turned in his seat and started the Caddy.

Hatch tried to reach up and rub his forehead. Assistant grabbed his wrist, twisting it downward. Again, he said nothing.

Back at the shop, Tattoo circled the block. When he had located the back entrance he stopped, telling Assistant to cover the back. He would wait in front. He told Hatch to stay in plain sight once he entered the shop. "We don't want anything unfortunate to happen to you," Tattoo warned, "or to the owner."

Hatch dreaded the moments ahead. He had worked hard for Sylvia. He had lived a flawlessly responsible life for the past two months and felt he had made great strides in pulling his life together. He knew the debts still owing from his past would eventually catch up to him.

He had hoped that they wouldn't catch him so soon. Now he had no choice.

To say he was in an awkward and embarrassing spot was a spectacular understatement. He was also in danger and had put Sylvia in danger as well.

When he walked into the shop, Sylvia came toward him. Fortunately, there were no customers present. "Where did you go? I thought you'd tell me if you had to leave."

"I didn't have a choice," Hatch replied.

"What's that mark on your forehead?" She stepped closer and reached up to touch the mark from the pistol barrel.

Hatch backed away. "It's nothing," he said.

"It's a circle. It looks like it's bleeding a little. What happened?" The concern on Sylvia's face pained Hatch.

"I need to talk to you." Hatch hoped his voice conveyed his apology in some measure.

"Let's go into the office." Sylvia turned.

"We can't," Hatch blurted out more forcefully than he intended.

"Why not?"

"There are two men watching us. They say they're bill collectors. But they're really muscle for a petty gangster in Seattle I once borrowed a few thousand dollars from."

Hatch looked down at the highly buffed wood floor of the shop. Sylvia said nothing.

"Uh . . ." Hatch didn't know if he could say more. But he also knew he had to say what must be said. "My past is catching up to me." He smiled wanly. Sylvia's eyes narrowed, and she began showing signs of a growing anger.

"So what now?" she asked.

"These guys are dangerous. I've got to find ten thousand dollars." Then he said with emphasis, "Now."

"Ten thousand dollars?" Sylvia's voice rose. "That's a lot of money. Do you have it?"

Hatch just shook his head.

"Let's call the police." Sylvia turned once again toward the office.

"No!" Hatch fairly shouted this. When Sylvia turned back toward him, he gestured in exasperation, "These guys know I can't call the police. This is an illegal gambling debt. They know I can be disbarred for this. And frankly, that's the only thing I've got left to fall back on."

Sylvia folder her arms across her chest and tapped one foot in a sort of "because I'm your mother" stance. "Hatch," she said, "you are a really sweet guy. You've been working hard. I like you, and I want you to succeed in putting all of your demons behind you. But I am not your mom. Take this thing somewhere else."

Hatch admired Sylvia. He admired her more now. But he knew that couldn't be the final answer for him.

"Look," he said, "I know you're right. I came here with nothing. You owe me nothing. In fact, I owe you. But I don't have any other option but to ask you to loan me some money. I hate to beg. It is humiliating. It's not my style. But I don't have a choice."

"Hatch, I don't have ten thousand dollars lying around. I'm a small business owner. This has been a good year, and things are going well now. That is partially thanks to you. But it can all turn around in an instant. Adding ten thousand to my debt could spell the end of this whole enterprise." Sylvia gestured around the shop with her out-stretched arms.

"I know. I'm sorry. I will pay you back—every penny and more. I'll help you make this work."

"What if you don't pay them?"

Hatch pointed at the mark on his forehead. "This was made by the muzzle of a pistol."

Sylvia closed her eyes and sighed. "If this creditor has found you, how many more are out there?"

"I don't know," Hatch answered honestly. "But all the others are legit. This is the only one that was under the table."

"You are asking so much, Hatch. I can't tell you how much. And it's all on your word. Other than that mark on your forehead, which you could have put there yourself, there isn't one piece of physical evidence that what you are telling me is true. You could work here on best behavior for two months, then con me out of ten thousand dollars and disappear. It's happened before. I'm sure it will happen again."

Sylvia's observation was spot on. Everything she said was well within reason. But it stung Hatch deeply. He had never had to beg, though he had often borrowed. His family name had always been his collateral. Even Patty had loaned him money after their divorce as he slid down the long mossy slope toward destruction. Now, in desperation, he was begging. He also confessed to himself that he had never repaid well, not even to Patty. Here he was, promising Sylvia something he had never really done in his life. He didn't blame Sylvia for her doubts. But he could still see that huge pistol in front of his eyes, could still feel it boring into his forehead. Fear drove him onward.

"Of course, you're right," he replied. "I can only give you my word." Then he added impulsively, "I love you and appreciate your generosity."

"Oh, Hatch. Please." Sylvia's voice was cold. She was furious. "That's an insult. What do you know about love? A man in love doesn't ask the woman he loves to bail him out of his troubles by putting her into trouble. He takes the heat. He pays the price to protect her from paying it."

Sylvia looked at him and shook her head, tears coming to her eyes. "Hatch, you're a good guy. I like you. I don't think you are a con man. But this is pathetic. Somewhere along the line you missed out on some important lessons."

Hatch was convicted. There was nothing else he could say. He hung his head, resigned to the truth.

Just then the bell on the shop door tinkled and a customer walked in, a young woman with a girl who appeared to be a preteen daughter.

"You wait on our customers. I'll see what I can do about solving your problem." Sylvia strode toward the office.

sixteen

Sylvia Rencher made one telephone call before she left the shop, walking the three blocks to Cascade Bank where she kept her business account. As she stepped out the front door, she looked for the black Escalade Hatch had told her about. The Escalade was there, parked about five stalls down the street. The windows were darkly tinted. She could see one man in the driver's seat but could not distinguish his features.

Seeing the Escalade partially confirmed her faith in Hatch's story. She was tempted to walk to the car and confront the driver but did not want to make a bad situation worse.

She had thought about calling the police, even against Hatch's objection. That could save her ten thousand dollars, money that she really needed. But she couldn't bring herself to take from Hatch the prospect of returning to legal practice, which could eventually help him dig his way out of trouble.

Sylvia was angry. She was angry at Hatch. Angry at the unseen villain waiting outside the shop. Angry at fate. She knew how anger felt. But she was not discouraged.

Sylvia felt strong. She was pleased with where she was in life. Pleased with what she had accomplished. She worked hard. She lived responsibly. She had learned and then mastered many important lessons.

At the same time, she did not like unwelcome surprises, she did not like to be manipulated, and she especially did not like parasitic men. She knew how it was to live with one. She had barely survived a decade with a male parasite.

The ordeal began in her early twenties. By the time she extracted herself, with help from a few wonderful friends, she was already thirty-something and felt like an old woman. But from that moment on, she had steadily pursued a vision of herself that would eventually put her beyond the reach of parasites.

As for Hatch, Sylvia didn't think he had those parasitic tendencies. She was assured by Trevor's confidence in Hatch. Hatch certainly had his own problems. Today's crisis was ample evidence of that. But he didn't visit his problems on others constantly. He wasn't always reaching for sympathy or incessantly thrusting his challenges to the forefront and crowding others' concerns into the background by trumpeting his own. He owned his weaknesses and didn't blame his misfortunes on others. The maddening characteristics of the human parasite were missing in Hatch's makeup. Sylvia felt she could cope with almost any other demons, but she could not—would not—subject herself to parasitic manipulation ever again.

Could she ever love a man like Hatch? Hatch had come into the shop in ill-fitting, unattractive clothing. He later told her that Trevor had done his shopping for him. He was also overweight by maybe seventy-five pounds and gave her the impression of having way too much confidence in his own charm.

In just two months, Hatch had shed some pounds but still had a long way to go. Still, he was gloriously handsome. His lustrous black hair was naturally wavy. His beard, which never got more than a day old, was equally dark and set off his intense eyes. His face did not have a mark on it, until that small red circle suddenly appeared on his forehead a few minutes earlier.

But, in some ways, Sylvia was very old fashioned. Her marriage to Walt had exaggerated the tendency. When she asked herself, *Could I love this man?* the question was immediately followed by a more important question: "Is this a man?" That was key. Every gorgeous face, every exciting body didn't make the man. They were male, all right. But to Sylvia, a man was something special. Real men were trustworthy. They were strong, reliable, kind, generous, and constant—sort of like modern Boy Scouts. Real men were also romantic—and, of course, attractive.

A man like that could be both a great business partner and a life-long companion.

Sylvia had already tried the parasitic kind. No more of that.

Sylvia's name was good on credit—not because she had inherited the name, but because she had earned it. In less than half an hour, Karen Markham, the small business loan officer at Cascade Bank had approved Sylvia's signature loan and cut her a cashier's check for ten thousand dollars. Sylvia felt slightly sick over the whole transaction. Her whole future could easily be riding on the actions of this day. As she walked back to the shop, she steadied herself emotionally, relying on her confidence in Hatch—and Trevor. She hoped she wasn't setting herself up for disaster.

seventeen

I F HALLOWEEN WAS A DAY FOR HORROR shows, this would qualify as one of the most horrible for Hatch. Sylvia had returned to the shop, wordlessly handed Hatch a cashier's check for ten thousand dollars, and then closed the door to the office behind her. She wore an impenetrable mask of neutral emotion. Hatch did not dare speak.

He carried the check to the driver's side window of the Escalade and waited for Tattoo to power it down. Tattoo was alone. Hatch had been planning his delivery speech, something that would head off any further contact with Tattoo and Assistant, and something that would discourage James Quan from ever coming back for more.

When the window came down, Hatch started his speech. "Here's the money. Tell James . . ." That's as far as he got.

Tattoo raised the pistol so that just the barrel was visible to Hatch. He extended his hand and took the check from Hatch, saying, "Shut up, stupid. I won't tell James anything. But I will tell you something. You're alive, and that's all you need to know. Don't go anywhere in case I need to find you again. If you're not here, I'll have to ask the pretty lady for your forwarding address. I'm sure you don't want that."

With those words, Tattoo raised the window, backed the Escalade out into traffic, and was gone.

Hatch cursed under his breath. He hated Tattoo, but he was also furious with himself. He wanted to blame this whole ugly morning on a deteriorating world. He wanted to blame it on ruthless, lawless people like James Quan and Tattoo. But his own reason convicted him. He had broken the law. He had put himself at the mercy of this scum. He was weak, frightened, and impotent. He felt like he had been raped, and he could do nothing about it. By far the worst of it was that he had dragged Sylvia into it with him and put her in danger. Happy Halloween, indeed!

eighteen

T REVOR MARTIN WAS NOT FEELING WELL. HE didn't sleep well these days and was concerned about the headaches and occasional dizzy spells. He'd been to his doctor with the complaint, but there was no immediate indication of any problems he should worry about.

He was free for the afternoon and thought he might indulge himself in a rare nap. He had already finished the paperwork for the morning shift and was leaving the Seattle yard when his cell phone rang.

"Martin," he answered.

"Trevor, this is Sylvia Rencher. I'm sorry to bother you. Hatch just told me that two thugs are demanding ten thousand dollars from him to pay off a gambling debt. They threatened to kill him. He's asking me to get the money for him. I think I can probably borrow it, but I hate to do it. And this feels too much like things from my past. I can't be sure he's being honest with me."

Trevor let Sylvia talk until she was finished.

When you pick a guy out of the gutter, you pick up his problems with him, Trevor thought. "Listen, Sylvia, I want you to be careful. We need to keep this as far from you as possible. Everybody touched by this kind of business is tarnished in one way or another. I will stand behind you on this, so don't worry about the money. I suggest you ask for a signature loan and try to get the funds in a cashier's check. Give it to Hatch. Let him deliver it. Don't go near these guys."

"Okay," Sylvia replied breathlessly.

"Are the bandits on foot or in a car?"

"Hatch said they are parked outside in a black Escalade."

"Take your time getting to the bank and back with the money. I'll see what I can find out. If anything goes wrong with the loan, let me know."

As an afterthought, he added, "I think Hatch is okay. He's done some dumb things, but I don't think he'd try to steal from you."

"Okay, Trevor. Thanks, as always."

"You're welcome, Sylvia."

Trevor could trust Sylvia to be smart under pressure. He still wasn't sure about Hatch. He headed east out of Seattle, knowing he had nearly thirty miles to travel up I-90. He exited at North Bend twenty-four minutes later and drove directly to Sylvia's shop. He parked around the corner on East McClellan Street, left his security badge and equipment belt in the car, and changed his uniform shirt to a civilian shirt he carried on a hanger for running off-duty errands.

Then he put his hands into his pockets and walked down the alley behind the shop. As he expected, he found a young man hanging out in the alley, smoking a cigarette. Sylvia hadn't given him any description of the men, but Trevor didn't need one. The man was in his twenties, powerfully built, and dressed to show off his muscles. Trevor nodded as he wandered down the alley. He turned toward North Bend Way and continued past the front of the shop. Part of the need for this tour was to determine how many men he needed to keep track of.

The Escalade was nose first in an angled parking spot. That meant the bandits were confident they had nothing to fear from Hatch. Trevor smiled grimly. They were probably right about that. Hatch didn't pose much of a threat. He also couldn't be counted on for any support.

Trevor did not make eye contact with the man behind the wheel of the Escalade. From the corner of his eye he could see that there were no others inside the SUV.

He stopped to glance briefly in a shop window and then continued his stroll.

The Escalade did not have a front license plate. He would need to get the tag number from the rear. Once back in his car, Trevor pulled out onto North Bend Way and drove behind the Escalade writing down the plate number. He continued north for two blocks before turning east again. Doing so, he passed Sylvia walking south. She had apparently been to the bank and was returning to the shop.

Trevor knew that he faced a dilemma. Once Hatch delivered the check, and assuming that the money was all that the bandits wanted, they would likely hit the freeway and travel directly back to Seattle before stopping. He knew he could find them again from their plates, but if possible, he wanted to deliver a message before they left town today. It was important to leave a bad taste in their mouths that they would associate with North Bend forever after. He knew that people like them were likely to go into the livestock business. The defenseless victims became a sort of underworld cash cow. Once they found a victim, they would come back over and over. Certainly, reasonable people avoided any contact with these unsavory characters. But plenty of people are too stupid to stay away from illegal gambling. As Hatch had, they ignorantly stumble into a deadly game.

Trevor was not sure he could protect Hatch from himself, but he was determined to protect Sylvia from these and any other bandits who came looking for Hatch.

He couldn't be sure how this would go down. He would have to rely on luck. He drove down Bendigo Boulevard across the river and parallel parked about two blocks from the freeway entrance. He would watch for the Escalade in his rearview mirror, pull out of his parallel position to block the street, and then take it from there.

Trevor waited and watched. Perhaps six or seven minutes passed. To his relief, he saw the Escalade round the corner two-plus blocks behind him. He started the engine and put his car in gear. Fortunately, there was no car parked ahead of him. He could pull out fast and swing wide across the traffic lane. He counted on the men in the Escalade to think he was just a thoughtless or unaware driver. That might buy him enough time to get out of the car and to the driver's door of the Escalade.

As the Escalade approached, he looked up and down the street to ensure there were no city police who might interfere. Trevor's heart began to pound. He felt a sharp pain in his head and dizziness washing over him. *No time for that now*, he thought. He took one last look over his shoulder. The Escalade had vanished. Trevor twisted in the seat and saw the back end of the Escalade as the driver swung south from the street and pulled into a Burger Barn parking lot.

Trevor could hardly believe his good fortune. He switched off the engine and leaped out of the car, running behind the back end and through the parking lot. He was a little winded but standing still when the driver's door began to open.

These two clowns are so sure they've got this thing buttoned up that they are stopping for lunch right here in town, he thought.

As soon as the door cracked, Trevor wrenched it fully open with his left arm and stepped beside the driver, shoving his service revolver up under the man's chin so hard that the bandit bit his tongue. The move caught both men completely by surprise.

"Don't move, or your friend dies on an empty stomach," he hissed at the passenger. He ripped the sunglasses off the driver and threw them to the ground. He pressed the gun upward with all his strength. The driver's head was cocked against the headrest, and he couldn't breathe or swallow.

"I have a message for you squirrels. You are on my ground. Don't ever come here again. Before you can sell this truck, I'll have a fix on you. I'll know where to find you. Your client gets his money. You tell him there is no more. Stay away from this town and stay way from that woman."

In a flash, he whipped the pistol back and smashed the butt into the nose of the driver who gasped and grabbed his face with both hands.

Waving the pistol toward the passenger, Trevor asked, "You understand me? Or do you need a piece of this?"

The passenger replied in a heavily accented voice, "I understand."

The whole bloody exchange had taken half a minute. Trevor placed the pistol in his waste band and pulled his shirttails over it. Then he slammed the door of the Escalade and crushed the driver's sunglasses under foot.

Trevor was shaking but not frightened. His system was charged with adrenalin. It was all he could do to restrain himself from running or yelling. He understood the impulse athletes feel to do a victory dance.

That will probably leave a bad taste, he thought as he walked away.

nineteen

I T WAS DARK BY THE TIME HATCH walked to Trevor's house after closing the shop. The temperature was crisp, but the evening was not wet. A few neighborhood kids were on the street in their costumes trick-or-treating. A light burned in Trevor's living room, and the porch light was on.

Approaching the walk, Hatch could see that Trevor was sitting on the porch step with a bag of treats in hand. Two small children were holding their bags up to Trevor while an adult escort watched from the sidewalk.

Hatch waited until they got their candy and passed him before sitting down beside Trevor. "Happy Halloween," Hatch said without enthusiasm.

"Hello, Hatch. How'd your day go?"

Hatch was startled. It was only the second or third time Trevor had called him by name. The two had gotten along well, though to say that they had a good time together would be exaggeration. Hatch was being cautious in every aspect of his life, like a man walking on a knife edge.

"I've had better Halloweens," Hatch replied.

"Then have a Snickers." Trevor held the sack up in front of Hatch.

"Thanks," answered Hatch, waving off the offer. "It might ruin my girlish figure."

Trevor actually chuckled. Hatch looked at him askance. "You're in high spirits this evening," he said.

"I like Halloween," replied Trevor. "I like children, and Halloween lights them up. It's fun."

"Wow." Hatch was really amazed. "Somehow I don't think of you as a fun seeker."

"You have kids," Trevor replied. "Don't they get excited at Halloween?"

"Yeah, they do."

"Didn't you enjoy watching them do their Halloween thing?" This conversation was unlike Trevor, but it seemed perfectly natural at the moment.

"Did I ever enjoy it? Hmm. You know, I don't think I knew how to enjoy anything."

"That's too bad." Trevor voice was genuinely warm and friendly. His white teeth shone through his smile. "You must have missed a lot."

"I missed more than I can tell you."

Hatch was sensible of Trevor's gazing at him. Then Trevor shuddered slightly.

"It's getting a little chilly out here for these old bones," he said. "Let's go inside and see what we can find to eat."

Hatch scratched his head. Trevor's mood was actually helping him to start feeling better. He had planned to tell Trevor what happened at the shop, but now he was reluctant to break the festive mood. Maybe he would bring it up later.

When they had washed up and set out a few items from the refrigerator on the table, Hatch said, "Today is rent day. Let me pay up before we eat."

Trevor waved him away. "We can take care of business after dinner."

"I think I'll enjoy the food more once I've paid."

"Okay," replied Trevor. "As you wish." He took the bills as Hatch counted them out, walked to the secretaire desk where last month's rent still lay in plain view, and put the new payment on top of the old.

"Thanks," said Trevor. "Now let's eat." As always, Trevor bowed his head, clasped his hands, and said a short grace over the food. Hatch watched him, thinking, *This is a good man*. Hatch didn't join in grace. It was not a matter of being ungrateful to God for providing. It was that somehow Hatch was still uncomfortable saying thank you. The words seemed so hollow coming from him. So insincere. So hypocritical. For now, he was more comfortable watching.

After dinner, Hatch began to feel mellow on top of the self-recrimination he had been heaping on himself all day. As the two men relaxed for a few minutes in the living room, Hatch said, half in jest, "It's the beginning of the holiday season. Seems like a good time for a bottle of wine."

Trevor glanced over at him and kept rocking.

"Probably not a good idea." Hatch laid his head against the back of the sofa.

"Probably not," he heard Trevor say softly. Hatch became lost in trying to remember Halloweens with Jenna and Ryan.

twenty

NOVEMBER SEEMED TO CRAWL BY FOR HATCH. For one thing, he was constantly anxious about the possibility that Tattoo and Assistant would show up again in their Escalade demanding more money. Of course, Hatch regretted that he had ever heard of James Quan and that he had ever sat in on what seemed like a few harmless poker games. Poker was all the rage and was being legalized in more locations—but not in King County. Hatch hadn't thought that running up a five thousand dollar tab was that big a deal. After two months of sobriety he could see how foolish he had been. He was unemployed. His finances were in shambles. He was seldom sober enough to clean up the messes he was making. Now he was paying for all that in spades—so to speak.

Every time he walked to or from work, every time he left the shop, and every time he thought of his disastrous Halloween, he looked around for the black Escalade. His demons were never far from the door.

As expected, the days grew shorter, colder, and toward the end of the month, much wetter. While Seattle has only a few snowy days each winter, North Bend, at a higher elevation and just west of Snoqualmie Summit, has more. Mount Si, a couple of miles from town, rose to 4,300 feet. Snow covered the mountain's summit from early November on. Hatch's habit of looking up the valley toward the east became another source of anxiety.

He still felt driven to travel on. He felt that he was weaving himself into a tighter social fabric in North Bend that must soon be abandoned. He could not stay here permanently. In the first place, there was so much unfinished business in Seattle. Sooner or later, he had to return and pick up the pieces—financially, professionally, and, of course, with his family. He didn't feel that life with Patty was over. At least he hoped it wasn't. He had two kids there that he loved and increasingly wanted to be with.

But he could not go back now. He realized he was on a honeymoon in North Bend. He had found some great friends—rather they had found him. For the first time, he had established a healthy pattern for living. He was sober. He was saving money—though he now owed Sylvia. All these were positive steps. But Hatch didn't kid himself about being ready to return home. The real changes that needed to be made were on the inside. If he was daily hanging by a thread in this supportive environment, how long could he hold on if he were thrown back into the chasm from which he had been lifted? A day? Perhaps a few? He wasn't ready.

But why travel eastward? Hatch couldn't answer that. He did know that fate had singled him out and had already worked miracles in his behalf. Trevor was a miracle. Sylvia another. The space of time in North Bend was a third. He had to keep going. Something lay there where the sun rises. When he found that, he'd have the strength he needed. Or so he hoped.

But he couldn't leave now. Each day the weather worsened. He was committed through the end of the year, and he was now morally obligated to stay until he had repaid Sylvia.

Hatch worked tirelessly in the shop. He and Sylvia hardly talked about anything other than work. There was little to say. She had stuck her neck out in a major way for him, possibly saving his life. She didn't remind him of it, but she did give him the impression that she didn't want any more of those sorts of opportunities.

He felt like a man on probation. This must be the way people feel that dodge bullets. Or receive last minute reprieves from the governor. Or receive chemotherapy that brings welcome remission of the cancer. He felt grateful to her. He felt respectful of her. He felt a huge obligation to make things turn out right for her.

When payday came, Hatch found his pay envelope by the cash register just as he had before Halloween. He took it to the office, laid it on her desk, and said, "You keep this. It's my first payment." Then he added, "Of many."

"No, you take it," she replied in a very business-like manner. "You need that to live on."

"I hardly need anything to live on," he replied.

Sylvia looked him up and down, then said simply, "Go buy yourself some decent clothes. *Your* appearance is bad for *my* business." She turned back to the online order form she was completing.

"Ouch." Hatch didn't dare say more. He took the envelope and retreated.

The following Monday, Hatch came into the shop wearing a new outfit. A burgundy stripe in the shirt and a very tasteful blue in his tie set off the camel colored slacks. His belt and tasseled loafers worked perfectly. His hair was freshly styled, and Sylvia could smell his subtle aftershave from several paces.

Sylvia caught her breath. Suddenly she wished she had never taunted him about his appearance. Now she had to live with him. Now she had to resist him. *I may have created a monster,* she thought.

This man was still too heavy for his size, but he really knew how to dress. She noticed that he was completely at home in the new clothes—as if he were born in them.

Without doubt, Hatch could knock out women in every direction. Sylvia found herself wondering about his ex-wife. At first, she asked herself, *How could a woman turn that loose?* But Sylvia was no schoolgirl. She had been around the block a few times. She knew that looks sometimes conceal dangers. Still, her prevailing thought as she watched the new Hatch was, *There is more to this man than I thought. And maybe more than he knows.*

"Good morning," Hatch said casually. He turned immediately to his work. "Now let's see what we can do for *your* business."

"Ouch," she said. But she did not dare say more.

Trevor was away through the Thanksgiving holiday. Sylvia had a bad cold and asked Hatch to tend the shop. Business was slow. High gasoline prices were slowing road travel, and the ski season was not yet underway. The shop was tidied, and Hatch had plenty of time to think. His thoughts drifted to Patty and the kids.

twenty-one

WHEN TREVOR RETURNED FROM THE THANKSGIVING HOLIDAY, something had changed in his demeanor. He seemed more preoccupied, though Hatch didn't feel free to quiz him about what he might be thinking. Closeness had grown between the two men, but it was not based on the sharing of information. Hatch felt he knew the older man well, but still knew almost nothing about him.

Whereas Trevor's earlier style had married the capacity for vigorous and dramatic action with almost infinite patience, he now seemed somewhat impatient. Never one for words, he now seemed willing to say things only once, and cryptically at that. He spent much of his time at home corresponding, longhand. Trevor did not own a computer. As the days of December passed, Hatch felt increasingly that his welcome was wearing thin. He began preparing himself for this period of repose to end.

Hatch felt himself increasingly pinched between the inclination to get out of Trevor's way and the obligation to stay at the shop through the holidays. He tried to be invisible when at home with Trevor. He tried to be upbeat and energetic when at the shop. Sylvia had gradually rebounded from the Halloween crisis and her bout with illness at Thanksgiving. The shop had a festive air and business had picked up in advance of the coming holidays. Sylvia was clearly feeling at the top of her game.

In many ways, the chemistry between Hatch and Sylvia had become decidedly more friendly and in some respects more intimate.

Hatch could not be sure what Sylvia was feeling and did not want to bring things too close to the surface by discussing them outright. He continued to walk a fine line. He liked her a lot. Even though she was older than he, Hatch could easily imagine living with her, working with her. She was a great catch. A man looking for companionship would be insane to pass her by. But, deep within, he knew there was no future for them as a couple. His growing sobriety and more constant responsibility had reawakened feelings for Patty long masked by addiction and all the related forms of self-destruction. While he liked nearly everything about Sylvia, what he enjoyed most were the many ways in which she reminded him of Patty. This, of course, he would never say to her. Sylvia was a remarkable woman in her own right. He began feeling a need to protect her and to protect himself from her—not from her aggression in any sense, but from her innate beauty, her goodness, and her vulnerability.

twenty-two

"LET'S CLOSE UP AT 4:00 PM AND go home." Sylvia stood at Hatch's elbow as he dusted the hardwood beneath a rack of Pendleton shirts.

"Are you expecting visits from any Christmas ghosts tonight?" Hatch asked in a playful fashion.

"Do I seem like Scrooge to you?"

"No, not at all," he replied with a chuckle. "It's more a matter of my seeming like Bob Cratchit."

"Cratchit went home to a loving family and a pudding that smelled like laundry," Sylvia said, standing her ground. She usually talked to Hatch in passing, never standing still, never very close.

"Trevor's place doesn't offer the loving family, but it does smell something like laundry." Hatch leaned on the long-handled dust mop.

"What will you two bachelors do to celebrate the occasion?"

"With Trevor, every day is like the next." Hatch's brow furrowed a little as he thought about the recent changes in Trevor. "I don't think Trevor is feeling all that well. I expect tomorrow will be a quiet day at the homestead."

"Well, if things get too quiet, come over to my place, and I'll treat you to some of my homemade lemon pudding soufflé."

"Wow, that sounds fantastic. Is that an invitation?"

"I don't know. In legalese, does 'Come over to my place' constitute an invitation?

"If not explicitly, then certainly by implication," Hatch answered. "What time?"

"Tonight or tomorrow?" Sylvia was serious.

Hatch felt a tinge of caution. He didn't know where she was in her feelings about him, but he finally had some sense of where he was and felt he was beginning to know where he must go. Any serious complication to that evolving plan at this point might set him back light years. He knew he should say *tomorrow*, but reasoned that they were both stable enough to spend a friendly evening together without any complications. He would enjoy her company. He hoped she would enjoy his.

"Tonight sounds great. What can I bring?"

"Just yourself. I think I have enough in the pantry to see us through an evening."

❧

Hatch allowed himself a late afternoon nap before going to Sylvia's apartment. He felt refreshed when he awoke. It was dark in his cubbyhole under the eave, the only light coming in through the partially open door. As he lay for a few minutes, he thought back to the morning he first awoke in the cubbyhole to see Trevor standing over him. He had felt so constricted by the close spaces and the dingy appearance of everything in the house. Nearly four months later those feelings had vanished. So much good had happened to him as a result of his stay here that he had developed affection for the little room. Perhaps he would need to leave soon. He hoped that whatever came next would lead to as much good.

Dressed and leaving the house for Sylvia's, he saw Trevor sitting in the parlor. As usual, the older man was sitting at his secretaire writing.

Hatch was feeling festive and was grateful he had a place to spend the evening. He stepped into the parlor and said, "I hope I'm the first to read the novel when you finish it."

Trevor turned in his chair, took off his reading glasses, and asked, "Headed out?"

"Sylvia invited me over to sample her holiday pudding."

Trevor looked at Hatch thoughtfully. "You look good. I hope you both have a pleasant evening."

"Thanks. You too. I don't expect to be late."

Trevor nodded and turned back to his desk.

twenty-three

Hatch had been to Sylvia's apartment two or three times before, delivering items from the shop. He had never been inside. Sylvia greeted him in a moderately-cut black evening dress covered by an ornamental apron. The apron did not hide her eye-catching figure but added a charming touch of domesticity to her otherwise irresistible appearance. A careless lock of hair graced her forehead. She looked exquisite.

"Hi, Hatch. Come in."

"Wow," he said spontaneously. "You look gorgeous."

He could see Sylvia blush slightly, the way she had the first day they met in the shop. In the presence of this beautiful, alluring woman, Hatch's knees began to quake a bit.

"Your place is charming," he said, looking around. "Mind if I take off my jacket?"

"Please." She reached out for the jacket, touching Hatch on the upper arm. He felt electricity.

"Thanks," he said.

As Sylvia walked the jacket to a closet, Hatch knew this was wrong. For anybody else, maybe it would be a dream come true. But for him, no. Sylvia was a glorious, wonderful person. He did not want to hurt her in any way, and he didn't want to derail his plans. He needed them to survive.

His voice of reason told him to ask for his jacket, excuse himself, and leave, if not walking, then running. But looking around the apartment he could see with what care it was decorated. He already knew with what care Sylvia had prepared herself. He had no doubt that she had made painstaking efforts with any food or refreshments. He could not bear to hurt her. He must be on guard against himself, for her sake, for his sake, for the sake of others who were not here but whose interests were clearly at stake.

"Sit, Hatch." Sylvia gestured toward the couch and then sat beside him at a respectable distance crossing her legs, leaning back into the cushions and facing him.

"I used to say that to my puppy when I was training him. His name was Hatch, too."

"Sorry," she replied with a smile. "Guess I brought a little of the shop home with me."

"No, you didn't. I'm just making small talk to catch my breath."

"Are you uncomfortable?" she asked.

"You have the home court advantage. You're gorgeous. You're the boss. I may be a little intimidated."

Sylvia looked down at her nails for a few seconds. Then she looked steadily into his eyes. He blinked first and looked away.

Sylvia smiled and put her hand on his leg. "Relax, Hatch. You know that I like you. I consider you a friend as well as a fantastic employee. You're the best thing that has happened to the shop. Your coming has been extremely good fortune for me. I will miss you there when you leave. I will miss you more as a friend. I have really enjoyed you, even though it's been a little difficult understanding your feelings for me, if you have any."

She rose from the sofa and walked across the room to turn the volume down on the background music playing. She didn't turn it off, just softened it so they could visit without straining to be heard.

When she sat back down, she turned toward him, her knees touching his. "But I want you to know that I am not coming on to you tonight. I invited you this evening to enjoy the holiday. That's all I have in mind."

Another pause. Another smile. "I think that is all that can happen between us. And that is enough for me. You still have another life that is important to you. I envy you for that. Can we enjoy each other and the evening like that?"

"Sylvia, you are marvelous. A guy won't meet many women like you in an entire lifetime. Even once is a miracle."

Her smile showed a hint of sadness. "But, in your case, you've met at least one other. Is that right?"

"It is." Hatch nodded.

"And she was smart enough to grab your heart and hold on to it."

"She did. I rewarded her with a lifetime of sadness." Hatch spoke barely above a whisper.

"Maybe things aren't as bleak as you think." Sylvia patted his leg and folded her hands in her lap. "If she is near your age, there is still a lot of life ahead." Sylvia sighed. "Tell me about her and your life together."

Hatch looked at this magnificent lady and loved her for her genuine goodness. He smiled and placed his hand on hers. "You know, mine is not a pretty story. I'm hoping for a better ending. Instead, tell me about you."

"Oh, now there's a story," Sylvia said, laughing. "Let's try the soufflé while we try to think of something more inspiring to talk about." She rose and walked to a dining table spread with holiday refreshments. Hatch followed.

❧

Hatch awoke the next morning on Sylvia's sofa. His tie was loosened and his shoes on the floor nearby. He didn't remember falling asleep but lay for a few minutes getting in touch again with the pleasant surroundings. They had visited late into the evening. Sylvia had enjoyed two glasses of red wine but had not offered any to Hatch. Rather, she provided him a glass of delicious red grape juice. He had laughed. "I think I can handle a glass of wine."

"How long since you've had any alcohol?" she asked him.

"Labor Day," he replied.

She reflected on that for a few moments. "Well, you're not having any at my place. I made a special trip to get that grape juice. I hope you'll enjoy it."

"Of course," answered Hatch, sipping the juice. "Very tasty. Thanks for thinking of me."

Hatch had said thanks. He was glad of that.

Hatch listened for Sylvia but didn't hear her moving about. As he stood and stretched, he saw a note and a small gift in one of his shoes.

Dear Hatch, the note read. *What a thoroughly delightful evening we spent together. Thanks for your kindness. I will be away visiting through the day. I'm hoping to see you at the shop. Have a Merry Christmas. Love you. Sylvia.*

Wrapped in a gift box and bow were a pair of sterling cuff links inlaid with mother of pearl.

Hatch read the note again. "There's more than one way to grab a heart," he said out loud.

twenty-four

HATCH WALKED BACK TOWARD TREVOR'S HOUSE. THE streets were deserted. The sun was up, but as always, Hatch's gaze was drawn toward the mountains east of town. A higher band of clouds was moving in that direction. The peaks were snowcapped. He realized that a moment of decision had arrived, or would soon. Should he travel eastward as had been his plan for the past four months? Or should he stay here, perhaps until spring? Or should he go home to Seattle and start trying to pick up the pieces?

He stood a long time, hands in pockets, sunbathing his face off and on as the clouds rushed up the slopes of the Cascades. If he was really honest with himself at this moment, and he must be, he did not have confidence that he could go home and maintain the positive strides he had made. He reviewed his past history with alcohol realistically.

For many years, he was able to go without a drink for days at a time. He committed himself to quit whenever the heat was on from Patty or from his mom. He considered himself a binge drinker rather than an alcoholic. Binges were easier to hide, not so much from family, but from work associates and casual observers. Unfortunately, the binges had gotten closer together until they became one long binge.

Hatch had once spent three weeks in a detox center with only mild to moderate symptoms of AWS. He got sober and continued in therapy for more than six months until the world started closing in around him and he took a drink or two to calm his nerves. Of course, when you open the gate to let one horse out, all the horses follow.

Standing now in North Bend, he was grateful for his four months of sobriety and for Trevor and Sylvia who had helped him stay sober. But he didn't kid himself about his future. He had been here before. The real question was whether Hatch had made the break—permanently. Could he go back to Patty and assure her that he would never tumble off the wagon again? In his heart, he didn't think so.

He now felt at home in North Bend. He had friends whom he could trust and who were learning to trust him. Should he stay here permanently? No. Never. Not as long as there was a chance of repairing his relationship with Patty and with Jenna and Ryan. Should he stay until spring? Probably. Winter really wasn't a season for walking, hitchhiking, and looking for jobs.

With the options tumbling around in his head, but now resolved to ask Trevor and Sylvia for a few more months of their hospitality, Hatch reached Trevor's and stepped through the kitchen door.

Trevor was sitting at the kitchen table, reading the weekly paper. While he would normally nod a greeting to Hatch in coming or going and then return to his business, this morning he turned in his chair to face Hatch.

"Merry Christmas," Hatch said, smiling at Trevor.

"Sort of expected you home last night." Trevor's face and voice conveyed a sternness that Hatch had not expected. He didn't feel a need to check with Trevor when he planned to be out late. He was a renter, not Trevor's son.

At the same time, Hatch did not want to antagonize his benefactor.

"Have a nice evening?" Trevor asked.

"We did," replied Hatch.

"Am I guessing right that you have gotten to be a little sweet on Sylvia?" Trevor pursued the matter.

"She's a lovely, loveable woman. As you know." Hatch was giving forthright answers to forthright questions but was uncertain where Trevor intended to go with the conversation.

"She's been pretty good to you, hasn't she?"

"She's been very good to me. Why do you ask?" Hatch was

becoming a little alarmed, not that Trevor was asking anything Hatch was unwilling to share, but that it was so unlike Trevor to do so.

"Do you think you could take care of a woman like Sylvia?"

Hatch thought before answering. "Good question." He sat down across the table from Trevor, determined to carry the conversation through, wherever it might lead.

"She's a lot of woman. They don't come much better."

"I agree." Hatch nodded.

"I ask again, could you take care of a woman like her?"

"I hope so."

"Would you ever put her in danger? Ever expect her to bail you out of troubles you created?"

Trevor's meaning was now clear. Hatch had not told him about the crisis on Halloween Day. It was possible that Trevor could find out about it. Possibly Sylvia would have told him. If so, Trevor hadn't said anything for two whole months.

"What are you getting at Trevor? Ask me a straightforward question. I'll give you an honest answer."

"I thought the question was straightforward. Could you take care of a woman like Sylvia? Protect her. Solve your own problems without dragging her into them?"

Hatch's chin dropped to his chest. "No. In that respect, I'm not man enough to take care of a woman like her."

"Why not?" Trevor's tone was not cruel or aggressive. It sounded like he was really asking for an answer.

"Wow," Hatch replied. "You've put me on the spot."

He looked up at Trevor who sat silently.

"I promised you an honest answer. Here goes. I've never been a fighter. I want to be. I want to stand up for things that are right. Stand up for people who are in the right place. But I guess I've always been a coward."

Hatch was being honest. Brutally honest. Tears came to his eyes. He wiped them back with his sleeve.

"What's the worst that could happen to you?" asked Trevor.

"I guess to be killed."

"How many times in your life have you been in danger of being killed?"

"Maybe once?"

"Tell me about it."

Hatch returned Trevor's stare momentarily and then looked away. "I'm guessing you know about it. Halloween day. Two guys came to the shop demanding ten thousand to cover a gambling debt. They threatened to mess me up or kill me if I didn't pay. I asked Sylvia to loan me the money. She did. I gave it to them. For the rest of my life I'll wait for them to come back asking for more."

Trevor was still silent.

"You asked for the story. How'd I do?" The conversation had turned an otherwise pleasant Christmas morning sour.

"What are the chances they would really have killed you?" Trevor continued the interrogation.

"They held a gun to my forehead and threatened to use it."

"What would they have missed out on if they had pulled the trigger?"

"They wouldn't have gotten the ten thousand."

"Do you think they really intended to kill you?"

"No, probably not. But it seemed that way."

Discussed after the fact in the light of day, Hatch realized that his life probably hadn't been in the peril he feared.

"If they weren't planning to kill you and go home empty-handed, what else could they have done?"

"Beat me up?" asked Hatch.

"Ever been beat up before?"

"Not really," Hatch answered. "I was in a few scrapes as a kid."

"Did you enjoy them?"

"No, I hated them."

"Why?"

"First, because fighting is stupid. There are better ways to settle disagreements."

"Like getting a woman to buy your way out?"

"Ouch!" Hatch sighed. "You're right. There are probably times when a man needs to fight."

"Was Halloween one of those times?"

"Probably," admitted Hatch.

"Hatch, it seems to me that you live with a lot of probabilities."

"Probably." Hatch smiled.

"Let me ask you again, was Halloween a day to fight?"

Hatch nodded. "Yes, Halloween was a day to fight."

"Why didn't you fight?"

Hatch shook his head. "You've got me pinned here. I guess I didn't fight because they had a gun. There were two of them. They were big guys. They looked mean. I was afraid."

"Afraid that . . . ?"

"They would hurt me. Break my bones. Bust up my face. I didn't know, and I didn't want to find out."

"So you dragged a woman into it to save you from being hurt. To save your face from being busted up. A woman who had already done a lot for you. Maybe as good a woman as you will ever meet. Did you think at all about what they might do to her if you didn't give them what they wanted?"

Hatch shuddered. He rubbed his face and ran his fingers through his hair. "You're right. It was a miserable, cowardly thing to do."

Trevor leaned forward, elbows on his knees. "Of all the places they could hit you, which one worries you the most?"

Hatch's head was down. "I guess in the face."

"You guess?"

"No, I know. I don't want to be hit in the face."

Trevor nodded as though they had finally gotten to the heart of the matter. "I've been looking at your face," he said, searching Hatch's face. "I don't see a mark on it." Hatch nodded.

"Your face has been an important asset to you in your social and professional life, hasn't it?"

"Yes," Hatch replied.

"You've protected it well. And it is an impressive face. It makes a great first impression. But it's not your greatest asset, Hatch. In fact, on Halloween day, it was your worst enemy."

"What do you mean?" asked Hatch.

"Stand up for a second." Trevor stood up facing Hatch.

Hatch assumed that Trevor was going to give him a self-defense lesson. Actually, he welcomed that. He was not proud of his Halloween day behavior. He stood facing Trevor, his hands at his sides.

Without further warning, Trevor's right fist flashed in front of Hatch's face, striking him full in the mouth. Hatch's hands went instantly to his face. He stumbled backward, crashing into the door-jamb leading to the parlor.

"Aggh!" he screamed as he turned his back to Trevor. A few seconds later when the searing pain in his mouth started to ease, he looked into his cupped hands and found them covered with blood. The blood was dripping onto his clothes. He felt the inside of his teeth with his tongue to see if any were missing.

After a minute of damage assessment and control, he turned back to Trevor, his hands still over his mouth. "Geez, Trevor. What did you do that for?"

"How did that feel?" asked Trevor quietly.

"It hurt." Hatch's voice was up. He could feel the anger rising in him.

"It hurt, but it didn't kill. Think you'll recover?"

"Very funny." Hatch's sarcasm was clearly audible through his hands.

"Let me see it." Trevor motioned toward Hatch's mouth.

Hatch dropped his hands so Trevor could take a look at the damage.

"Doesn't look too bad," reported Trevor. "A couple of small cuts."

Again, without further warning, Trevor's fist, this time the left, flashed. This time the blow landed beside Hatch's nose below his right eye.

Again Hatch reeled and covered himself. "What are you doing?" he yelled.

"I'm showing you that you can survive having your face busted! I'm hoping you'll discover that your face is not the most valuable asset you have to protect."

"Thanks for the lesson." Hatch was enraged. He turned toward the bathroom. At that moment, Trevor grabbed him by the upper arm and swung him around, hitting him again, this time in the sternum. All the air exploded from Hatch's lungs. He dropped his hands as he gasped for air. Again, Trevor hit him in the face, striking him in the brow over his left eye.

Hatch fell to the floor and curled into a fetal position. He was crying, gasping for air, and pleading with Trevor to stop.

Trevor grabbed him by the collar and dragged him into a sitting position. "This doesn't end until you make it end." His voice was stern, demanding.

"Please," Hatch pleaded.

"No words," Trevor replied. "From here on out, you speak with your body. With your fists."

"No," cried Hatch.

Trevor slapped him hard on the side of his head. Hatch could hear his jaw pop.

"This is domestic abuse." He looked up at Trevor towering over him. "You'll go to jail for this."

"Don't think so," replied Trevor. Trevor slapped him again on the neck. The slap burned.

Hatch cried out. His emotions were in turmoil, his rage building and going out of control.

"Stop!" He struggled to his feet. Trevor hit him in front of the ear.

In a blinding rage, Hatch charged Trevor hitting him in the mid-section with his shoulder and driving hard with his legs. He pushed the bigger man backward, crashing into Trevor's prized secretaire. Trevor rolled to his side and came up standing beside the shattered secretaire. Hatch was slower in rising. Trevor hit him again. Hatch whirled, driving his elbow into Trevor's side and then hitting the warrior in his rock-hard stomach. Hatch felt the knuckles in his hand pop and pain shoot up his arm.

Another blow from Trevor hit Hatch in the back, on the shoulder blade. He knew now that he was struggling for his life. He had to look up. He didn't think he could beat Trevor, but he had to make his punches count. The only way to do that was to get Trevor on the floor. He gripped Trevor around the waist and tried to throw him to the floor. Impossible. Trevor hurled him to the side. Hatch hit the wall and felt every joint in his body recoil.

Again he charged Trevor. That had worked once but would not work again. Trevor's elbows came down on Hatch's back driving him to the floor.

Hatch wanted to lie still and die. But the battle had ignited a spark in him that would not extinguish. He rolled to his side and staggered to his feet. A third time he charged Trevor and hit him in the chest with his head. This rocked the big man backward. While he was off balance, Hatch drove his fist into Trevor's groin.

Trevor groaned and turned away from him, breaking contact with Hatch and stepping to the other side of the sofa.

"Okay." Trevor held up his hand. "You got in a good shot there. Let's call it a draw."

Hatch hurt everywhere. He was trembling all over and struggling for breath. He burned. He was covered with blood. "I'm not done!" he roared at Trevor.

Trevor smiled. "That's more like it," he said in a placating tone. "There's a man in there after all. You've kept him in prison for thirty-six years, but you just set him free."

Hatch glowered at him. He spit blood through his clenched teeth. "You ever try that again, and I'll kill you."

"Whoa! Back off, youngster," Trevor warned. "You did well. But know that I am just getting warmed up. You should be cooling down. I wouldn't die easily."

Hatch turned toward the kitchen. "What a mess." He wiped the blood from his face on his shirtsleeve. He sat on the kitchen chair and put his head in his hands. Increasingly, he felt a consuming sense of exhilaration spread through him. He couldn't tell which he wanted to do worse, laugh or cry.

Trevor laid his hand on Hatch's shoulder. "Let's take a look and see where the blood is coming from."

Hatch wrenched away violently. "Don't touch me," he warned.

"You think I'm your enemy, boy, but I may be the best friend you ever had. I won't touch you, and I won't hit you. Just let me take a look at things."

Hatch still refused. Trevor handed him a damp dishcloth and told him to go into the bathroom in front of the mirror and clean away the blood. When Hatch had done so, Trevor prevailed on him to put a butterfly bandage on the cut over his eye. The inside of his upper lip was badly cut, and Trevor thought it needed stitches. Two of Hatch's knuckles looked like they needed to be x-rayed, as did his jaw.

Hatch let Trevor drive him to a first-aid clinic, knowing he would have to pay cash for the treatment. The rest of Christmas day was spent in mending themselves and Trevor's belongings. Hatch would not talk. It seemed Trevor could hardly be quiet.

Finally, Hatch asked him, "So now that you've wrecked my face, what asset do I have to protect that is of more value than that?"

"I hoped you'd ask," replied Trevor. "Your greatest asset is your character. But since it has been hiding behind that pretty face all these years, it has sort of shriveled up. With the face out of the way, I think the character is going to come out of hiding."

"I hate you," said Hatch coldly.

"Go ahead. Keep saying all those things that you are going to regret." Trevor smiled.

twenty-five

THE DAY AFTER CHRISTMAS FELL ON A Friday. Trevor was off to work early. Hatch put his sheets in the washer and then threw them in the dryer before leaving for the shop. He would walk home at noon and remake the bed. He had decided that this would be his last morning at Trevor's house. He wrote a note, and left in on the now lopsided secretaire with his December rent. The note was scrawled with his bandaged right hand. It read:

Trevor, here is December's rent. I hate you. But I also owe you more than a little bit of thanks can repay. Still, thank you. I hope to see you on my way back to Seattle—whenever that may be. Hatch.

Before leaving the house, he took one last look at his image in the mirror. The stitches over his left eye were bandaged. His lip was still badly swollen and the suture thread from the stitches inside his mouth showed a little when he parted his lips. His right eye and cheek and the left side of his face in front of the ear were an angry black and red that would resolve into very visible bruises and a classic shiner. Worst of all, one corner had broken off of his front tooth. He planned to buy a pair of inexpensive sunglasses to cover as much of the damage as possible. He wore the clothes that Trevor bought him on his first day in North Bend. Bloodstains had ruined his newer outfit. He would decide whether to drop them at the local cleaners or drop them into a trash bin. He had trouble escaping the feeling that four months of progress had been erased in ten minutes on Christmas Day.

❧

Hatch was on time to open the shop. He tried to relish every step of the walk from Trevor's to the shop, knowing this would be the last morning he would make the walk. He was conscious of his appearance as perhaps never before. He tried to imagine what Sylvia would say, how she would look when she first saw him. While he had trouble shaking the feeling of doom that the fight had left inside him, Hatch admitted to himself that he was unexplainably proud of his battle scars, ridiculous as that seemed. It was not as though he had survived a near-death experience. He couldn't explain Trevor's motives, but when the heat of battle wore off, he realized that in some twisted way Trevor had intended the beating to do Hatch good. Already he sensed that it *had* done him some good. He felt differently about himself this morning.

Sylvia's reaction was much as he had expected.

"Hatch, what on earth happened to you?" She came to him immediately and stood on her tiptoes, her hands on his chest, and inspected the damage at close range.

"Just trying to pay off some of my bills," he responded as nonchalantly as possible.

He had not expected her next reaction. "Was it the men in the Escalade? Have they been back?"

Her anxiety showed on her face. He understood immediately that she was not only concerned for him but for herself. "No, not those guys. Are you worried about them?"

"A little," she confessed. "People like that are hateful. They are a plague to the rest of us. It's like the change in America after 9-11. They say that once you have been a victim of terror, the world is never really the same again. I think that has been true for me. I'm afraid they'll come back. It seems so unfair."

"That was my fault," Hatch answered. "I should have kept that away from your doorstep instead of dragging you into it."

Sylvia surveyed the damage he had sustained the day before. "You are being too tough on yourself. After all, they were the bad guys. They were the ones doing wrong."

Hatch looked at her earnestly. "That will never happen again. I'm sorry I betrayed you."

"Oh, stop!" she cried. "You are giving me chills. You know I have a soft spot for strong men—meaning *strong* in the good sense. But I do appreciate you saying that.

"Now," she continued, "are you going to tell me what happened?"

"It's a guy thing," he replied. "And actually, the time has come for me to give you my notice. I think I should be on my way."

"Right," she said, "in one more week."

"A problem has arisen. I don't have a place to live here any longer."

"I see," she replied after a pause, her brow wrinkling.

"Can you do without me this last week?"

"No, Hatch. Actually, I can't. I'm not sure what is happening, but we have a deal that you will stay to the end of the year. I have to hold you to it."

Hatch nodded. "You're right. It's my problem. I'll find a way to solve it."

"You can't stay at my place," Sylvia said, thinking out loud. Raising her eyebrows she continued, "But you could sleep on the cot in the storage room for those few nights. It won't be very comfortable, but certainly better than a bench down at Riverfront Park."

Hatch nodded. "Okay, I guess that could work."

She touched him on the arm and smiled. "Really, Hatch, you know that I don't want you to go at all. I will fight to keep you here every possible day."

"You've been so good to me, Sylvia. There's no way I can thank you enough. Thank you for the thousandth time." His eyes began to mist slightly. He blinked it away. "Shall we make the thirty-first the last day?"

"Unless I can talk you into staying longer," Sylvia replied.

twenty-six

O N JANUARY 1, HATCH STEPHENS ROSE FROM the storeroom cot where he had spent the night. Sylvia had invited him over the evening before to see the New Year in. They watched the festivities on television and toasted the event without alcohol—the first time that had ever happened in Hatch's life so far as he could remember.

Sylvia asked him what time he intended to leave and asked him to drop the key to the store at her apartment.

Hatch shivered as he walked the few blocks to Sylvia's. There was a dust of new snow on the walks and lawns. It was light by 8:00 AM. The sky was clear. That seemed like a good omen. But the sun had not yet crested the mountains. He was excited to see it rise. He could not help congratulating himself on making it this far. Four months ago his life was in the tank. That was Labor Day. He had remained sober since that day. January seemed like the wrong season to go walk about, but he felt this was the right thing to do and the right time to do it. He had no idea what lay ahead, but he also felt an internal sense of confidence that whatever came was meant to be and would do him good. That all seemed very cheesy, but real.

Sylvia was dressed and waiting for him.

"Just came to say good-bye," he greeted her at the door.

"I've changed my mind. You can't go." She wasn't smiling.

"Gotta go," he replied.

"All right then, a compromise. It's a holiday. The shop is closed. I haven't been out of town for a long time. I'll let you go if you let me drive you to Yakima."

"No way," he said, laughing. "This is like a pilgrimage—a crazy, unexplainable pilgrimage. Something I have to do alone."

"Nice try." She smiled as she locked the door to the apartment behind her. "You're making that up. Everybody knows that pilgrimages are usually done in groups. Dorothy, the Scarecrow, the Tin Man, and the Lion were all seeking Oz. The Knight, the Miller, the Monk, and the Wife of Bath were all headed to Canterbury together."

As Sylvia headed east on I-90, the sun crested the Cascades and shown brilliantly through the windshield. Hatch felt a thrill that he could not share. The pair visited pleasantly as they approached and passed over Snoqualmie Summit and started down the east slope of the Cascades. When finally they reached the exits to Yakima, Sylvia asked, "Well, Pilgrim, where do you want me to drop you?"

"This convenience store at the exit might be a good place to start. Sylvia, I know I keep thanking you over and over, partly because you have been a wonderful friend, and partly because it feels so good to be able to say *thank you*. I owe you so much. The same for Trevor."

"Hatch, you have also brought something precious into our lives. Business is better and life has been, well, livelier while you've been in North Bend."

Hatch stepped out of the car. "I think I'll be back."

"Come and see me."

"I have to. I have to deliver a check."

"That's very flattering. The kind of assurance every woman wants to hear."

Hatch smiled at her, still conscious of the stitches inside his lip. "Thanks for bringing me this far."

Before he closed the door, Sylvia said softly, "Hatch. I hope everything will work out for you. I really do. But, if you find that she has moved on in her life, please come see me." Then she smiled. "I may still need help in the shop."

Hatch pulled the coat tight around his throat as he watched Sylvia Rencher drive away.

twenty-seven

HATCH TOOK A DAY AND A HALF reaching I-84, the main east-west interstate from Portland that he thought would carry him most directly to Denver. He could not explain to himself why he was drawn to Denver, but from the first moment he awoke on a Seattle street the day after Labor Day, he had more or less constantly been preoccupied with the rising sun and traveling eastward. Denver seemed to be the gateway to the West, therefore the gateway to the East as well. He didn't have any idea where he would go from Denver. Just getting there seemed a large enough undertaking at the moment. Of course, he could just buy an airplane ticket and be there by afternoon. But this entire journey, slowly as it had unfolded, was instinctual, and his instincts told him to cover the ground between where he now stood and Denver. The thought had often occurred to him that the impulse he was heeding might carry him beyond Denver to somewhere else. New York? London? Athens? Calcutta? Sydney? Honolulu? Seattle? Could this quest carry him around the world? Would he or anyone he cared about still be living by the time he traversed the globe? And to what purpose was all this?

These unanswerable questions were on his mind again as he stood with thumb extended near the freeway entrance to I-84 East next to a truck stop outside Hermiston, Oregon. The sun was shining, but the day was bitterly cold. He had reached Hermiston late in the previous evening by a series of rides. Fortunately, his last ride, an independent trucker headed down the Columbia River to Portland, had dropped him in front of a seedy Hermiston motel showing a vacancy sign.

Hatch was slow to rise in the morning and walked most of the way to the freeway before a kid in a local market delivery truck picked him up. Hatch suspected that his appearance was hindering him from getting rides with motorists who, for the most part, were inclined to be suspicious of anyone thumbing a ride anyway. All of his rides thus far were with men. He could understand why women were afraid to chance picking up a hitchhiker, but that did not bring him much comfort while he shook from the cold.

The coat and gloves he bought at the thrift store in North Bend looked okay, and the coat was warm enough. He found, however, that the gloves just did not protect his fingers from the biting cold. He kept switching thumbs in order to warm a hand in his coat pocket.

I-84 is a major freeway. From Hermiston it crosses the state of Oregon with only a few population centers enroute. These include Pendleton, LeGrand, and Ontario. Hatch felt that if he could get a ride, chances were good it might carry him to the next town. That was far better than being dropped at some obscure exit where few or no rides might surface for the next leg. All in all, he admitted to himself, hitchhiking was no picnic. In warm weather, he might prefer to just begin walking, but that was impossible under present circumstances.

He was about to walk back to the truck stop and warm himself when a big Dodge Ram pickup with a crew cab pulling a flatbed trailer passed him as the driver picked up speed on the freeway entrance ramp. Perched atop the trailer and covered by a tarp was the profile of a car that Hatch knew by heart. He dropped his thumb and watched the procession, his mind flooded by old memories.

Lost in thought, he hardly noticed that the pickup slowed to a stop partway down the entrance ramp. Hatch had turned back toward the oncoming flow of traffic and raised his thumb once more when he heard the pickup driver honk. Realizing that the truck had stopped for him, he began jogging toward it. As he reached the trailer, already out of breath, he could not resist the temptation to raise the cover just enough to see the paint color of the car being transported. His heart leapt. The finish was gunmetal gray. The wheels were vintage. He knew most of the rest of the car even without seeing it. He dropped the cover. Reaching for the door handle, he noticed that the truck belonged to Lester Auto, LLP, of Nampa, Idaho.

Pulling the door shut behind him, Hatch turned to face the driver. "Thanks for stopping."

"Hey, not at all," came the booming voice. "Where are you headed?"

The truck's driver was a man of about Hatch's age. His appearance was unremarkable, except that his round face lit up in a smile. He was clean shaven, with a day's growth about comparable to Hatch's. He wore a checkered flannel shirt and down vest above denim jeans. In the roomy cab of the Ram, Hatch could see that he wore a pair of high top leather boots. Country pop music played in the background. The man extended a hand toward Hatch.

"Toward Denver," Hatch replied drawing off his glove to shake hands.

"Long flippin' trip for this time of year," returned the driver as the truck gained freeway speed. "I'm not going that far, but I'm headed in that direction. My name is Mark Lester."

"Lester Auto, Nampa Idaho" said Hatch, nodding.

"Right," Mark said over his right shoulder. "I noticed you checking out the XKE. Know anything about them?"

"I've owned two Jaguars over the years." Hatch blew on his hands and then held them up to the heater vents on the dash.

"No joke?" asked Mark. "Tell me about them."

"The first was a '71 V12 coupe just like the one on the trailer. It had 317 horses and four on the floor. Gunmetal finish and black skins." Hatch shook his head as he recalled the details. "I loved that car. My dad bought it for me while I was in college. Trying to keep me from going over the edge, I think."

"Really?" Mark replied. "We'll have to check the title history of the baby on the trailer and see if it's your old car come home." The constant smile on Mark's face seemed at home there.

"I sold the '71 when I started law school," Hatch continued. "My girlfriend, Patty, had an uncle who owned a '59 XK, one of the original 150s with 245 horses. It was a beauty, but he and earlier owners had let it run down a little. It needed some pepping up. So I bought it with the proceeds of my sale."

Hatch had almost forgotten how good it felt to talk about these cars that were the first loves of his life. All present concerns faded as he spoke. He was transported into that bygone era.

"I'm amazed that you can still remember the names of your college sweethearts," Mark said, laughing.

Mark's laugh was contagious. Hatch found himself replying with a laugh. "In this case, Patty became my wife and the mother of our kids."

"So, she is Mrs. . . . ?" Mark asked with a shrug.

"Sorry, the name is Hatcher. Hatcher Stephens."

"Okay. Hatcher and Patty Stephens, of?"

"Of Seattle."

"Hatcher and Patty Stephens of Seattle," Mark said with finality. "And the little guys?"

"Little guys?" asked Hatch. "Oh yeah. The children are Jenna and Ryan, ages eight and six."

"Hatcher, Patty, Jenna, and Ryan. The Stephens. Gotcha. Back to the '59."

"I had a friend who was into muscle cars. His family had means so he had a garage with tons of tools and a paint bay. We gave the '59 a face-lift. I eventually sent it out for paint and upholstery."

Hatch completed the story with the appraising tone of a wine connoisseur, "British Racing Green with tan hides."

Hatch sobered. "I owned it until three years ago. Sold it for $85 K when we got into a little financial scrape and needed the money."

"Shoot, sorry to hear that," replied Mark good-naturedly, but with a nod that signaled he understood how those things happen. Hatch doubted that he understood.

"What are you driving now?" Mark asked.

Hatch's voice softened. He no longer felt his earlier exuberance. "I was making payments on a new BMW Z4. Lost that too."

"Sorry, Hatcher," replied Mark. "Sounds like you hit a heck of a stretch of rough road."

"Thanks," said Hatch. He hadn't been called Hatcher since Trevor changed his name. He liked the ring of it, but he also realized that the name, like his face, had become a façade he was prone to hide behind.

Not going to do that anymore, Hatch thought. He forced himself to smile. "Anyway, things are looking up." Hatch laughed. "The Z4 is a nice little car, but it has no provenance, no savoir-verve like these prestige cars." His tone became reflective.

Mark nodded but continued to smile. "Well, Hatcher, sounds like we have a lot of interests in common. Fortunately, we have a long drive ahead of us. I want to hear more."

Mark turned out to be a great listener. He had a knack for seeking information a bit at a time. By the time they gassed up in LeGrand, Oregon, Hatch had told him about the alcohol, the divorce, and losing his position with the firm. Mark received each new revelation with thoughtful respect. After many months, even years of hiding his life from himself and others, Hatch found this long and comfortable visit with Mark to be therapeutic. Hatch was sure that Mark had noticed the cuts and bruises still clearly visible on his face. Though he must have been curious about them, Mark seemed careful not to mention them.

Mark's wholesome demeanor and careful attention inspired Hatch to explore some of his thoughts and feelings out loud. Mark's own candor and self-disclosure helped Hatch feel a bond of trust beginning to grow between them. He realized that he was not able in four months to know Trevor as well as he knew Mark in eight hours. He had been away from North Bend for only two days, but it seemed a lifetime. Hatch missed Sylvia and Trevor already.

By the time Hatch and Mark crossed the Snake River into Idaho, it was late in the evening. Hatch now knew Mark to be the owner of a small auto restoration business in Nampa, Idaho, a suburb of Boise. Mark was a family man. He and his wife, also named Patricia, had a large family of seven kids, two dogs, and a parakeet.

Like many people in southern Idaho, Mark was a Mormon. He had started the business in his early twenties after filling a two-year mission for his church in Monterey, Mexico. His dream was to restore some of the old muscle cars. He loved the first generation Chevy Camaro, '67, '68, and '69. He had restored a handful of Plymouth Furys, a number of Corvettes, and a long list of Ford Mustangs.

"I was never good in school," Mark confided. "But I loved cars and thought I might have a good head for business. So far, being in the car business hasn't killed my love for cars, but I *have* discovered that I don't have much of a head for business, ya know? Dang! Isn't that the way it goes?" He laughed and pounded on the steering wheel with the heel of his hand.

"For example," Mark continued, "I moved from muscle cars to

the prestige market because of the bigger margins. Restored Mustangs could sell for $15, $20, to $30K. But Porsches start there and go to $70K. Jaguars, Aston Martins, Ferraris, Maseratis, from there to $150K. And the prestige market is worldwide. I know the business is there. But Lester Auto has grown steadily by 8 to 10 percent a year for ten years. That's nice, but I can't get the flippin' thing to take off."

As they talked, Hatch began to think about the night ahead. "I've really enjoyed our visit," he said with sincerity. "I am indebted to you. If you could let me off at a motel near the freeway, I would be very grateful."

Mark was quiet for a minute or two. "Say, Hatcher. I have been thinking these last few miles. As I said before, I need to turn a corner in my business. I'm thinking I need to hear a fresh perspective. How about staying in town overnight, and then coming down to the garage tomorrow and taking a look at things? I would be dang pleased to consider any thoughts you might have. You know these cars. It sounds like you know something about the buyers. I'm needing a little help with this flippin' thing."

Hatch was elated by the distance they had traveled in one day. He was eager to push on toward Denver. At the same time, he had just told Mark that he owed him for his generosity. He couldn't decline the man's request now. Spending a few hours in the morning would still leave ample time for him to catch a ride further east.

"Sure, I'd be glad to," he replied. "Mind you, I am not a businessman. The only item on my resume that is even remotely related would be four months as sales help in a retail shop. But I would love to see what you are doing."

"All right!" Mark had managed to smile for eight hours. "Tell you what. Patricia and I own several rental properties around town. One of them is a furnished one-bedroom not far from the garage. Why don't we put you up there over night? That'll save you a few bucks and will be an easy pick up for me in the morning."

Mark's apartment was tidy but tiny. Hatch wasn't sure what kind of people might constitute the renter pool. Newlyweds? Students? Widows? The single bedroom provided one double bed. Hatch's first item of business was a pit stop. The second was to crank up the electric wall heaters. One was located in the kitchen, the other in the bed-room. In a few minutes the hard chill in the air began to thaw.

Hatch sat on the edge of the bed, removing his shoes but leaving his socks on. Reflecting upon the day, he could hardly believe his good fortune. Traveling all the way from North Bend to Nampa, Idaho, a trip that could have been a horrid ordeal in the dead of winter, had gone too smoothly. He was beginning to suspect that a providential hand might be guiding his destiny. The four blessed months spent under the care of Trevor and Sylvia were far out of the ordinary. How could he have suffered a long and seemingly inexorable slide over many years from a position of privilege and now suddenly be lifted through the benevolent efforts of complete strangers? Hatch had placed little credence in matters of fate thus far in his life. But sitting this evening, well and whole, in a cheerful apartment in Nampa, Idaho, was suffi-ciently startling to prompt serious thought about the possibility that his life was not, after all, left completely in his fumbling hands.

twenty-eight

MARK LESTER ARRIVED AT THE APARTMENT EARLY the next morning. He had been away from home for three days buying and returning with the XKE from Portland, but said he wanted to have the car in the garage when his crew arrived for work. This being a Saturday, the crew would work only half the day.

Hatch helped him uncover and unload the XKE and roll it into a bay at the front of the garage. The garage was located off the Franklin Avenue exit from I-84 on Eleventh Avenue North. The location had been carefully selected years earlier to give quick access to parts dealers and had matched the company's original muscle car image. Now, the light industrial-commercial zoning didn't fit the business's revised image.

The garage was well organized. The floors were cleaned to the bare concrete and free of oil or grease. The walls were concrete block, left unfinished. Fluorescent light fixtures hung from exposed steel roof trusses. The windows were washed. Parts, supplies, and the more expensive tools and electronics were stored on open shelves along the walls. The front end of the elderly brick building featured a display window with a fully-restored 1990 Porsche Carrera on display. The front also housed a business office and small but comfortably furnished conference room.

Besides the newly-acquired '71 Jaguar XKE, the company's present inventory included a '67 Series One XKE, an Alpha Romeo, two Corvettes, and a second Porsche 911.

The crew of eight arrived a few minutes before 8:00 AM. One mechanic, the transmission specialist, called in just before eight saying that she was sick and would like the day off. Peter Berk, an Englishman, was the shop foreman. One of the mechanics and the two painters were all Mexicans. "All three are legal," Mark explained in front of them as he introduced them to Hatch.

In addition to the shop crew, Mark's office manager and sister-in-law Karynn was on hand for the shop meeting that began promptly at eight.

"As you can see, we brought in the '71 this morning. The papers are in order, and I looked it over as carefully as I could in Portland. Peter, inspect it carefully. If I missed something big, we have seven days to return it. We don't want to do that if we don't have to, but the dang thing has got to pay for itself, and us."

Mark was smiling as usual. "I'd like to introduce Hatcher Stephens of Seattle. Hatcher has consented to walk through the business with us and see if there are any things we can do to improve our customer base and profitability. Please cooperate with him."

Members of the crew nodded, some smiling, some already thinking about their next task. Hatch wondered whether the Mexicans understood what was said. Judging from first appearances, the only coolness exhibited by crew members was from Peter, the foreman, and from Karynn, the office manager. Hatch could imagine that they might be a little resentful of a visiting consultant, coming in to snoop around and make a few suggestions and then leave without any accountability for results.

As work got underway in the shop, Hatch could feel that the atmosphere was friendly but businesslike. He stood at Mark's elbow as Mark and Peter carefully inspected the '71, comparing notes, asking each other questions, and estimating costs. Almost immediately, Hatch felt the excitement of this enterprise. It was a small but highly-fired team of people willing to pit their know-how against all market forces and competition, just for the love of craftsmanship. The place fairly hummed with industry. Hatch watched Mark with envy. Mark was unassuming, happy to let others show their stuff. He referred most of the technical questions to Peter.

Hatch caught up to Peter during the morning break and tried to strike up a conversation but could feel Peter's resistance.

"Tell me about your background," Hatch asked Peter.

"What do you want to know?" Peter asked, his tone aloof, emphasizing his British accent.

"Where were you trained?" It was the only question Hatch could think of at the moment.

"I started as an apprentice with Bentley when I was sixteen years old. They stumbled in the late-1970s. I could have moved to one of the other major manufacturers, but they were all a bit dodgey at the time. The whole industry was on the skids in the 1980s and early '90s. So I took a chance on a small company like this one in Surrey. It was called Prestige Restorations. Perhaps you have heard of them."

"Indeed, I have," replied Hatch.

"After a dozen years with Prestige, learning all aspects of restoration, I fell upon the chance to come to the States working for a family prominent in auto restoration near Miami."

Peter sipped on a soft drink. Hatch had not noticed until now that none of the crew was smoking. Some drank coffee from thermos containers.

Peter continued, "Didn't like Miami. Didn't like the family. Didn't much like the States. Thought of going home."

He paused as if considering how much to say. "By sheer happenstance, I spoke on the telephone with a startup competitor in far away Idaho. I didn't even know there were autos in Idaho. I had thought beforehand that Yanks in the West were still riding horses. But I was taken with Mark. He impressed me as being down-to-earth. He flew me out for a look-round. We hit it off. Been here for the better of nine years."

Peter smiled only perfunctorily and seemed to be saying as little as possibly, trying to honor the boss's direction to cooperate with the visitor.

"So you came to Idaho, bringing thirty years of world-class experience with you." Hatch hoped he didn't sound too patronizing, but he needed to penetrate Peter's reserve—or resentment.

"Something like that," Peter replied in no softer tone.

Hatch kept thinking back to his conversation with Peter as he watched and quizzed other crew members through the morning.

Though he had planned to wrap up his visit by noontime and be on his way, he found that by the time the crew was ready to quit work he wanted to know more about the business. He didn't think he had much to contribute, but he wanted to know how people made businesses like this work. Most of all, he loved being around the cars. Parts, interiors, systems, even lubricants and tires excited him.

Mark was away through much of the morning. When he returned just before noon, he brought his family with him. His two oldest children, a girl and a boy, came into the shop and talked freely with the crew. Hatch noticed that they did not touch anything, but they looked without restraint.

Mark beckoned Hatch to the front end. There he introduced Hatch to Patricia. Mark and Patricia stood together, his arm around her waist. She was a petite woman with long blond hair, casually dressed, no makeup. She held a toddler in her arms. Six other children were actively engaged in doing something or other. Just the sight of seven children together took Hatch's breath away.

"Hatcher is from Seattle," Mark began. "He has two children, Jenna and Ryan. They are the same ages as Trina and the twins." Patricia smiled pleasantly but plainly.

Turning to Hatch, he introduced the children. "The two out in the shop are Gina and Scott. This is Trina, age 8, Tiffy and Tyler, age 6, Nate, age 4, and the baby is Angela. That's the whole fam." Mark smiled proudly as he introduced his brood.

"Hi, everybody," Hatch said. Reaching a hand to Patricia, he said, "They are lovely children."

"They can be a handful," she answered.

"But we love them all, don't we, sweetie?" Mark was quick to insert.

"We do," Patricia replied.

Aunt Karynn rubbed Nate's unruly hair and put an arm around Tiffy's shoulder, leading her into the office.

Nate, hands on his hips, looked Hatch directly in the face and asked, "What happened to you?"

"Whoa, Nate." Mark stepped in to interrupt the question. "That may be pretty personal."

Hatch suspected that Mark was secretly as curious about the cuts and bruises as his son but chose to stay on the right side of propriety.

"It's okay," replied Hatch. Looking to Nate, who was rounder, seedier, and more blunt than the other children as though he came from another family, Hatch explained, "I had to save a princess from a whole gang of bad guys. They beat me up pretty badly, but they all look worse than I do."

Nate screwed up his face as if in doubt.

"That's a lie," said Hatch, smiling. "But it's a much better story than the real one."

Nate shrugged matter-of-factly and walked away.

Mark left Karynn to close up. "How did you make out this morning?" he asked Hatch as Patricia shepherded the children toward the door and the waiting minivan.

"Well," replied Hatch. "I have a couple of ideas that may be helpful. But I would like to know a little more."

"Take your time," said Mark. "Stay in the apartment until we wrap this up. And don't worry about the rent. We'll square when we're done."

"Karynn," Mark called to his sister-in-law. "Will you give Hatcher the keys to the parts truck so he can get around until Monday? Thanks, kiddo."

Turning to Hatch, Mark explained, "Hatcher, Patricia and I have a busy day tomorrow or we would invite you over for dinner. I'll see you here Monday morning. We can talk more then." Mark followed his family out the door.

twenty-nine

Hatch hadn't been behind the wheel since Labor Day. Driving back to the apartment on Saturday afternoon, he wondered again what might have become of his Z4. He knew he had left it on the street in Seattle. The city had doubtlessly towed it to their impound lot where it had probably stayed until the finance company came looking for it. The finance company had doubtlessly filed a bad credit report on Hatch. Nothing new there. It would have sold the car to a dealership or at auction, turning the unpaid balance over to a collection agency. Hatch guessed they were looking for him to the tune of fifteen thousand dollars.

He did a little math as he washed up, deciding to get his dinner at a buffet. Fifteen thousand for the car, ten to Sylvia, three credit cards maxed out at six each. All in all, he was looking at nearly fifty thousand of outstanding debt. He had been gone four months. All his creditors but Sylvia were looking for him now. He had to pay. He wanted to pay. He would develop a plan and get started soon. But he still had unfinished business in the east.

Hatch ate at a buffet, not because he liked the food, not because he liked the atmosphere, not because it was inexpensive, but because buffets normally did not serve liquor. Especially now that he had wheels again, he had to be careful as he established new patterns. The places he frequented, the routes he drove, all of these had to be carefully chosen to bypass any possibility of stopping to get a drink.

Hatch knew that he needed to establish healthy, constructive patterns that excluded alcohol. He needed to fill his life up with positives so that no room was left for the destructives. After eating, he drove around to get acquainted with Nampa. He was looking specifically for a public gym. As he looked, he passed several watering holes. He made mental note of their locations. These were streets he would never drive down again.

He finally found a Gold's Gym in a strip mall. Parking in the nearest empty stall, Hatch walked in to check out the prices. All facilities like this one were fairly similar. Since he would only be in town for a few days he wanted to start making a daily workout part of his healthy pattern. He would need to do the same everywhere he stopped as he traveled eastward.

He liked what he saw at the gym. They allowed daily admission and he had a free evening, so Hatch decided to start immediately. He asked the girl at the desk for directions to the nearest sporting goods store, which happened to be a few doors away in the same strip mall. There, paying as little as he could, he bought a pair of cross-trainer shoes, a pair of shorts, and a workout shirt.

Returning to the gym, Hatch saw himself in a full-length mirror for the first time in many months. He had probably lost a little weight while living in North Bend. Perhaps as much as fifteen pounds. He expected the weight to melt of, when he stopped drinking. He was disappointed.

Surveying his bulk, he felt sorry for Patty. When they married, Hatch was a trim 165 pounds and very fit. In a dozen years of marriage he put on an additional hundred pounds. During that same time, Patty didn't add any weight. She kept herself in shape for him. He let himself go for her. That was not what she deserved. That must also change.

Hatch noted from a posting on the wall that the gym offered sparring sessions. A photo showed two men in boxing gloves and headgear squared off with each other. He decided to try sparring as soon as his facial wounds were healed. *Next time I get into that situation, I'll know how to take care of myself,* he resolved, thinking back to Halloween.

After his dinner digested, Hatch did what he thought of as a light workout. He used the circuit machines to exercise each of his muscle groups, using only enough weight or resistance to discover a starting point for future workouts. He could build from there.

Returning to the apartment, Hatch was pleasantly fatigued. Furthermore, he felt good about his first evening alone. He had done what he must. He would set healthy patterns, avoid pitfalls, and pray that no crises would overwhelm him in the meantime. He meant praying in a figurative sense since he had not actually prayed to deity since reaching his teen years.

With nothing else to do, Hatch went to bed early. On Sunday, he worked out again, ate sparingly, and bought himself a copy of Victor Hugo's *Les Miserables* that he spent the remainder of the day reading.

Thirty

Eight o'clock Monday morning and Hatch both arrived at Lester Auto at the same instant. The workday began as it had on Saturday morning with a crew meeting. Mark made a few comments about the vision of the company and then gave Karynn time to talk about accounting, inventories, time cards, and paychecks. He also gave Peter time to make assignments and talk about production schedules. All this was handled very efficiently and the crew was soon off to work.

Hatch noted clearly from the discussion that the company watched its pennies. They were working hard to keep costs down and productivity up. Hatch was mystified by the generous and casual treatment he was receiving from Mark. Hatch was aware, for example, that he had driven several dollars worth of fuel out of the little parts truck. He had lived several days in Mark's rental property without paying. When he had a chance to sit down with Karynn on Monday morning, he asked how Mark handled such matters.

Karynn was younger than her sister, Patricia, Mark's wife, by several years. She was also a pretty woman, and she took care of herself. Of course, Karynn was single and was not caring for a husband and seven children. That doubtlessly made some difference in their lifestyles, Hatch reasoned—some huge difference. Still, not knowing either of them well, Hatch could only guess that Karynn did not have the temperament to fill a house with children and dedicate her life to nurturing them. She seemed more outgoing and more outward thinking. And she did not seem to like Hatch.

For a man like Hatch, who had always wanted to be liked—always needed to be liked—by others, unprovoked interpersonal resentment was both a mystery and an annoyance. Why was it that some people disliked him before ever speaking? It happened more with men than with women, he reasoned, mostly because of his face and his manner. That had been more true when he was younger and more physically attractive. The hundred pounds had cost him dearly in terms of his self-confidence with women. At the same time, those pounds had protected him from a string of aggressive and unscrupulous women. He could not deny that in some regards he had welcomed the weight to make himself less attractive. At the same time, he knew the need for female attraction was—or at least had been—an essential element in his makeup.

His present condition clouded the picture. He could not tell whether some women now disliked him because he was fat and repulsive to them, or because he had a pretty face and they did not trust him.

Trevor had done his best to simplify the riddle by rearranging the pretty face. Since his face was now scarred and bruised, Hatch concluded that Karynn, who was shapely and clearly body-conscious, did not like him because he was fat. He decided that since he was going to be in the business for only a day or two longer, he had little to lose by asking Karynn about her feelings. At the last second, however, he cowered and opted to use Peter as a straw man.

"As I have visited with some of the crew," he explained to her, "I have the impression that Peter doesn't like me being here. Either he doesn't like me personally, or he thinks I am a threat somehow to him or to the company. Any thoughts about that?"

Karynn smiled slightly but answered Hatch directly. "I can't really speak for Peter."

"How about speaking for yourself? Am I sensing the same thing from you?"

Her face blanched slightly. "In my case, it is not you as a person. It has to do with your being here." She fell silent.

"I guess that is comforting. I'm not sure what it means. How is my being here uncomfortable for you?"

Hatch was now on familiar ground. He was trained to interview.

He liked to ask questions. He always wanted to understand what others were thinking and feeling. At one time it had been a key to professional success. Now he considered it key to his personal success.

Karynn answered, "My brother-in-law is a great guy. He is good to work for in most ways. All the members of the crew like him, respect him, would do almost anything for him. And they believe in the company. He pays us all well. At the same time, he has very big dreams. I mean, here we are in a Podunk town, and he is talking about marketing prestige autos around the world. I think he would eventually like to manufacture his own cars. He's always drawing up his ideas, talking them through with us. We all have a profit sharing arrangement, so if things go great and the company gets big, it could mean a lot of money for us."

She paused to let Hatch catch up to her thinking. He nodded.

"That is especially true for some of the crew. We have three Mexican nationals who have become naturalized citizens. They send most of their earnings home to family members. They are exceptionally skilled, and they work very hard. They are as loyal as workers can be.

"But the kind of growth he dreams of keeps eluding us. He asks our opinions, but he doesn't trust them. It's frustrating. At the same time, he keeps bringing outsiders in who don't know the business. You're not the first. He seems to trust them more than us. For my part, I just don't want to play that game anymore. No offense, but if you don't know the business, I'm not interested in your suggestions. I can't say for sure, but I think Peter feels the same way."

Hatch sat silently, looking at this woman and realizing how capable she seemed. She was another in a lengthening line of similarly able women Hatch had known—women like Patty, Grace Cunningham (and his other associates at Austin, Stephens, and Park), Sylvia, and now Karynn.

"I can't argue with your view of things. In fact, I would likely feel the same way were I in your shoes. I'm wondering if Mark is seeking my ideas, not as someone who understands the business—he has you for that—but as someone who understands the clientele. I have owned every one of the cars you have in the shop right now, and several others. Seattle is a bigger city, and all my life I've been rubbing shoulders with people who drive or could drive these cars if they wished to."

He paused to let Karynn think about this. She nodded. "That could make sense, but I've talked to most of our customers on the phone from around the world. I've taken their orders and answered their questions. Why do you think you know them better than I do?"

"I'm not sure I do," Hatch replied. "But let's think for a second about what you just said. You are thinking of customers. I guarantee you that these people do not think of themselves as customers. Customers just buy. They are nothing but talking checkbooks, or to be more contemporary, talking credit cards. Clients, on the other hand, are temporary financial partners. They not only hope to get something of value from the business, they also intend to make a contribution, financial and otherwise. They are seeking social as well as commercial exchange. The idea that you are taking an order from them or answering their questions would be offensive. Most of them would come to a purchasing negotiation very well informed—or they would bring with them someone who is very well informed."

Karynn was silent. Hatch hadn't intended to lecture her. "I'm sorry," he told her. "I'm telling you things you already know. I'm just trying to illustrate the kind of issues that may seem small to us but can be big for your clients."

Karynn remained silent. Hatch saw her swallow hard and take a deep breath. Then she nodded. "No need to apologize. Maybe I need to broaden my thinking."

In Hatch's judgment, her acknowledgment showed very favorably on her. People do not like to be corrected. He had done so fairly directly but, he hoped, tactfully. She had borne the brunt of correction and seemed ready to move forward. He hoped she wouldn't lay in wait for him, seeking a sweet revenge. She didn't seem that type. Hatch would wait and see.

Thirty-one

B Y NOON ON THURSDAY, HATCH CAUGHT UP with Mark as he was leaving for a Chamber of Commerce luncheon. "I think I'm ready to talk when you have a few minutes," he told Mark.

"Great," replied Mark with his trademark smile. "What if we get together with Peter and Karynn about four. Are you okay if they sit in?"

"Of course. They're your team. I think their reaction would be critical. They may have better ideas than I do."

By the time four o'clock rolled around, Hatch had dipped into all the soft aspects of the business. He had nothing to offer regarding fabrication, mechanics, electrical, body restoration, or accounting. All he could possibly comment on intelligently would be in the realms of company image, marketing, sales, and client relations. But he did think there were a number of ideas in those areas worth discussing.

He met with Peter and Karynn in the little conference room before Mark came in. He had been exploring Lester Auto's website and listening to some of the client contacts Karynn made throughout the afternoon. Now it was his turn to speak. He had always been good at client presentations and felt he could do well this afternoon. He didn't have much to lose since he would be on his way by morning. But he had been in the business for nearly a week and knew enough about the company and the people who made it succeed that he had started to care. Even though he wouldn't be around to see it happen, he wanted to leave a few suggestions that could move Lester Auto up to the next level.

"What I have to say today will be brief, and not earthshaking," he said to Peter and Karynn. "It's probably no different than what you've been telling Mark all along. But I do believe the approach I'm going to share is legit. We don't have time to review all the points before he gets here, but I'm open to discussion in every direction. Is there anything we need to say to each other before he comes?"

Peter and Karynn looked at each other. Karynn shook her head. Peter spoke up. "Just stick to the truth. We've already seen a string of experts come hat in hand, promising the sky. Between where we are and the sky are lots of dents and dings, lots of bad weather and bad luck, lots of early mornings and late nights. Don't try to impress Mark at the expense of what can realistically be achieved."

Hatch admired Peter, even if the feelings weren't mutual. Peter's was the kind of advice a business owner should hope for from his production supervisor. "I'll try to stay honest. Help me stay there," he said genuinely.

Mark came in. He was still dressed up from his noon luncheon. He smiled and nodded to Hatch to begin. "We'd better get this dang thing goin'. I'm bettin' you have a lot for us to chew on."

"A few suggestions that I hope are worth considering," Hatch began. "I'm an attorney and not a businessman, though in the final analysis we're all about business. And business is all about sales.

"You know your business far better than I. Coming to it as an outsider, I suggest that you first take a fresh look at your image. Your name, your building, your website, and to some extent, your business processes all seem like they would have been ideally suited to your muscle car beginnings. But when you started transitioning into the prestige market, I'm not sure you remade yourselves completely.

"For example, and please don't be offended by this," Hatch spoke directly to Mark. "The business name, Lester Auto, has a muscle car feel. It is straightforward, sparse, and efficient. That doesn't fit as well in the prestige market. The word *prestige* speaks to your new clientele. They understand it. They value prestige. They are the sort of people who want their possessions to be distinctive. They treasure precision craftsmanship. A name that reflects that value will attract the clientele you are seeking. *Classic Restorations, Precision Restorations, Prestige Restorations*—these are names that might work better for you."

Hatch waited and watched for Mark's reaction. Across the table, Peter was nodding slightly.

"We'll have to think about that." Mark's face was neutral. "There is quite a cost associated with a business name change, and it might stall our growth in the short run. What else?"

Hatch waited for Mark to turn to his associates, Peter and Karynn, and seek their reactions. Mark did not do so.

"Sharpening your image to appeal to more of the prestige market probably means an overhaul of your website and your facility. For example, if you jump online and look at the websites of your competitors, they not only feature their cars but also of their facilities and personnel.

"First, I would makeover the production area. Paint the floors an off-white color. Paint the walls. Upgrade the lighting to sweep away any visual shadows. Consolidate the parts and supplies in a closed-off area to keep the clutter out of sight. It may be a little less efficient in terms of the steps your workers take to get a part, but it will look better to clients peering into the inner workings of the business. Let them in. Let them see you at work. Put your lead workers in white lab coats with the company logo on the pocket. Put all of your mechanics, body, and paint craftsmen in matching coveralls. Pay to have a logo designed and display it everywhere.

"Let your brighter, crisper image show on your website. You're in a worldwide market. Reaching additional clientele in Europe, Canada, Australia, and parts of Asia could give you the sales boost you're seeking. You can still be distinctively North American, but you have to employ all the conventions that belong to the social and economic set that your potential clients are comfortable with.

"That also means an overhaul of your operating language, the ideas you convey, and the terminology you use." At this point he was speaking directly to Mark. "Client-oriented language should pervade the business and be common tender for all your associates."

Hatch knew he was slaying sacred cows on every hand. But he also knew he was right, so he pushed on to his conclusion. "What we're discussing here is total image enhancement. Keep the good that you already have. Enhance it to broaden your appeal to the prestige clientele. I'm suggesting that the reason you have not been able to break through into the upper crust might be that you have not yet met their standards.

"You see, the clients you are seeking do not want their autos worked on in a shop. They want autos that are products of a lab. Shops have germs. Labs are sanitary. A greasy fingerprint will make them shudder. So will slang communicated over the telephone or Internet. Cleanliness. Tidiness. Precision. Quality. Distinction. Luxury. Orderliness. These values have to pervade. They have to reach into every nook and cranny, echo from every tongue, in every ear, on every scratch pad—because they are you. That's the prestige market."

Hatch rested his case.

No one spoke.

Mark, whose eyes had been fixed on Hatch's face during his lengthy explanation, blinked, and his gaze went to his hands folded in front of him on the conference room table.

Then Mark looked at Peter. Peter was nodding his assent. He shifted his gaze to Karynn. Karynn returned his gaze but gave no indication of her reaction.

Mark broke the silence. "You are saying that the reason we have not reached cruising speed is that we have just been dabbling in the market. If we want to play with the big boys, we have to become fully committed. Burn our bridges behind us. Become our competitors."

"The best of them, at least," Hatch added with a nod.

"Dang! Flip! Shoot!" exclaimed Mark. "That means I need to overhaul my language. Doesn't it?"

"Yeah!" replied Karynn. "Hello!"

When the meeting ended on Thursday afternoon, Hatch felt he had delivered his message well. He had made a genuine effort to provide something of value and, in doing so, repay Mark's generosity. He liked being back in a thinking role. The gig he now had as consultant to Mark was temporary, and in most ways felt artificial, but it returned Hatch to the stage. He ended his presentation feeling stronger. He reflected on how good it felt to be sober and back in the mainstream where people were trying to create realities and make good things happen.

Mark was respectful of Hatch's ideas. "I need to think this over and talk to Patricia about it. I think you're right about us needing to make a decision. I also need to talk to Peter and Karynn, and maybe others on the crew." Mark sighed, and then smiled. "Can we talk again tomorrow?"

"Of course," Hatch replied.

The Friday meeting never happened. "I need some more time on this," Mark explained. "Can you hold on until early next week? Just continue our arrangement until then?"

Hatch was happy to stay on for a few days longer. The winter weather was brutal. Hatch's face essentially healed. He was learning more about the business by the day. Mark had asked him to start handling some of the incoming queries. And Hatch had signed up for his first sparring session at the gym for Saturday afternoon. He was anxious about learning to fight. He dreaded coming to grips with his fears. But he was determined to carry through.

Thirty-two

H ATCH ARRIVED AT THE GYM WITH PLENTY of time to spare on
Saturday. He was dressed in his regular workout duds. He had
worked out daily for a week and was beginning to feel some benefit
from his efforts. He was trying to cut back on carbs and sweets in his
diet. There were no visible changes yet, on the scale or in the mirror.
But he was elated by following through with his commitment to himself.

The sparring sessions were in a side room with a large window.
The combatants were visible through this window to the customers
working out in the main exercise room. Similar rooms were set aside
for aerobic dance, pilates, and spinning classes. There was no boxing
ring in the sparring room. The floors were covered with blue cushioned pads. In each corner of the room hung a punching bag.

Sparring sessions were scheduled at twenty-minute intervals.
Hatch wondered if that would be long enough to get a good work out.
While he waited, he watched the two young men scheduled before
him. Both wore boxing gloves and the standard issue headgear. They
bobbed and weaved, each covering his head with his gloves and the
midsection with his arms and elbows. Both moved about strategically
and jabbed as opportunity allowed. In one corner of the room, another
boxer punched and kicked a heavy hanging bag.

These were all young men, much younger than Hatch. They were
very light and extremely fit. Their muscles were chiseled, their stom-
achs rippled. As they sparred, sweat poured freely from them, wetting

the mats. Periodically, they would stop sparring and draw a couple of towels from shelves on the opposite wall. With these they wiped the water from the mats and then resumed their spar. There was no referee in the room. The participants regulated their own combat.

All three of the men in the room were shirtless. Hatch was far too embarrassed about his present condition to take off his shirt. He simply tucked it into his trunks.

When a buzzer sounded the end of the workout, the two men touched gloves and came out the door talking in friendly tones to one another.

Hatch entered the room. He put on the headgear he had checked out from the service desk, securing it with the Velcro chinstrap. He slipped on the gloves. The gloves used in the gym were fastened with elastic wrist straps and did not need to be laced. He looked around the room, now from the interior. The other fighter still punched and kicked the bag.

Hatch waited for the sparring partner who had signed up opposite his name. He couldn't recall his partner's name and didn't know how to contact him.

Knowing that time was precious, Hatch stepped to one of the unoccupied hanging bags and tried striking it a few times. The gloves cushioned his hands well enough. It felt good to lean into the bag and hit it as hard as he could. He started to dance a little as he punched. The whole experience was new to Hatch. But, like most Americans, he had watched bits of televised fights and thought he knew about what to do.

By the time Hatch had punched the bag with increasing force and speed for perhaps a minute he was winded. He stopped to rest. His arms were already tired. He leaned on the bag and breathed deeply.

Across the room, the kick boxer called to him. "You here to spar?"

Hatch looked over. The speaker was just a kid, maybe twenty years old. "Yeah," Hatch replied. "You?"

"Yep. I'm ready to go." He was now sitting on the mats, tying on his shoes.

Hatch walked to the center of the mats. He tried to look respectable, but knew it was little use, as he danced and jabbed to loosen up.

His opponent approached.

"Hi, I'm Hatch."

"Diego."

"Take it a little easy on me. This is my first time."

"Really. I couldn't tell." Diego's reply had an edge to it. He looked like a kid who took his fighting seriously and didn't want to waste a sparring session babysitting somebody's grandfather. His fierce and somewhat resentful expression put Hatch on notice that he couldn't expect any quarter from this adversary.

"Right," Hatch mumbled.

Diego held his gloves together in front of him. Hatch did the same. Diego bumped them, then fell back a step or two, and started to dance.

This whole thing looked so completely different to Hatch when viewed up close. He was looking over and around his gloves, trying to keep his eyes on Diego, who was moving about with the speed and agility of a mosquito. Hatch could see every muscle in Diego's shoulders and abdomen.

Hatch, on the other hand, could feel the flab on his stomach, chest, and the back of his arms bouncing up and down as he tried to dance lead-footed. His movement felt awkward and embarrassing.

So far, no one jabbed; no punches were thrown.

Hatch saw Diego's eyes go to his left, so he bobbed to his right. Instantly, Diego threw a punch with his left that struck Hatch's right glove and drove it back into his face, smashing his nose.

Hatch was stunned. The blow hurt. It had come so fast that he could not possibly have defended himself against it. He stepped back and shook his head, realizing that he had to do more than cover his face with his gloves.

Hatch covered up again and moved in closer, determined to jab at Diego. Again, so fast that Hatch saw only a blur, Diego threw a combination. One glove hit Hatch on the side of the face in front of his ear. That spot was still tender from the beating Hatch received from Trevor. The other glove hit his left glove and bounced off.

This time, instead of stepping back, Hatch swung as hard as he could with his right hand at Diego's head. Diego avoided the punch completely, and Hatch's momentum carried him around exposing his side to the younger fighter.

In a flash, Diego landed two blows in Hatch's rib cage on the right side. These punches were thrown hard and took Hatch's breath.

Again he stepped back. He was no longer dancing. No bob. No weave. He was breathing so hard that was all he could concentrate on. He was tempted to walk away and chalk this up as one of his worst ideas ever. But, in the midst of his wanting to seek asylum, he thought of Sylvia. He thought of the two bullies in the Escalade. He thought of Trevor's beating. He nodded at Diego, took a deep breath, covered up, and waded back into the fight.

During the next ten minutes, Hatch never did hit Diego. But he did throw a couple of jabs that landed on the younger man's gloves and arms. In return, Diego showed Hatch every reason why he should take up golf or go back to tennis.

When they finished, they touched gloves. Diego gaze was dismissive. Hatch nodded. "Thanks, that wasn't much of a workout for you. But I had to start somewhere. Thanks for helping me."

"No problem," replied Diego impersonally as he sat down to remove his shoes. His workout would continue on the bag.

Hatch thought about punching the bag for a couple of minutes, but his arms felt like rubber bands. His nose was bleeding a little. He could see the blood smeared on his glove. His lip was puffy. He was afraid that one of Diego's blows to his mouth might have ruptured the stitches inside his lip.

He realized that what he was doing wouldn't make much sense to a bystander. But it made perfect sense to him. That was all that mattered at the moment.

Thirty-three

M ARK WAS READY TO TALK ON MONDAY morning. He asked Hatch into the business office before convening the crew meeting.

The conference room was carpeted. The central feature was a large oblong table with a dark laminate finish. The business had sprung for six decorative wooden chairs with upholstered seats intended for visitors. They were supplemented by folding metal chairs during crew meetings. On the paneled walls hung promotional posters from some prestige auto manufacturers. In the muscle car world, the room would have passed well enough. In the prestige auto world, it was barely reaching toward respectability.

Mark offered Hatch a seat. They were alone. Mark looked weary. The expression on his face was not unpleasant. Unpleasant seemed to be impossible, given Mark's native cheery temperament. But his eyes looked puffy and his face drawn. He looked emotionally exhausted, if not physically.

"Hatcher, I've had a terrible weekend. I have thought my way through your presentation over and over. Patricia and I have discussed the implications. Dang, it's hard to make changes when you have given your life to something for a dozen years.

"Even worse, I'm a naturally confident guy. But in this case, I admit to being frightened. Five years ago, when we moved into the prestige market I had no idea what that really meant. I was just looking for bigger margins. But, after hearing you, I realize that really succeeding in that market will require a major change of approach. I not only have to decide if I want to make those changes, but if I'm able to make them.

"Look at you. It would be easy for you to achieve the prestige image. You've grown up with it. You're educated. You think like the customers—or clients—or whatever. You know how to talk to others who think that way.

"Look at me. A stinkin' hayseed. No education. No culture. No connections in that world. I belong in muscle cars, with people who love muscle cars. For me to talk and act like you would be totally phony. But muscle cars are not going to take us where I want to go. I'm really feeling trapped here."

Hatch watched Mark struggle and knew there was truth in what he was saying. But he also believed that Mark could succeed at transforming the business.

"Mark, you are selling yourself short. First of all, anyone can see that you are exceptionally able as a business manager. Everything you have built testifies to that." Hatch swept his arms wide to include the whole building, business, and enterprise.

"Second, where you come from does not completely determine what you can become. You may not want to be like the prestige elite, but I have no doubt you are capable of doing it. Just look at me. I'm a refugee from their camp, learning lessons in yours. I'm not sure I can change completely. I don't know that I want to. But I know it is doing me good. You can do the same. Visit my camp for a while. Learn a few lessons. Learn the language. Learn the customs. It doesn't have to be permanent. Become crossover capable. It can't hurt you, and it could do you some good.

"Finally, you are not really that far away. Your language is a little colloquial, but you are good with people and make a great impression. You still have to be you. It would just mean polishing a few corners. Same for the rest of the crew."

Mark was silent for several minutes. He closed his eyes; his breathing deepened. Finally, he said, "You're right. This is something that has to be done. I can do this. *We* can do this. I talked to Karynn and Peter about it. Karynn is willing. Peter is already converted to the idea."

Mark's smile was returning, though he was clearly working on himself, forcing his optimism to the surface. He continued, "Picking you up on I-84 may be one of the most valuable things I've ever done for the business—if we're successful. If not?" Mark paused. "Flip, we just need to go forward. We are stuck in our tracks. No risk, no reward."

He looked at Hatch intently. "I have a proposition for you," he said. "I know you're wanting to be on your way to Denver and whatever that brings, but I need your help to make this leap. It will be second nature to you, trial and error for me. Will you stay with us for a while? Work on a retainer for six to eight months? You have the vision and the know-how to help us pull off this transition. If not you, then I have to go searching for somebody else. None of us has what it takes.

"But I think we can learn quickly. If you could stay for six to eight months, you'd be on your way by early fall, and we'd be on our way as well. I'll pay you fifty thousand dollars, give you a place to live, and provide the parts truck for your use after hours and weekends. In addition, I'll set aside two hundred thousand to make the changes you outlined. That's a quarter mil. A quarter mil is a lot of money to a business our size. But I believe we can recover the costs in a year to eighteen months."

Both men sat silently while Hatch pondered this offer. He felt some urgent reservation, mostly because of time. He had already been out of touch with his former world for four months. Nobody knew where he was, not Patty or the kids, not his creditors, and now, not Trevor or Sylvia to whom he owed much. If Patty thought he was dead, she might make permanent changes in her life that would take away forever what he wanted most in this world. Perhaps he could let her know what he was doing. He thought she still cared a little. Maybe if she knew that he still cared a lot, it could buy him the time he needed.

At the same time, he had to face the reality of his debts. Fifty thousand dollars could help him clear up much of what he owed others, and let him return to Seattle in a position of personal strength.

By the time six to eight months had passed, he hoped to be sober for a full year and to have fixed himself into a healthy pattern that would keep him that way forever. He could not go back unprepared. He could not disappoint Patty or the children again. He could not. He must not. At the end of a year, maybe the driving force within him to go eastward would have left him. Maybe the rising sun would no longer draw him.

"It is good of you to offer," Hatch replied at length. "I need a little time to think about it. Can I give you an answer tomorrow morning?"

"Shoot, yeah!" The smile in Mark's voice matched the smile on his face. "That's a better answer than I expected."

Mark stood and extended his hand, "If you buy into this, I'll do everything I can to make it pay off for both of us."

"So will I," Hatch replied.

✺

Hatch went to the gym right after work. He felt unexpectedly elated. Maybe it was the prospect of having a job and a certain income. Weighing in lifted his spirits even higher. He had reached 239 pounds. Still a long way from his goal, but it was a move in the right direction. He worked out hard and went home tired.

That evening he wrote a note to Patty. He hadn't spoken or written to her for nearly five months.

Dear Patty,

Please excuse my neglect, as always. I am away from Seattle, and am doing well. I have finally taken the drastic steps needed to get my life, hopefully our lives, back together. I have been sober for nearly five months. I am working. I'm trying to vanquish the demons.

I can't say how soon I'll be back, but I will be good while I'm gone. I'll come back the man you believed you were marrying. It's do or die time for me.

Please give my love to Jenna and Ryan. I miss you desperately. I miss them desperately. I think of you constantly. Will you please tell Jenna and Ryan that I have written? If you could, I would appreciate you telling Doris as well. No man ever had a better mother.

I would like to tell you more but am afraid of getting either of our hopes up too high yet.

Love you dearly,
Hatcher

Hatch addressed the envelope to Patty but put no return address on it. He read the note several times before sealing the envelope. It was honest. In some ways it was understated. That was probably best at this point. Patty would recognize the phrases *drastic steps, I will be good, the man you believed you were marrying,* and *getting our hopes up,* and would know what they meant without further explanation.

Hatch took great care in creating and mailing this message because there would be no way to know how well it was received for many months to come.

The following morning, Hatch entered into a verbal contract with Mark, concluding it with a handshake. They worked out a system of minor advances so that Hatch would have enough to live on while the work was being completed.

Then Hatch asked Mark to post his letter to Patty from Pullman, Washington, that evening while Mark was in Pullman inspecting and possibly buying their next restorable auto.

Mark glanced at the envelope. "Patty Stephens. I'll get it to her," he said with a smile and put the letter in his shirt pocket.

Mark was good to his word in all regards. Hatch tried to do the same. He worked hard, helping to craft the new business image and train the crew, now known as associates. "Do we get a pay raise along with the fancy title of associates," asked Marcus Ortiz, a body man, to a round of chuckles from the other associates. "No," replied Peter, "just unlimited personal satisfaction."

The appearance of the facility and dress of the associates was upgraded, all business forms and stationery were revised, the website got a major face-lift with professional help from a Boise web design firm.

Everyone in the business found some relief in the early returns from publicity in implementing the business name change. Instead of falling off as feared, website hits, client-initiated contact rates, and revenue all began to climb slowly. By early summer the rate of climb increased.

Alarm spread through the business in June when notice came of a suit for trademark infringement filed by Prestige Restorations of Surrey, England. A hasty settlement was reached when a trademark search by a firm in New York showed that the words *Prestige Restoration* showed up in some form in the legal names of at least six businesses in the United States.

Involved as Hatch was in every aspect of the business, he felt he was receiving a first-rate education in small business operations. His love affair with cars continued. But Hatch no longer worshipped them as possessions. He didn't long to own one. He now viewed them as a means to get in touch with the broader values the business was built around. He had never known the elation of pouring his soul into something and then walking away from it to find another thing worthy of pouring more soul into.

While the transformation of Lester Auto into North America Prestige Restorations advanced, Hatch's healthy life pattern also progressed. By the beginning of summer, he had dropped an additional twenty-nine pounds. He now weighed a little over 210 pounds. He lived frugally, ate sensibly, worked out daily, and above all else, he was still sober. He had consumed no alcohol for nine months, the longest continuous stretch since age six. He felt good about this accomplishment but kept constant vigil.

The other aspect of his pattern that was returning great satisfaction was sparring. *Who would have guessed*, he thought, *that after running away for thirty years, I would become hungry for battle.*

After his first miserable humiliation at the hands of Diego, Hatch picked up a copy of *Boxing for Dummies*. He started reading about fighting. He badgered the other fighters at the gym for information and techniques the way an aspiring golfer does at the nineteenth hole. He watched videotapes of matches at the gym. As he learned, he improved.

Hatch had no desire to become a professional fighter. He was far too old for that when he began. And he was not ignorant of the dangers. But he was growing to love the idea of manly self-defense. His determination grew. As he promised Sylvia, he would never lean on a woman again to do a man's job. He still was no match for his more advanced sparring partners and realized that even they were amateurs in the sport. But he had learned to fight without fear. He could think while acting. Hatch grew more confident in his ability to defend himself against serious injury.

His increasing skill did not come without cost. At times he was so bruised that there was no comfortable side to sleep on. His mouth, nose, and eyes were repeatedly cut. The brow of his left eye began to develop a knot of scar tissue. He persisted, however, in the belief that his old friend-enemy Trevor had spoken truth when he told Hatch that he had something more important to protect than his face. Character! If Hatch had developed a mantra since walking away from Seattle, it would be something like *character is everything*. He heard those words in his mind many times each day. They comprised his answer to every dilemma, every decision, every conquest, and every disappointment.

Thirty-four

HATCH THOUGHT OFTEN OF HIS FRIENDS. HE wondered and endured anguish about the well-being of his family. At times he practically forgot that he and Patty were divorced. He felt more like he was away on an extended business trip. Still, he realized that precious time was passing. He knew the possibility existed that Patty had remarried—or would. He knew that she might have divorced him emotionally as well as legally. He knew that the children were growing up without him.

He was beginning to feel strong. Maybe it was time to go home and face the realities. To be strong in the absence of the crucial challenges of life is no strength at all. He remembered from a college English course John Milton's assertion, *I cannot praise a fugitive and cloistered virtue.*

Still, to go home too soon, to mistakenly think himself cured, to underestimate the challenges he would continue to face, and then to fail at them once again—this he could not do. If even now there was the slimmest chance that he could convince Patty to try once more, if there was any hint of life left in their love, then one more failure would certainly extinguish it.

His only hope lay with Patty. She was not an ordinary woman. With any ordinary woman, chances of reconciliation would have long since vanished. No. Hatch could not go home yet. His hope had revived, the future looked more optimistic, but he could not risk the last vital contest.

So, he stayed on, working ever nearer to completion of his contact with Mark. He wrote to Sylvia and told her all was well. He asked her to convey his regards to Trevor. His feelings toward Trevor had softened as he increasingly realized what a great gift Trevor had given him.

The only real difficulty Hatch faced in Nampa was the tension that arose with Karynn. They shared the business office. When Mark was in the office, space felt a little tight. But Karynn and Hatch were there almost constantly.

Karynn was a physically attractive woman, and very likeable, though a little abrupt in her manner. In their close quarters, Hatch couldn't help noticing her repeatedly throughout the workday. During the winter, a close friendship grew between them. In moments when the pressure was off for Hatch, they visited. Karynn liked to share her thoughts. Hatch liked to listen. While Hatch had recently been through a similar friendship with Sylvia and had a good grip on this thoughts and feelings, Karynn was not accustomed to working closely with anyone but her brother-in-law, who treated her much the way older brothers treat younger sisters.

Hatch began to suspect that Karynn was developing romantic feelings toward him. Guesswork like that by men can be mistaken and often dangerous. But, as time passed, his suspicions seemed securely founded. Karynn invited him to a social event with other young adults at her church. Hatch accepted the invitation feeling that a public setting would afford enough safeguards so that nothing awkward or hurtful could happen. Trying to be honest with himself, and considering the possible dangers, Hatch knew he could be attracted to Karynn. This situation was terribly similar to the Christmas Eve at Sylvia's apartment. The big difference was that Sylvia was a mature and together woman who had already experienced a failed marriage. In that regard, she was likely less susceptible to irrational romantic impulses than Karynn would be. At the moment, Hatch wasn't sure there were any other romantic impulses but the irrational.

The whole of Treasure Valley, from Boise on the west to Ontario on the east, was dotted with white church steeples. The residents seemed to be a very church-going population.

The evening began well. Among perhaps a hundred young adult men and women, Hatch was the oldest. Young adults are generally thinner than their older, married counterparts. So Hatch was also aware of his appearance. The demeanor and appearance of the young people he met impressed him.

The social activity was a simulated Olympics in which all contestants moved from station to station joining in a series of games. Some games were eye-hand coordination and physical skills like shooting free throws, popping balloons with darts, and jumping rope. Some were word games, matching games, and puzzle solving. A third variety brought young couples into physical contact. These games included such activities as passing an orange to a partner without the use of hands, by grasping the orange between one person's chin and chest and holding it so the partner could grasp it and pass it on in the same way. At another station, blindfolded young men were asked to identify the faces of their women partners by touch. At still another, couples cooperated in chewing pieces of licorice candy from both ends until they met in the middle, in effect kissing one another. Hatch noticed that some couples returned to that station over and other. Others passed it by altogether.

Approaching the candy eating station, and watching the couples having a great time, Hatch could clearly see that one of the overriding purposes of the social event was to bring young people together with others of their own faith and values in such a way that romance could result. He didn't blame the organizers for taking that approach, but he began to feel anxious about how he was going to handle such moments.

Karynn took his hand and led him toward the licorice station. He noted how much younger Karynn seemed in this setting than she did at work. Here she was among peers. Hatch felt like an old, lamed racehorse among young contenders coming to the post for their first race.

Yikes! exclaimed the voice of Hatch's inner character coach. The coach, effectively silenced by alcohol and bad choices over many years, had not been dead after all, but merely gagged. Now the coach was yelling orders. *Act sooner than later to avoid hurting her feelings. If not, walk away. Get a drink. Go to the john.*

But Karynn had maneuvered him into the line before he was aware of the dynamics of the game. To back out now would be apparent to other couples and potentially embarrassing to Karynn. Hatch wanted to avoid that if possible. He tried excusing himself by making a self-effacing comment, "I hope you won't be too embarrassed if my false teeth pop out while we're doing this." The comment earned him a giddy giggle from couples close by. Hatch found it ironic, but not altogether condemnable, that he would go to the gym regularly hoping to beat some guy's head in and still be reluctant to bruise this young woman's delicate feelings.

Before Hatch knew it, they were on the contest stand with two other couples. Partners in each couple placed the licorice between their teeth. The couple that ate their way through the candy first was promised a reward, as if the kiss were not reward enough.

Karynn could chew away with the best of them. Looking down over his nose, Hatch could see Karynn's lips and teeth maniacally gobbling up the distance between them. He began laughing and let go the licorice once or twice. That slowed their progress. When the winners were hailed, he let go altogether, and Karynn ate the remainder. They had come within perhaps an inch of the fated kiss. Hatch laughed aloud, and in an effort to conclude the moment without being assessed a social foul, he said to her, "I'm sorry to laugh. Now you can see why I've never been a very good competitor. It just doesn't work to laugh at the guy across the line who wants to tear your head off."

Karynn replied with a perceptive half-smile. "Hatcher, you're not a coward. You just try so hard to do what's right that you don't know how to have fun."

After an enjoyable evening of games and refreshments, Hatch drove Karynn to her parent's home and walked her to the door. They stood visiting for a few minutes, but the evening was cold.

"Thanks for inviting me," he said genuinely. "It must be a little threatening to take a stranger to meet your friends. I enjoyed them, and you, and the evening."

"Like you're going to say anything embarrassing," Karynn replied. "Who in this town ever met someone so polished as you?"

Her compliment touched Hatch. He needed an honest way out of this. "Unfortunately, I have a very dark and sinister past. I have as many enemies as you have friends."

"I find that hard to believe."

"Maybe sometime I can explain it."

Karynn looked over her shoulder. "I think my parents are probably

out of the living room by now. Want to come in and start explaining?"
She smiled her lovely smile.

"That might ruin an otherwise successful evening for me. I'd
better leave you whole," he said, returning her smile. "Good night,
Karynn. Thanks for taking pity on an old shut-in."

She slapped him on the arm. "Neither of us believes that, Hatcher.
Thanks for going with me." She stepped forward and hugged him,
putting her head on this shoulder. He hugged her back.

"See," she said. "Even your cold shoulder is warm."

With that she turned toward the door.

Hatch thought about that comment as he drove back to his apartment.

Thirty-five

THROUGH THE HEAT OF SUMMER, MARK AND Hatch met often to
assess the company's progress. The revenue figures verified that
Hatch's instincts for reaching a broader market for prestige autos were
correct. Two big sales at the end of July and receipt of four special
orders brought projections for the company's best year ever. In his
thirteen previous years of business, Mark had never received a special
order for an auto restoration. All the earlier restorations were done on
a spec basis, meaning that finished cars would sometimes sit for months
before being sold. The financial advantage of special orders was that
the company received an advance on the estimated total cost and that
the sale was consummated on completion of the work.

Mark made no secret of his enthusiasm for the new direction the
company was taking. He praised the associates and acknowledged
Hatch's contribution in particular. These successes were particularly
sweet to Hatch. As he and Mark reviewed the third quarter revenue
projections, Mark commented, "How does it feel to really hit a home
run on this thing? It's like you were looking into a crystal ball."

"Really, it feels great. Even though the credit goes to you and the
other associates who did all the work, it is gratifying to see a vision
become a reality. In all my years at the firm, that really never happened. They didn't hire me to think. They hired me to carry out other
people's thoughts. This is fun. I want to do this again. Thanks for
giving me a chance."

Mark put his hand on Hatch's shoulder as he spoke. "I can't believe what good fortune you have brought us. We won't forget you soon. By Labor Day our contract will expire. I think we can carry the ball from here, but we'd rather have you stay. Come to work for me full time. Handle the marketing end. It's clear that we need someone to carry on there full time. You're our first and best choice, and I will make it worth your time."

"Thanks, Mark. You know how I admire you and love the business. But I still have some unfinished business of my own."

"I understand," replied Mark. Then with a big smile, he added, "Actually, I've been hoping to make you my brother-in-law." He glanced toward the business office. "We could end up being partners."

"There's nobody I would rather work for or with," replied Hatch. "I've been thinking about how to wrap this up gracefully. You're headed for Grand Junction the day after Labor Day, right?"

"Right," said Mark. "Come with me. Help me pick up that Ferrari. If you like what we see, come back with me, and I'll get you more into the production end. If not, you're that much closer to Denver."

"It's a deal," Hatch said. "I was hoping you'd ask me. I'd love to travel that far with you. After all, that's how we started."

"That's right. I was coming back from Portland with the '71 XKE. You won me over right there."

On Labor Day, Hatch went to work out at the gym. It was to be his last sparring session. In eight months he had made several good friends at the gym. Diego signed on as his sparring partner. Hatch cracked the 200 lb. mark for the first time and was feeling his oats. He was still no match for Diego, but he was respectable. He was in control. He landed a half dozen good punches and drew a little blood from Diego's nose. When they finished the session, they touched gloves.

"I'm gonna miss you, big guy," Diego said, smiling. "I still remember our first round. All the guys in the dressing room were laughing at you. Nobody wanted to sign on as your partner because it was a waste of time. But you showed us all. When I get to be a grandfather, I want to be just like you."

They laughed as Hatch pulled on his shirt. He had lost sixty pounds in a year and had maybe forty to go. He felt good. His muscles were hard. He had tossed his fat clothes and knew he looked much better. Leaving the gym, he took a careful look around. This place had been good to him. He would have to find a gym at the next place as well.

Hatch spent the rest of the afternoon cleaning his apartment. He wanted to leave it in top shape for Mark's next renters. Then he settled down and read the last fifty pages of *Les Miserables*. He had worked steadily away at the book for eight months. He read some sections several times hoping some of the great ideas and noble feelings in Hugo's book would sink into him and stay.

The reading likely accounted for his mood. He was feeling extremely tender. His last act in Nampa was writing Patty another letter.

> *Dearest Patty,*
>
> *I'm probably making a fool of myself and don't even know it. It has been eight months since I wrote you last. Of course, I didn't hear back since I didn't give you an address.*
>
> *I hope beyond all else that you, Jenna, and Ryan are well. I miss you all every day. Please tell the children that I have written.*
>
> *I have been away for one year. I am sober. I have been good. I have worked steadily. I'm beginning to believe that the old Hatcher is dead. I hope so. I'm starting to like the new one.*
>
> *I can't say how soon I will return. I assure you this, when I come back, I will come back whole—or not at all.*
>
> *You are always in my dreams.*
> *Hatcher*

Thirty-six

RISING EARLY THE MORNING AFTER LABOR DAY, Hatch watched the sun rise over the mountains on the east end of Treasure Valley. The sky was cloudless. It would be another hot day in a hot and dry summer. He thought it remarkable that in a year's time, he had not risen once without thinking about the sunrise. For most of those three hundred sixty-five days he had restrained the desire to get up and go. He kept his word to Sylvia and then kept his word to Mark. He had no regrets. He had been true to them. They had been good to him.

He also thought it remarkable that in a year's time he had not acquired a single possession. He owned only the clothes he wore and a copy of Hugo's *Les Miserables*, which he had promised to Karynn.

Hatch's Washington state driver's license was still valid. He had no other ID. He had cut up his credit cards in North Bend. He had no bank account, no mailing address, no telephone. But he was no longer penniless, either. Mark had agreed to hold his check for $42,000, plus a bonus of $10,000 until he returned. Hatch carried about four thousand dollars in big bills in his socks.

In addition to sixty pounds of unwanted fat and a miserable drinking habit, he left behind cherished friends: Trevor, Sylvia, Mark, Karynn, Peter, the associates at the business, and sparring partners at the gym.

He turned his thoughts ahead. First, he would enjoy a pleasurable business trip to Grand Junction with Mark. Then, he would find his way to Denver. How much further he would need to go to find the place where the sun rises he did not know. But he was eager to go—no longer afraid.

Mark was waiting when Hatch arrived. He and Patricia had taken the children and members of the extended family water skiing on Labor Day. They finished up with a barbecue that lasted late into the evening. A great day, according to Mark's report.

"You should have come," he said to Hatch. "The water and the watermelons were great. The kids had a super time, but I'm sore this morning. I may be getting too old for that kind of excitement." Mark would be thirty-five on his next birthday. Hatch would turn thirty-eight in November.

"Why don't you drive the first leg," Mark offered. "I think I may go for a little shut-eye."

Mark slept for two and a half hours until Hatch pulled off the freeway at Burley, Idaho, to stretch his legs. They had passed southern Idaho towns like Bliss, Wendell, Jerome, and Twin Falls. On both sides of the freeway, men and boys on tractors were mowing and baling hay. Irrigation sprinklers pumped a seemingly endless supply of water onto the thirsty crops. Unlike the dry farms of eastern Washington and Oregon, and the sugar beet fields of the Treasure Valley that Hatch became so familiar with while living in Nampa, these were intensively irrigated, multi-harvest fields. Hatch admired the industry and productivity he saw all around.

As they resumed their travel, Mark drove. They turned south onto I-84 and headed toward Ogden, Utah. For another hour they climbed and descended low brush-covered hills and passed through fertile agricultural valleys. They talked casually for most of that hour; then, having said all that had to be said, or could be said, they fell silent. Mark searched through the menus of CDs in the big truck's built-in changer to find some of his country pop favorites. Hatch watched the crops go by and marveled at what difference water makes in the arid West.

Soon after they crossed the Idaho state line into Utah, they rounded the shoulder of yet another hill. They could see a straight stretch of freeway ahead. They noticed a long line of what appeared to be stalled traffic on their side. The line stretched all the way past an upcoming exit to the hill beyond. At the far end of the line flashed the lights of half a dozen emergency vehicles.

"Whoa," said Mark, moaning. "Looks like there's a problem up there. Shoot, I hope the freeway isn't closed." Then he added sheepishly, "Oops. Not sure how that 'shoot' got in there. Wouldn't be good for business, huh?"

Hatch laughed.

They soon came to a halt behind the car ahead of them. The line wasn't moving at all. Mark shut off the engine. Ahead, they could see drivers and passengers getting out of their cars to walk around a bit.

"Doesn't look good." Mark's disappointment was audible. "The traffic isn't very heavy today. It must have taken a couple of hours for this many cars to stack up."

They sat still for a while. Mark turned on the radio searching for a local station that might give traffic information but could find nothing. They were nearing the middle of the day, and the temperature outside was too warm to sit comfortably without the benefit of air conditioning. Mark started the engine and let it idle.

Eventually, both Hatch and Mark began to feel impatient. They noticed that an increasing number of cars and trucks were swinging onto the outside shoulder, driving slowly forward to a freeway exit, and crossing over into a small town north of the freeway.

"Shall we follow them?" Mark asked.

"May as well. Better to sit this out indoors," answered Hatch.

They followed the line that was now becoming a flow. They crept forward, patiently awaiting their turn to cross the overpass and headed down into town. The sign beside the freeway read "Snowville."

Snowville wasn't much of a town at first glance—two filling stations, a diner, a small motel, a farm equipment repair shop with accompanying parts store, the national forest office, one church, a town hall, and an elementary school. At first glance, Hatch guessed there were maybe fifty homes scattered among the big cottonwood trees.

Closing the freeway had flooded the little town with visitors. Vehicles parked in every spare inch of shade. Mark had to drive north on one of the two main streets of the town past the elementary school to find a place to park his truck and trailer. The town looked like it might when a holiday crowd came to watch a rodeo.

They got out of the truck, stretched, and headed toward the filling station and convenience store. Enroute they passed a small cluster of travelers standing beside a Chevy Suburban. Mark approached them and asked, "Any idea what happened up the freeway?"

A young, husky male with close-cropped black hair, wrap-around sunglasses, and a chin beard replied, "We hear there were two big rigs and at least two passenger cars in a crash. One of the big rigs was a gas hauler. It caught fire and pretty well burned things up. Even the road surface. There have been ambulances back and forth for the past couple of hours. Looks nasty."

"Sorry to hear that," replied Mark. "Any idea how long the freeway will be blocked?"

"We just heard that somebody called the Highway Patrol. They say a couple of big wreckers are on their way from Tremonton."

"Thanks for the info." Mark waved as they walked on.

Reaching the intersection of streets that constituted the business district of Snowville, they looked at the crowds seeking refuge from the heat of day.

To their left was Madge's Diner, a large wood-sided building attached to the older of the two filling stations. The frame windows showed red- and white-checkered curtains. A neon *Coors Beer* sign shown in the window.

"Let's try the diner," Hatch suggested. "I'll buy the burgers. We may have to wait a while. I hope it's cool."

Hatch was right about the wait. The diner was packed beyond capacity. Travelers were standing in clusters in every available space. He was also right about it being cool. The building had evaporative cooling. The interior was minimally decorated, with wooden tables and booths. A moose head hung over the clock at the far end. The kitchen was to their left, the restrooms behind.

Because the accident had come unexpectedly, the small service staff normally covering the diner at midday was swamped by business. Two or three waitresses hustled at top speed, their faces red with exertion, wisps of hair flying in unruly reaction to this wrinkle in the normal schedule.

After a pit stop and hand wash, Hatch and Mark found a spot where they could lean against the wall until seats became available. Hatch asked a woman standing next to him, "How long does the wait appear to be?"

"I'm not sure," she replied, voicing her impatience. "They've carried three people in the last stages of starvation out on stretchers."

Hatch laughed. "Tragedy everywhere we look."

"Isn't that the truth?" She shook her head.

⋙

Hatch gave up counting the number of times he shifted from foot to foot before one of the waitresses signaled for them to sit at a two-person table in the corner. Reinforcements had arrived, and the food and drink were flowing a little more freely.

"Hi, boys," said the waitress in a low voice. "Here are your menus. I'll be back with water." By the time they could look up, she was gone.

When she returned, they were ready to order, not wanting to risk losing their place in the queue. The waitress was a woman who appeared to be in her fifties. She was heavy on her feet and hobbled a little as she moved from table to table.

Trying to be pleasant for her sake, Hatch said to her, "Busy day."

"Tell me about it, Hon."

"You better ask Madge for a raise," he continued.

The waitress put her hands on her hips, tapped one foot, and returned with a smile, "Hon, I am Madge, and it takes more than this to get a pay raise around here."

Hatch laughed. Smiling at Mark, he said, "All right! We got the boss woman herself."

They all laughed. "What'll you have?" she asked.

"Two number one burgers with fries. An ice tea for me and a root beer for him."

"It'll be right up."

Madge was a little too optimistic in her promise. "Right up" turned out to be about twenty-five minutes."

"Sorry," she said with a weary smile. "I'm moving about as fast as a fat, old lady can move."

As she put the plates in front of them, Hatch kept the conversation going, "People sure do like this town."

Off-handedly, Madge replied, "Of course they do. This is where the sun rises."

Hatch's head shot up, his eyes wide open. He felt a stunning charge of electricity course through him. Madge had turned away.

"Madge, wait!" Hatch said this so loudly that people at surrounding tables turned to look at him. Madge turned back with a puzzled expression on her face.

"Madge," he asked urgently, "what did you just say?"

She thought for a second. "Oh, just a local saying." Busy as she was, she put the round serving tray under her arm and leaned forward so that the men could hear without her having to raise her voice over the clamor of the crowd.

Hatch could feel the blood rushing out of his face and began to feel a little light-headed.

"Let me get this next big order up, and I'll tell you about it." She walked away.

Mark looked at Hatch with concern. "What happened just now, Hatcher? You look a little pale."

"I need to hear her story. I'll tell you later if it makes any sense."

Hatch had difficulty eating. He was no longer hungry. He also had difficulty carrying on a conversation. Madge's comment and the electric shock it had elicited in him kept replaying in his mind. "This is where the sun rises," she had said.

Hatch was confused. Surely this was not where the sun rises. Not in this little town surrounded by sage-covered hills. He had never even heard of Snowville, Utah. Still, he could not deny the physical sensation he had just experienced. Somewhere inside him was the memory of a similar jolt.

Furthermore, when the thought crossed Hatch's mind that he should forget what he was feeling and go on to Denver, he felt physical revulsion. He must not go to Denver. He felt it. He knew it. What he must do was talk to Madge.

"Hatcher, are you okay?" Mark's voice penetrated Hatch's depth of thought.

"Yeah, Mark. I'm okay. Sorry. I can't go to Grand Junction with you. I've got to stay here and talk to Madge."

"What?" Mark looked incredulous. "Have a sip of your ice tea." He leaned toward Hatch. "You don't want to stay here, friend. You'll never catch a ride out of this place."

Hatch looked at him resolutely and repeated, "I've got to talk to Madge."

Mark was still smiling, but his eyes showed concern. "You're worrying me a little. Have you had a stroke or something? You're not sounding quite rational."

"I know I'm acting strange. But this is important to me. It has to do with my unfinished business."

Mark looked stunned. "Well, that's a surprise to me. You are a capable, cultured man of the world. What could ever interest you in Snowville?"

"I'm not sure," Hatch answered honestly. As an afterthought, he added, "What could induce you to run a worldwide prestige auto business out of a place like Nampa?"

"Got me there," said Mark.

"I'm not belittling Nampa. I'm just saying that sometimes smaller might be better. Simpler might be more profound. I don't know. I only know what I have to do."

Madge was long in getting back. "Sorry, boys. I'll need a month's vacation when this is over."

Just as she spoke, an older man leaned in the partially opened door and said loudly enough for most in the diner to hear, "The freeway is open. Traffic's starting to move."

An audible cheer rose from the crowd, including Madge.

"Hallelujah," she said. "I love the business, but I need my health more." She dropped the bill on the table. "Thanks, boys. Pay at the register." She was gone again.

Mark looked at Hatch. "What do you want to do?"

"Can we drag our feet for just a few minutes to see if the place clears out so I can talk to her?"

"Sure," replied Mark. He continued to pick at the crunchy little French fry ends left from his order. Hatch shoved his fries to Mark's side of the table. He had not touched them.

When the freeway opening was announced, most of the travelers waiting for service left immediately. Those who had finished their meals also left. Activity began to die down and two of the waitresses had enough time to stop and compare war stories.

Soon, Madge noticed Hatch and Mark. She returned to the table. "Anything else, boys?"

Hatch smiled at her. "You promised to tell us how it is that the sun rises in Snowville."

"Oh, I forgot." Madge looked around to see that business was being covered, and then she pulled a chair from the next table and sat down. "Oh, my aching dogs," she said, laughing.

"That's just something we say to each other here. The town sweetheart is Molly Lewis. When she was just a little flower, her mama, Cindy, died and left her with her daddy, Art Fields. You'd see the two of them walking along the street hand in hand. She was the most darling thing ever born. She would ask her daddy, 'Why do we live in Snowville?' And he would tell her, 'Because this is where the sun rises.' 'Really?' the little doll would ask. 'Yep,' Art would tell her, 'it comes over these hills every morning. It stays over Snowville all day. Then it goes to bed over those hills when it's time to go to bed. This is the most important town in the world, because this is where the sun rises.' "

Madge wiped a tear from her eye on the back of her hand. "Molly says it is so, and there's not a person in town who doubts it."

"Does Molly still live here?" asked Hatch.

"She does." Madge was beginning to cry. She reached for an unused napkin on the table and wiped her eyes. Then she said with a catch in her voice, "But not for very long."

"Anyway, that's the story," Madge said, rising. "I'd better get going." She moved to another table where Hatch could see that she was still wiping her eyes.

Hatch looked at Mark. "Please forgive me. I can't go further. Looks like I need to meet Molly."

After paying their bill, they walked back to the intersection. Hatch hadn't left anything in the truck that he planned to keep, so the friends shook hands to say good-bye.

"I'll stay in touch," Hatch promised. "Could you do me a couple of favors? Give the book in the truck to Karynn. And when you get to Grand Junction, mail this letter for me. Will you?"

"Of course, I will," said Mark. Then he grabbed Hatch and gave him a mighty hug. Stepping back from the hug, he smiled and poked Hatch in the ribs. "You're only half the man you were when you came to Nampa."

Thirty-seven

THE MOTEL IN SNOWVILLE PROVED TO BE larger than Hatch had guessed. It appeared to have just six rooms. In reality, there were a dozen, with doors in both the front and back of the building. He registered for two nights, not knowing how long he would be in town.

Each room had a window-mounted cooler, so the temperature in his west-facing room was tolerable. Hatch wanted to talk to Madge again, and he wanted to meet Molly Lewis. He decided to rest for an hour and try to catch a bite for dinner at Madge's, since he had eaten almost nothing for lunch.

When he walked into the diner at about five o'clock, he asked if Madge was in. A taller, thin woman with weathered complexion told him that Madge had taken the rest of the evening off since she had been on duty during the whole of the afternoon's unexpected rush. Madge would be in when the diner opened at seven the next morning.

Hatch told the waitress that Madge had mentioned a Molly Lewis. "Where would I find Molly?" he asked.

"Molly owns the parts store. You can find it across the street to the west," she said, pointing in the general direction.

"Any idea how long they are open?" Hatch asked.

"I think until six," was her answer.

"How late are you open?" he asked.

"Until eight this evening," she replied. "But, if you want dinner, be here by seven."

Hatch nodded his thanks and left, walking toward the parts store.

⁓⁂⁓

Farmer's Grange & Supply was located in a long, weathered frame building. The equipment repair end had a lofty roof and high overhead doors, presumably to allow big pieces of farm machinery or trucks with high clearance to be pulled in for repairs. Indeed, as Hatch walked past, both of the business's bays were open to view, the high doors being pulled up. Each bay was occupied by a big piece of machinery. One or two mechanics worked each bay, hands and arms in the machine, elbows and fannies out.

The parts store was on the west end. The building sat on a high concrete foundation, so the door was four feet off the ground at the top of a set of concrete stairs. The door had been painted recently, but the remainder of the building was badly weathered. The only window on the store's face revealed two large promotional posters for John Deere machinery and a Help Wanted sign. One of the posters pictured a tractor-mounted mower, the other a self-propelled baler. The heavy door stuck when Hatch tried to enter and then popped open with a jolt. He stumbled in.

A service counter extending almost the entire width of the room divided the interior of the store. On Hatch's side was a row of stools up next to the counter. Behind the counter were rows of parts shelves perpendicular to the counter. The walls behind him and the ends of the counter were adorned with equipment posters and at least three large calendars showing more equipment. The calendars were doubtlessly the generous gifts of equipment vendors.

Three customers sat at stools along the counter. From behind the counter, two men faced Hatch, a younger man of slight build in his early- to mid-twenties and an older potbellied man. Obviously they were the sales help. Except for Hatch, every one in the room was dressed the same—blue denim jeans, a sweat-soaked, long sleeved, western cut shirt, and a cheap polyester ball cap advertising somebody's agricultural service or product. Hatch was struck by how much advertising was being done everywhere he looked, and by how little attention any of the customers—who were the targets of the advertising—seemed to be paying to it.

Hatch stepped to the counter and waited to be helped. To his right, the slighter parts man seemed to be scrolling through an online catalog at an antiquated computer, searching for a part by brand and description while his customer looked on. A few steps farther down the counter, the potbellied parts man was re-emerging from the shelf area carrying what appeared to be a big water pump, possibly for a truck or tractor.

After what seemed five minutes, the slender parts man swiveled his computer monitor around so his customer could study a page of diagrams and then stepped over to Hatch. "How can I help you?" he asked.

"Wonder if I could talk to Molly," Hatch said quietly.

Slender looked down at Hatch's clothes. "Can I tell her what you want?"

Hatch hadn't prepared an answer for this question, but he was determined to meet the woman. On the spur of the moment, he responded, "I saw a Help Wanted sign in the window."

This answer startled Slender who looked at Hatch suspiciously. After a moment, he turned and yelled over his shoulder into the shelf area, "Mol! You've got a guy here looking for a job."

Instantly, every eye in the store was on Hatch. There was no answer from the back of the store. Customers and sales help kept staring at Hatch as though an alien from outer space had just landed.

There was a time when this kind of awkward focus would have embarrassed Hatch, and he would have dived for emotional cover. He was beyond that now. He looked back at Slender and smiled confidently.

Gradually, the others went back to their work. Slender drifted back to the customer he had been helping, saying, "She'll likely be here in a minute."

Hatch didn't know what he was going to say when Molly appeared, but he trusted himself to the moment and waited. When Molly finally appeared from the back of the store, she stepped out from between two rows of shelves, dressed like all the men, except that her clothes were the feminine version and were freshly laundered and ironed.

Molly was neat as a pin, a simile that seemed perfectly apt in this setting. Her petite frame was perhaps five feet four inches in height. Her long hair was dark with natural highlights resulting from prolonged exposure to clean air and lots of sunshine. Her eyes were dark, her features refined, and she was slim—slim enough to give the impression that she was not altogether well.

The only word Hatch could think of to describe her smile was *luminous*. Whether she would have been beautiful, or even pretty, without her radiant smile was unclear to Hatch from the first moment he saw her. After seeing her, it didn't really matter.

To reach the spot where Hatch was standing, Molly had to walk the length of the service counter. She moved with a sort of fluid grace. As she came, each of the men in the store greeted her.

"Hi, Mol."

"H'lo, Mol."

"Miss Lewis," a customer nodded and touched the brim of his ball cap.

"He's there." Slender pointed toward Hatch without looking up from his computer screen.

"Hi, Molly," said another.

Each of these greetings was uttered in a friendly and almost reverential tone. Hatch didn't know whether he had ever seen anyone so completely and effortlessly dominate a social setting. He would not have been at all surprised if each of the men in the room had prostrated himself before this unlikely royalty. As she moved, it seemed as though the flies trapped inside the store and bumping futilely against the windowpanes to get out had stopped buzzing out of respect. The ever-present noise of the nearby freeway seemed to fade into silence. Hatch felt as though he had unwittingly stumbled into a scene from Disney's *Cinderella*.

Hatch's first impulse in reaction to the deification of this young country girl was to scoff. He wasn't sure that her brightness and neatness warranted the suspension of the earthly standards we hold all other mortals up against. He was clearly not ready for the effect she was about to have on him.

When Molly stepped in front of him across the service counter, she simply said "Hi, I'm Molly Lewis."

Thirty-eight

HATCH HADN'T COME TO SNOWVILLE FOR LOVE. He felt he already had love in his life. But when Molly Lewis spoke to him, love is what he found. He had flirted with ideas of romance at various moments throughout life. He found what he considered to be true love with Patty. If he hadn't been truly in love with Patty, it was certain that she had been in love with him. Without being moved by love, no woman, no person, could have endured the hurt and disappointment Patty had encountered and have responded so consistently with kindness and respect toward him as Patty had.

Hatch admitted to himself that he did not have a great capacity for love. Or, perhaps, it was a matter of not having developed his capacity for love. Because he was anemic or perhaps maimed in this respect, he had managed to return only a fraction of the greater love bestowed on him by those who had greater capacity. Patty topped the list. She loved in the whole-hearted, clear-eyed, realistic fashion of a being that accepts imperfections and loves in spite of them. Jenna and Ryan loved him as their father with that love that nature craves—innocent and trusting. How Doris, his mother, loved him was still something of a mystery to Hatch. The love he felt *for* her could best be described as the comfort of familiarity. The love he felt *from* her seemed injured, perhaps so often that it was more scar tissue than flesh.

Hatch had felt love of various types and intensities for and from other men and women, but they were also fractional.

But when Molly Lewis spoke to Hatch, looked at Hatch, smiled at Hatch, he practically melted. His first overpowering impression was that Molly loved him. He felt instantly accepted, valued, and trusted by her. There was no accounting for the emotion that her smile moved within him. He suddenly wanted to warn her away. He felt like he was facing a person who had somehow managed to keep herself unblemished by contact with the mainstream of humanity. For her sake, he felt the urge to cry out, *No, you don't know me. You don't know what a failure I have been. You don't know how many times I have selfishly disregarded the well-being of others and indulged my own whims. You don't know what dirt, what filth, what degradation I have fallen among. You don't know how often I have turned my back on others who have loved me and requited their love with callous neglect and criminal indifference. You don't know how often I have slinked into the shadows to avoid the call to stand up for a noble and needful cause because I love my own comfort and worship leisure. You don't know how I have rationalized away every crime and sin I have committed and laid the fault on the doorsteps of others. You don't know what a coward I have been. Run from me. Leave me. Let me be the miserable wretch I am. I leave nothing but heartache wherever I go.*

As unreasonable as the impulse seemed, Hatch felt like he should beg her pardon and ask her to forgive him because he was unworthy of her. At the same time, he wanted to ask her to heal him, to unmake him, and to remake him like she was.

Hatch could feel a tear from the outside corner of his eye break lose and roll down his cheek. Quickly, he reached up to wipe it away. He swallowed hard.

"Hi, I'm Hatch Stephens." Awkwardly, he turned and pointed at the sign in the window. "I want to apply for a job." He watched Molly's face to detect the moment when she would recognize him for what he really was and turn away in terror or disgust.

Molly smiled easily. "I'm pleased to meet you, Hatch. Why don't you come back to the office where we can visit?"

Hatch felt wooden-legged and stumbling as he rounded the service desk and followed Molly through the stacks. As they walked, he lectured himself, *What is the matter with you? You're acting like a schoolboy. You're older than this woman, and you are acting like a ninny. Tell her why you're really here.*

The office was comfortably but simply appointed. On entering the room, Hatch noticed a young girl, maybe six or seven years old—about Ryan's age—sitting at a side table, drawing.

"Hatch, this is Rachel," Molly said. "Honey, this gentleman and I are going to talk about the store. You can stay but try to be quiet."

Rachel had long blonde hair, hanging in ringlets. Hatch was startled to see that the girl wore a dress. He had not seen a dress since he arrived in Snowville. Most of the women he had seen wore denims. Those who were dressier wore pants. Rachel turned back to her drawing, humming softly to herself.

"Well, Hatch," said Molly, motioning him to a chair and sitting behind her desk, "we are a farm equipment and automotive parts store. We supply the repair shop next door and sell to walk-in business. Do you have any experience in the parts business?" she asked.

"Not really," answered Hatch honestly. "But I do have some retail experience and I know quite a lot about cars."

Molly smiled. "There isn't a boy of thirteen in this community who can't say the same."

Hatch laughed. "You're right. But I am a very quick learner. At least as quick as most of those boys."

Molly was not at all unpleasant. "Have you ever been a farmhand?" she asked.

"Not really," answered Hatch again. "But I have some experience in assessing and improving business processes to improve profitability."

"Those sound like worthwhile skills." Molly seemed to be enjoying their visit, though it was immediately obvious that Hatch didn't have the skills needed for the job he was seeking.

"Actually, we are profitable as a business," Molly said. "We're really seeking additional service desk help. You're consulting skills might be needed more by some of the other businesses in town," she said, laughing.

Hatch knew that the moment of truth had arrived. He had been striving with his might for a whole year to discover the source of his rabid fascination with the place where the sun rises. His striving had led him to Molly. He was now sitting in the town where the sun rises, and Molly was decidedly connected to this chain of events that had begun to transform his life. He could not risk the possibility that she would dismiss him and this chance be lost to him. He knew he must speak. He looked across at her and felt that she would be willing to listen, to help. He took the leap.

"Molly," he said as steadily as he could manage, "I realize that I'm not a sterling candidate for the position. I know it's near to closing time for you, and I don't want to be a nuisance. But I would like to tell you a bit about myself. Maybe you could suggest my next steps.

"A year ago today, the day after Labor Day, I awoke from a drunken stupor on the streets of Seattle. I was down and out. My life was in ruins. I had lost my career, lost my family, lost my self-respect, and betrayed everyone who ever tried to help me. I had nowhere else to go and was planning to take my own life.

"Something happened inside me while I lay on that sidewalk, drooling like a lunatic, wet with my own urine. Something I can't explain. When I awoke, I was hungry for light. It was a hunger greater than the thirst for alcohol. So you know it was powerful." Hatch smiled sadly.

"I knew from that moment that to find myself I needed to go to the place where the sun rises. Of course, I had no idea where that would be, except that it was east of Seattle. So, I started walking.

"As I've walked, I've changed. I've slain some of the demons that bound me. I've been helped miraculously by a few saints—a few angels. I still have a lot of changing to do. But I believe that if you had seen me, known me, a year ago, you would be able to see the difference. It has not been easy. But I feel I'm coming to life again.

"This afternoon when the freeway was closed, a friend and I stopped at Madge's Diner to get a bite, and Madge happened to mention that Snowville is the place where the sun rises. I can't tell you what effect her words had on me. When I asked her about it, she told me about you. I knew I had to meet you."

Hatch's head was down. Tears filled his eyes and slid down his cheeks.

"I don't mean to trouble you, Molly. But I'm desperate. If you have any thoughts about what this town where the sun rises could possible mean to a man who had fallen as low as a man can go, I hunger to hear them. I beg you."

For a man who had been too proud through his entire life ever to ask for help from others, Hatcher A. Stephens III had now descended the full distance. When he heard in his own voice the words *I beg you*, a barrier ruptured within him. He put his hands to his face and began to weep. He was embarrassed to be crying in front of a woman he didn't even know, but each effort to bring the tears under control only intensified the flood of emotions beginning to spill from his chest through his eyes.

No one spoke. Hatch was struggling mightily to redeem his manhood, but with little success. He sobbed. Then he felt a cool hand on his cheek. Looking up through tear-flooded eyes, he saw little Rachel standing beside him, her face a study in pity. Pity for him. The pity and alarm a child might have for a wounded puppy. Pure, innocent, unabashed caring for another living being. Hatch could not help himself. Tears were flooding his eyes, spilling down his face, and soaking the front of his shirt. Little Rachel laid her head on his shoulder and put her arms around his neck as his chest heaved convulsively. He heard the door close partially behind him and realized that he and Rachel were alone with his boundless sorrow and endless tears.

After minutes had passed, Rachel released her grip on his neck, kissed him on the cheek, and left through the door. When Hatch's fits of sobbing began to subside a little, he looked around the office and spied a box of tissues. Taking a handful of them, he dabbed at this face and clothes to begin cleaning up the mess he was making. Periodically, he dropped his head again and cried as successive waves of sorrow swept through him.

Hatch no longer worried about time. He didn't worry about being left alone in someone else's office. He didn't worry about being red-eyed or puffy cheeked. He didn't worry about being embarrassed. He had exceeded all boundaries where embarrassment could possibly matter. He let his emotions go and cried openly, deeply, cleansingly until all of his remorse poured out.

Gradually, the storm abated. Hatch got himself under control enough to stand. He reached for another handful of tissues. As he did so, he noticed a note lying before him on Molly's desk. Taking it up, he read, *You're hired. Be here tomorrow morning at seven. Mol.*

Hatch took the note with him. Walking out of the office and across a little open space behind the shelving area, he found an outside door. He went out, pulling the door shut behind him. He walked around the building onto the paved street that headed back to the motel. He went directly to his room, pulled the blinds, cranked up the cooler, and lay on the bed. He took a towel with him from the bathroom to soak up the tears that continued to flow until a peaceful sleep enthralled him.

Thirty-nine

NEXT MORNING, MOLLY INVITED HATCH BACK INTO the office to work out the details for his employment. Molly looked physically fatigued. Hatch felt emotionally drained. No mention was made of the previous afternoon's discussion.

Molly told Hatch a little about the business. Molly's father had owned it until his early death five years earlier. At the time of his death, the business included both the repair service and the parts store. He left it to his two children, Molly, who was living in Tremonton at the time, and Dave, her younger brother. The children had later decided to sell off the repair business, though it still shared the same building, on lease from them. Dave proved to be none other than Slender, whom Hatch had met briefly at the service counter the day before.

Molly revealed to Hatch how little the position paid. Hatch countered that he needed only enough to live on. She asked him where he would live. The motel would be too expensive on his pay. Hatch asked if there were any rentals in town. Molly called Dave into the office to discuss the living arrangements.

Dave was nearly as slender as Molly. He was a handsome young man with mild manners. "I don't know of any rentals," Dave reported.

"We're trying to think of a place for Hatch to live while he gets settled in," Molly replied thoughtfully.

"Don't know." Dave shook his head.

Dave was very respectful and tender in his regard for Molly. He didn't seem to resist the idea of Hatch working at the store and didn't seem to be stonewalling in the discussion of finding a place to rent. He simply didn't know of a place.

"We don't really have room at the house for another person," said Molly.

"I guess I could stay at the motel until something opens up," Hatch replied.

"Way too expensive. You know," Dave spoke to Molly, "one thing we could do would be to clean out the old tack shed. It doesn't have air conditioning but it does have a stove and a bed. A guy could get by there for a while."

"Oh, my heavens!" said Molly, laughing. "It was a fun place to play when we were kids, but you wouldn't ask your worst enemy to live there."

"I wouldn't mind living there," Dave parried her reaction good-naturedly.

"Can I take a look at it?" asked Hatch.

"No, I won't hear of it," said Molly.

"There may not be any other choice right now," Dave said, shrugging.

That evening after the store closed, Hatch rode with Dave the two long blocks from the store to the old tack shed. Molly Lewis and Dave Fields lived with Molly's daughter, Rachel, in the old Fields place. Art Fields, their father, had owned a whole block of about six acres on the north side of town. The entire block was fenced as pasture and bounded on the east and west by the two main streets in Snowville. The family home faced south on a cross street just north of the elementary school. Twenty yards distant from the house was the tack shed where all the harnesses, saddles, shoeing equipment, and other gear needed in a horse culture hung on nails and from the exposed rafters.

The tack shed had one door and two windows, one in the front and one on the east side. The entire structure was made of wood. The interior of the shed was open with no partitions. Along the east wall was a dingy, sagging cot. In the northwest corner was an old wood-and coal-burning stove. Every inch of wall space was covered with tack. The interior looked much as it would have if it had been in existence a hundred years earlier.

Hatch decided to give the tack shed a try. In his humbled, penitent mood, nothing seemed too meager. He reasoned that life owed him nothing. Whereas in his first life everything had been handed to him, in his new life he wanted the satisfaction of building everything from the bottom up. If in the future he lost everything, he could never have less that he had now. Actually, he knew that was not true. He did still have several thousand in cash on him, and fifty-two thousand waiting for him in a Boise bank. But most of it already belonged to others.

The tack shed was reached by a series of paving stones from the swinging board gate at the street. Next to the gate was a telephone pole with the only streetlight on the entire street. The light was a single incandescent bulb in a green metal shade. At night it shone down to the ground in a brightly lighted circle about thirty feet across, casting little light into the dense darkness all around it.

Hatch and Dave cleaned out the tack shed that evening, meaning that they threw away a few old, unusable pieces of gear, and rearranged the rest so that Hatch would have a place to hang his clothes and keep a wash bowl with his toiletries. Once or twice a week he could come over to the house or walk down to the truck stop to shower whenever he wanted. The truck stop sounded like a better arrangement to Hatch.

He had one more night in the motel. That gave him enough time to buy a couple of blankets and other necessaries.

Next night, Hatch Stephens moved into the tack shed.

forty

WORD OF HATCH'S COMING GOT AROUND THE small town pretty well. Some of the townspeople seemed to accept him immediately because he was working for Molly. Others seemed to view him with a mixture of curiosity and ridicule. Those who came into the store for parts soon recognized that he was a speedy and accurate sales person. He also began to make friends among the customers because he talked little and listened much.

He became a regular customer at Madge's. The crowd of men who came in each morning for coffee and a sweet roll for breakfast soon began to recognize him and acknowledge him by name.

"How's things at the tack shed?" one would ask with a laugh.

"I'm thinkin' about chargin' the rats rent," Hatch replied to their laughter.

"Hatch, why did you stop at Snowville? If you'd have stayed on the freeway another half hour you'd have come to civilization."

"I tried civilization earlier," Hatch said. "Nobody's happy there."

"May not be happy, but at least they're not poor," came the answer. Laughter always followed.

When Madge had a few minutes she often sat down across from Hatch and shared the local folklore with him. There wasn't much that Madge didn't know. And what she knew, she was happy to tell. Hatch looked forward to their good-natured banter.

Of course, he was most interested in Molly, Dave, and their family. They were not only his employers—Hatch still felt that Molly held the key to the mystery dominating his existence.

Soon after establishing his domestic pattern for work, meals, showers, life in the tack shed, and walking around the town for exercise, Hatch learned from Madge what everyone else in town already knew. The reason Molly was so thin and tired was that she was suffering from congenital heart disease, the same disease that took her father before he turned fifty. But Molly's condition was more advanced than his had been when he was her age. Doctors had already told her not to expect a long life.

"Tell me about Rachel," Hatch asked Madge.

"Sweet Rachel. Have you ever seen a sweeter angel than her?"

"Not many," said Hatch, thinking of his own little girl. "I imagine she has a dad. Where is he?"

"It's a long, sad story," Madge replied. She stirred her coffee with a swizzle stick. "Molly was the Rachel of her generation. We don't have a lot of kids in town, and when somebody like Molly or Rachel shows up, they stand out. It goes back to Molly's mom, Cindy. She was the same way during my generation.

"First, they're beautiful. Second, they are good. Third, they love other people, and other people love them for it. Cindy, Molly, and Rachel are like royalty in this town, if you haven't already noticed. Molly's illness has really struck at the heart of the town."

"Yeah, I see that." Hatch was eating a half grapefruit that he had tediously carved up before starting in with his spoon.

"Cindy was lucky to marry Art. He was a good man from the time he was born to his last breath. But there wasn't a guy in town for Molly when she came of age. The kids are all bused into Tremonton for middle school and high school. That's how we lose most of our kids. They go to school, fall in love, and end up moving away.

"Molly fell in love in high school." Hatch detected a change in Madge's tone at this point. Instead of reflecting on the town royalty, she now seemed to be introducing the villain.

"She was gorgeous, vivacious, loaded with personality. She wanted to be a cheerleader. Art tried to talk her out of it, but there was no way. And he couldn't break her heart. So she tried out. Everybody in town was so excited, not because they cared much about cheerleading at Bear River High, but because they cared so much about Molly.

"Well, she became the romantic target for all of the big boys at school. You know, the jocks. She was too young to see clearly. She dated a lot, and I think she tried to keep her head on straight. But eventually, Mr. Big won her over. Chad Lewis. Captain of the football team. Son of a local attorney who of late has become a county judge. And honestly, Chad was a pretty good kid himself. They were king and queen of everything, most-likely-to-do-this and most-likely-to-do-that.

"They fell in love. As I understand it, they were good all the way through school. Then Chad went away to school up in Logan. Molly couldn't because by that time Art was getting sick. He needed her help in the business.

"I don't know everything that happened from there. I understand that Chad was on an athletic scholarship. He began to get a little big for his britches. Then he forgot how to keep them on. When he came home from school during the summer, he was away from all the pretty coeds and came to Snowville looking for Molly again. One thing followed another, and I guess they had to hurry the marriage along a little to keep peace in the families and in the community.

"But I'll tell you, by that time, people around here did not like Mr. Lewis. He was cocky. He was rude. He talked down to people. Ridiculed the town, its people, and the things that are important to us.

"They got married and Chad insisted they move back to Tremonton where his stock was a lot higher. Rachel was born there six or seven months later. Chad would never bring them home. Art was real sick, but he always had to drive into Tremonton to see his daughter, and even then he wasn't welcomed. It broke his heart. He loved Molly so much. He had such great hopes for her. And he wanted to love Rachel. But he just didn't get a chance."

Just then, the phone rang. Madge jumped up. "Gotta go, hon."

"Hey, I want to hear the rest of this tomorrow," Hatch yelled after her.

Hatch was at Madge's with time to spare the following morning. His waitress was Timmy

"Madge in?" he asked her.

"She's back there."

"Will you tell her I want to talk to her?"

Hatch ordered and received his breakfast before he saw Madge. She walked past his table but did not stop.

"Madge," he called out.

She turned around.

"Are you going to tell me the rest of the story?"

"Can't, hon. I got a call from an anonymous tipster telling me to shut my mouth."

"What? Who?"

"Can't say." She started away again.

"Madge, wait a second." She came back to the table but did not sit down.

"You've got to tell me the end. There's nobody else for me to ask."

"Maybe it's better that way."

"Just tell me one thing." Hatch was practically whispering. "Did they divorce?"

Madge nodded the affirmative and walked away.

forty-one

Work and life in Snowville, Utah, were pleasant for Hatch. The customers who came into the store were generally friendly and likeable. These were people who knew how to work hard. Hatch enjoyed being around them. Early in October, one of the churches in Snowville had its annual harvest social. It was billed as a dance, but most of the adults were just standing around socializing. The hired band was more successful playing music the teens liked. The refreshments were abundant and tasty. There was no alcohol to drink and no smoke in the air. That suited Hatch's taste these days. He hoped it always would.

Molly was there, always surrounded by a cluster of friends and admirers. Dave had brought a date. They danced several dances and then stood around visiting like the others. Hatch noticed that the social hall was filled with laughter, sometimes raucous. He wondered how these people could unwind enough to really have a good time without alcohol.

Most of the socializers seemed happy to include Hatch in their circles. He recognized many faces and knew a dozen or so people other than Molly and Dave by name. Madge was not there.

Hatch sat down on one of the metal folding chairs on the outside of the dance floor just to rest his feet. Sitting there only a minute or two, he was delighted to receive a visit from Rachel who had come with her mother. Children apparently were not invited, but a few were present, probably the children of young or single parents who had to choose between bringing their children or staying home.

"Hi, Hatch," said Rachel unselfconsciously, leaning on one of his knees.

"Hi, beautiful," replied Hatch. Indeed the little girl looked splendid in a classy dress, her blonde hair again in meticulous ringlets.

Rachel didn't appear to even register the word *beautiful* and certainly didn't react to it. "Do you want to dance with me?" she asked in an earnest tone that children use when asking adults to play with them.

Hatch liked to dance. He had been a passable dancer earlier in his life and was not afraid to try.

"Of course, I want to dance with you," Hatch said enthusiastically, and Rachel's eyes brightened.

They stepped to the floor. Only a few other couples were dancing, so there was plenty of space for additional dancers.

As they danced, Hatch thought about the long reach. Both watched their feet to make sure Rachel didn't get injured. Hatch looked down on her and was overcome with affection. An image flashed through his mind of her pitying eyes when she comforted him the first time they met. He thought about Jenna and how she must look by now. How he wanted to dance with Jenna like this. How he wanted to hold her and tell her how sorry he was and how she could trust him to do what was right forever after. Rachel wasn't even his daughter, just his little friend. But her trust in him, her love for him, made him feel noble.

Tears came into Hatch's eyes again. He looked up to blink them away. He noticed as he did so, that everyone in the room was looking at him, or at least at Rachel. He couldn't help smiling back. *It doesn't get much better than this*, Hatch thought.

forty-two

As OCTOBER WANED, THE NIGHTS GREW COLDER. Hatch began building a little fire in the stove after work. By the time it burned down and cooled off, he was in bed and slept well. However, be began to realize that rising in the morning was going to be a major challenge when the temperatures really dropped.

The Friday after the harvest social, Hatch walked over to the truck stop after work to buy a snack. He had eaten his big meal for the day in the diner at noon. As usual, Madge sat with him for a few minutes telling him what she knew about many of the townspeople. Hatch was beginning to realize that Madge was a social outsider in her own right. He thoroughly enjoyed her but heard from others that she was a gossip and a busybody. He considered her a friend and was determined not to let the opinions of others change the way he saw her.

The fact was that Hatch liked everybody in town. This was a new sensation for him, since throughout his life he had tended to put people in categories. Like all social category systems, his system ultimately resulted in one of two judgments, acceptable or unacceptable.

As he walked toward the truck stop he was mentally thinking through all of the people he knew in town to this point. Not one fell into the unacceptable category. He knew there were troubles in town, and troubled people, but he still liked them. He couldn't think of a single person he didn't like.

Aware that a car was approaching, he slowed his pace and stood waiting. A smoke-colored Lexus sedan with dark tinted windows passed him slowly. As it did so, the driver's window lowered. The driver was a younger man with blond hair, fashionably cut and groomed. He wore dark glasses, which he pushed up on his forehead as he passed by, showing Hatch his face clearly. At first, Hatch took the driver for a passing motorist, since he had never seen that vehicle in town. But the driver was looking directly at Hatch. Only one word came to Hatch's mind to describe the look on the man's face—*malice*.

After a prolonged passing, the driver put up the window and gunned the engine, shooting gravel and dust back at Hatch. The entire incident puzzled Hatch, but he shrugged it off and resumed walking.

Of course, there was no gym in Snowville. To stay fit, Hatch worked out daily, as best he could, in the tack shed. A workout included pull-ups from the rafters, pushups, and sit-ups. He developed a short routine lifting an anvil he found among the shoeing equipment in the shed. On his days off, Hatch jogged north up the Holbrook Road and back before hitting the showers at the truck stop. He also did his best to continue wise eating habits, which meant a lot of cheap salads and canned fruit dishes at Madge's Diner. Despite the obstacles imposed by his circumstance, he continued to feel well; his weight continued to drop, and his overall condition was as good as any man in town.

While Hatch was generally accepted in the community, there was one notable townsman who remained distant and cool toward him. That man was Deputy Paul Spanos, a Snowville resident employed by the Bear River County Sheriff. Paul's duties ranged throughout the county, but he was the resident official for the northwest end and lived in Snowville.

Paul didn't join in the general adulation of Hatch. Perhaps it was his natural skepticism, or perhaps he was trained to be suspicious of strangers until they were proven innocent. He was not aggressive toward Hatch, but generally stood off in social settings, arms folded over his chest to accentuate the sergeant stripes on his sleeves, doing what could accurately be described as keeping an eye on Hatch. Hatch probably fueled Deputy Spanos's suspicions, if indeed the deputy had any. Hatch was a little fearful that his past might unexpectedly catch up to him as it had in North Bend, and he found himself tensing up whenever Spanos was near. While Hatch's credit rating was doubtlessly flawed, there were no warrants out there waiting to be fulfilled. He tried to remain cordial toward the deputy and hoped that time would come to his aid.

The Sunday morning after Hatch's brief encounter with the Lexus driver, he happened to be visiting with Madge after breakfast. Since the store was closed on Sunday, he was in no hurry. The diner was practically empty. Half the town was in church; the other half was off recreating.

Madge steadily shied away from questions about Molly, but Hatch felt he already knew all he needed about the Fields and Lewis families. This morning he brought up Paul Spanos.

"Tell me about Deputy Spanos," Hatch said to Madge.

"What about him?" she asked.

"He doesn't like me. I'm not sure why."

"Maybe you are a little too close to Molly," Madge said quietly, as if she were just making a wild guess.

Hatch thought for a moment. "Ah, is he sweet on her? I hadn't noticed that."

"I thought we weren't going to talk about Molly." Madge deliberately kept her eyes on her coffee.

"We're not. We're talking about the deputy," replied Hatch. "Besides, you were the one who mentioned her name."

"Paul is the same age. He has been sweet on her since childhood. I told you that Molly went for Chad Lewis because there were no boys in town. That wasn't completely true. Paul was always there, and always interested. I don't think anything has changed. That's all I'm saying."

"What can I do to close the gap with Spanos?" Hatch had to ask the question.

"You're a guy. Figure it out. Gotta go, hon." She was off.

Hatch did try to figure it out. He decided not to leave the matter lying around. In his new mode of cleaning up problems in a timely fashion, he decided to talk to Spanos.

Walking back to the tack shed, he had to pass Deputy Spanos's little home across the street from the school. The Sheriff's Department SUV was in the drive. Hatch walked to the door and knocked.

Deputy Spanos came to the door in his uniform trousers and an undershirt. He nodded at Hatch but waited for him to speak.

"Got a minute?" Hatch asked.

Spanos hesitated, visibly deliberating his response, but finally said, "Sure, come on in." Spanos led him into a comfortably but simply furnished living area. It looked much like all the others in town. It was tidy, but Hatch noticed that a coffee table in front of the couch was covered by several road atlases spread open for Spanos's inspection. Hatch was going to ask if Spanos was planning a trip, but noticed that the atlases were open to maps of European countries.

"Are you interested in Europe?" Hatch asked in steady voice.

Again, Spanos was slow to respond. Hatch waited him out.

"Yeah," Spanos finally said with a shrug. "Yeah. I spent a couple of years in Belgium and still have friends there. I'm thinking of visiting them next summer. How can I help you?" he asked Hatch.

"I'm sorry to come unexpected and uninvited," Hatch said. "I was just walking by to my little place, and thought I'd try to get acquainted."

Hatch glanced around Spanos's room for any pictures or objects that might suggest that the two men had something in common. He saw nothing. He decided to be direct. "You're a public figure in town, known and respected. On the other hand, I'm new. I'm an outsider. You are paid to protect the residents. I'm guessing you are wondering why a guy like me drops into town out of nowhere. What would his motives be? Does he pose a risk to law-abiding citizens? And so forth. If you have any questions that might hang like a cloud over my head, I'm ready to give you some honest answers."

The two men were still standing. Spanos had not offered Hatch a seat.

"I do have some questions. I had more but have already satisfied a few," Spanos replied. "I know you come from Washington State, and I know there are no outstanding warrants for you there. But I don't know where else you've been."

Hatch was glad to get a conversation going with Spanos. "I'm a lifelong resident of Washington," he told the deputy. "In fact, I never lived anywhere else until January of this year. I spent eight months in Nampa, Idaho. I will be happy to give you contact information for my employer there if you'd like to talk to him."

"Why did you come to Snowville?"

"It was partially accidental," Hatch answered. "I was passing through on my way to Denver when the accident closed the freeway. I saw a Help Wanted sign and asked Molly Lewis for a job. She hired me."

Hatch looked at Spanos again. He was debating how candid he should be with the deputy. He decided to go for broke. "Look, I'm a recovering alcoholic. I've been away from home for a year, trying to rectify past mistakes. But I'm not a criminal. I'm not a con man. My credit rating wasn't good when I left home. But I've been sober for a year. I've worked hard and have saved some money. I don't think I pose a risk to anyone in town."

"How much did you tell Molly before she hired you?" asked Spanos.

"Most of that, and some worse," replied Hatch.

"I'll check your credit rating," Spanos warned. "And I'll warn Molly that she is taking a risk."

"I don't blame you," Hatch said.

Spanos, hands on his hips, looked hard at Hatch. "Stephens, you don't impress me by coming here and baring your soul. I'm not fooled by that. If you are clean, so be it. I'm not trying to persecute you. But I also know that con men are the first to say they aren't con men. They're the first to drop a few hints about past crimes, trying to convince everybody they have come clean. They want to be buddy-buddy. They come knocking on doors, like you are doing."

Spanos walked to the door and opened it, gesturing with his head for Hatch to leave.

"There's nothing you can do here to take the pressure off," Spanos continued, "except stay clean. I'm watching you. I'm not here to be your friend. I'm the law. Talk is cheap. We'll see how you do. If you go straight, great. If you don't, I'll be there to bust you."

Hatch nodded as he walked out the door. "Sounds fair," he said. Walking out into the street Hatch shook his head. *That went well*, he thought.

forty-three

LATE SUNDAY AFTERNOON, HATCH WAS TIDYING UP the tack shed. The day had been cool but beautiful. He did his laundry at the truck stop, built a little fire in the stove, and was spending a minute trying to get organized for the week ahead. He planned to take a walk around town before twilight vanished completely.

Without warning, he heard a voice from out on the street. "Hey you, in the tack shed. Come out here."

Surprised, Hatch stepped to the street-side window and looked out. There he saw the smoke-color Lexus parked in front of his gate. Standing under the street light that was just beginning to cast its circle of light in the darkening evening stood the driver Hatch had seen on Friday.

Hatch opened the door and walked to the street. He had no idea what to expect. As Hatch stepped though the gate and closed it behind him, the driver began to crowd him. He was obviously feeling aggressive, and Hatch could tell the man was half drunk.

The driver was taller than Hatch and had a bulky physique. Hatch guessed him to be near thirty, about the same age as Molly, Dave, and Paul Spanos. He was well dressed. Driving a new or nearly new Lexus meant that he had a significant source of income.

"How can I help you?" asked Hatch.

"You can get out of this town." The younger man's expression was jeering.

There was a time in Hatch's life when this kind of aggressive behavior would have caused him great alarm. He would have started negotiating for his survival immediately. That was the old Hatch. This was the new.

"Why would I want to do that?" Hatch stood his ground.

Driver put his hands on Hatch's chest and shoved, clearly trying to provoke a fight.

The shove barely moved Hatch. He could feel the adrenaline level rising in him. He was not afraid. In fact, this was the moment he had waited for, trained himself for. He began to feel the excitement of gearing up for combat.

He was sensing his next move when the back door of the sedan opened. Both men looked in the direction of the movement. Stepping from behind the door was little Rachel Lewis.

Before Hatch could speak, the driver said to Rachel, "Girlie, get back in the car 'til I tell you to get out."

Hatch was shocked. "Are you Rachel's dad?" he asked.

"You don't need to know. You need to get out of here. I won't tell you again."

Rachel had advanced a step or two, "But, Daddy," she began to speak.

"Girlie, you get in the car."

Hatch's eyes narrowed.

The driver started toward Rachel. "If you are still here the next time I come, I'll bust your head," he said to Hatch over his shoulder as he took Rachel by the arm and moved her back toward the car.

"Nice way to talk in front of your daughter," said Hatch.

The driver slammed the door when Rachel was inside. He said no more, just pointed at Hatch as if to say, "You have been warned." He reentered the car and drove the remaining distance to the house where Rachel again got out of the car and walked dejectedly to the door. She turned and waved timidly to her daddy whose car was already speeding away in a cloud of gravel and dust. She knocked slightly, and the door opened, admitting her to the home.

Hatch watched all of this from his vantage point in front of the tack shed. He was riled. He could feel the hair standing on his neck. He hoped the driver would return so they could continue their conversation. He wanted to run, or shout, or throw something. He was feeling an overdose of adrenaline and needed a way to dispel it. The sensation caused him to reflect on what he was doing. Now that he knew how to fight and had developed a taste for it, he suddenly realized that fighting could become just as addicting as alcohol had been. Just the thought of losing control over his emotions and actions frightened Hatch. Was this another in a long list of things he would have to bring under his control?

forty-four

Despite the head of steam Hatch was feeling, and regardless of his hunger to actually try out his hard-won fighting skills for a worthy cause, he was stunned by the encounter. He returned to the tack shed and put on his coat to warm him against the cold night air. A walk around town would give him a chance to clear his head and dissipate the adrenaline load he was carrying. Otherwise, he never would get to sleep.

He was already a ways past the Fields home when he heard the front door close and Molly's voice calling to him.

"Hatch." Molly walked to the street and came toward him. She was also wearing a coat. Hatch waited.

"Hi," she greeted him. "Are you going for a walk?"

"Yes," he replied. "Thought I should enjoy these fall evenings. I'm imagining the winters can be pretty hard here."

"They can." Her voice was light. As always, Hatch was amazed that Molly never seemed to have a care in the world.

"Have you had a nice day?" she asked.

"It was a nice day." He wanted to add, *Until five minutes ago when I bumped into a jerk that appears to be your ex. How could you possibly have married a person like that?* But he did not put those thoughts into words.

"I'm glad. This is such a pretty place. Such good people. Such a lovely time to be alive."

Hatch reasoned that Molly must know what he was thinking. She must have anticipated the hundred questions swirling around in his mind. There was a time when he would have asked them. He would have just blurted out, *Tell me about all of this. How did this ever happen to you? How can you stand to let your precious daughter go with that guy? Tell me. Tell me.*

But that was the old Hatch. This was the new. He would wait and let her make her move when the time was right for her.

"When I was a little girl, my dad and I walked around town every Sunday night. Just like this." She laughed a girlish laugh, but the laugh had a weary edge. Hatch heard it.

He wanted to answer, *I actually heard that. You are cheerful, but you're tired. You try with all your might to see the good in everyone and everything. But you see how imperfect this world is, and you are saddened and disappointed by it. I heard that. And you didn't even have to tell me.* Hatch savored this moment of realization, but he said nothing.

"You are very reflective this evening, Hatch." Molly looked up at him in the dim light and smiled.

You have a lovely smile, Hatch was thinking. *You are such a good person.*

"It has taken me a long time to learn to listen," Hatch answered her. "When I have the presence of mind to listen, I am always rewarded."

"You are very wise," she replied simply.

Partway around the block, they stopped and looked up into the stars. Without the ambient light of the city, the stars blazed away in the sky. They listened to the last songs of the curlews down by the creek. When the birds fell silent, the last crickets of the season took up their crippled symphony.

They extended their walk well into the darkness of the October evening. Hatch enjoyed every step, every moment. Eventually, Molly put her arm through his. "Do you mind?" she asked. "This is so like a million walks with my father. I have missed them dearly."

Hatch laughed. "It's not very flattering to walk with a pretty girl and realize she thinks of you as her father."

"It should be flattering," she replied. "You are a father. Not mine, but a little girl's who feels the same way about you that I felt about my father. Being a father is as close to being a god as you can get in this world. You couldn't wish for more in this life. You shouldn't wish for less."

"Do girls love their fathers?" Hatch asked.

"When they are small, they worship their fathers."

"What if their fathers are jerks?" He couldn't help asking the question, still thinking about his earlier encounter. The impulsive question shattered the mood they had enjoyed. Hatch immediately regretted having spoken.

They walked in silence for a minute or two. "Are you asking about you as a father or about someone else?" Molly asked.

Hatch's breath caught in his throat. Molly's simple question was so incisive. Hatch had been thinking about poor little Rachel whose father was a jerk. Molly's question moved his thinking to poor little Jenna whose father was a jerk.

"Thank you for asking that," he said.

"Your daughter worships you. I have no doubt."

"How did you know I have a daughter?" he asked.

"Just a guess," she said, smiling. They had reached the walk to the Fields home. "What a lovely, wonderful walk this has been. Hatch, thank you so much." She patted his hand and then extracted her arm from his. "See you in the morning?"

"Sure thing, Boss." Hatch walked back down the street toward the tack shed, the gravel crunching under his feet. His thoughts were on Jenna. Did she still think of him? Would it be possible to still enjoy the fragments of her worship? Or had he missed it altogether?

forty-five

WEEKS PASSED WITHOUT HATCH SEEING RACHEL'S FATHER again. Hatch fell hopelessly in love with Rachel. She came to the store each day after school and read or drew on the counter next to his station. She was equally close to her uncle David. She often sat on David's lap and questioned him about his blossoming love affair with Sarah Jensen.

"Do you love her?" Rachel asked.

"None of your business," answered David with a smile.

"Do you love her as much as me?" Rachel persisted.

"I don't love anybody as much as you," David answered in a romantic voice.

"Yuck," Rachel said and pushed him away.

"Are you going to marry her?"

David looked at the girl thoughtfully. "If I do, do you want to come and live with us?"

"Where will you live?" she asked.

"Probably in Grandpa's house for a while," answered her uncle.

"No," Rachel replied as she finished writing her name on a picture she had drawn. "I want to stay with Mom."

David looked up at Hatch who had been listening to this exchange. The worry showed in his face.

On Sunday evenings, Hatch stopped at the Fields home to invite

Molly to walk with him. Increasingly, she was too weary to do so. She was also absent from work more often as winter neared. David assumed more of the responsibility in the business.

"How's Molly?" Hatch asked David on a Monday morning when she did not appear at the store. He had stopped by the previous evening hoping to walk with her, but she had declined because she wasn't feeling well.

David was a little misty-eyed. "She's losing ground, Hatch. The blood is pooling in her system. Her heart can't keep up. Her doctor has her on the list for a heart transplant, but the chances are not good. Demand is high. Supply is limited."

"I'm sorry," Hatch replied, sharing her brother's concern. "What do you need from me?"

"Just remember her in your prayers. We've got to keep her calm."

"Let me help where I can," Hatch asked earnestly.

"We will. You've already helped. You've sort of filled a hole here. It's a good thing you came along when you did. Molly has missed Dad so much. I think you've kind of been filling Dad's shoes."

"That would be an honor," Hatch said. Then turning his thoughts to David, he asked, "What's up with the wedding plans?"

"They're up," David replied with a smile. "I think we're going to get married during the holidays. She'll be back from school for Thanksgiving, and I think we'll make the announcement then."

"Terrific," said Hatch. "Do you need a best man?"

"If we do, you'd be a good one."

"Keep me in mind."

Hatch thought often about his earlier run-in with Chad Lewis. He hadn't come back, which was just as well. Hatch increasingly realized that he had to stay away from Rachel's father. Maybe that was just a bad weekend for Lewis. Maybe not. At any rate, Hatch knew he would have to back away from a fight. There was no way he could hit Rachel's father. If the girl worshipped Lewis, and Hatch was sure she did, then fighting Lewis would be hurting her. Hatch could not do that.

One afternoon, when David left Hatch to mind the store, Rachel came in after school. She took up her spot next to Hatch. All of the customers who came in knew Rachel by name. They all delighted in talking to the bright little girl.

Hatch shouldn't have done it, but he couldn't restrain himself from asking Rachel about her father. "Rachel, do you love your father?"

She looked up at Hatch thoughtfully. "Yes. Do you love your little girl?"

You're just like your mother, Hatch thought. Then he said to her, "Of course I do. Tell me about your father."

"He's sad," answered Rachel.

"Is that all?" Hatch asked.

"Yes." Rachel climbed down from the stool to visit the bathroom.

Hatch had learned through patient discovery that Chad Lewis had bi-weekly visitation rights with his daughter. While Lewis could have enjoyed her company every other weekend, he actually saw her about every six weeks. David, like everyone else around Hatch, was reluctant to talk about personal matters, but he briefly complained that Lewis sometimes called to announce that he wouldn't be by to get Rachel. Sometimes he didn't even call. Rachel was broken-hearted, David related, but as was her custom, she quickly looked for something to cheer herself. That usually involved doing something nice for another person.

Hatch could see David's affection for his niece. Hatch admired him for that.

It had seemed to Hatch only a matter of time before he must face Chad Lewis again. He had no idea why Lewis had singled him out as a target for his malice. Maybe Rachel had told Lewis about dancing with Hatch. Maybe she had related that they had become close friends and spent time together at the store after school. Possibly that would stir jealousy in the father. Maybe Lewis resented Hatch's closeness to Molly and had heard of their Sunday walks. Like everything else in a small town, these things were known.

Snow fell on Thanksgiving weekend. The town was buzzing with the announcement of a Christmas-time marriage between Sarah Jensen and David Fields. Molly invited Hatch to Thanksgiving dinner. The gathering was festive but quiet. Rachel was away at Lewis's family. David and Sarah were there for dinner, but left soon after to visit her family as well. Hatch cleaned up the dishes. Molly rested on the couch. Not wanting to intrude further, Hatch slipped out the door and returned to the tack shed.

The shed had been passable as a residence in warmer weather. In the cold, it was totally inadequate. The little building had no insulation. Hatch kept a good fire going in the stove. He lay on his cot still dressed as darkness descended. He was thinking about the future. He had been sober for fifteen months. Alcohol, which had dominated his life, was now more distant from his thoughts. He felt the time was nearing when he could return to Seattle to settle his debts and set about picking up the pieces of his shattered life. He felt he was not the same man and would never be again. He longed to see Patty. He longed to see Jenna and Ryan. His only real fear was that his former life had vanished and that tenuous emotional ties with his family had completely dissolved.

As he lay thinking, a mighty whack on the front of the tack shed caused him to sit bolt upright on the cot. He rose and looked out the window. His heart sank. Parked in the circle of his own little street lamp was Lewis's grey Lexus. Lewis and another man were standing at the gate. Apparently they had thrown something against the door.

Hatch knew he could not hide in the shed. He dreaded going out, not because he was afraid of Lewis, but because he had no idea how to get past Lewis without hurting little Rachel.

forty-six

HATCH PULLED ON HIS COAT, FASTENED IT, and put on his newly purchased gloves before opening the door and going out into the night. He pulled the door tight to keep as much heat as possible in the tack shed. He was thinking of the previous Christmas, which seemed a lifetime earlier. That was the day he discovered he could take a hit in the face and survive. He might need to repeat that lesson tonight. He didn't think he was going to forget these holiday experiences.

The two men in front of him were of about equal size. Lewis wore an expensive leather jacket. His companion wore a ski parka. Both men were stamping their feet and blowing their hands in the cold weather.

"Happy Thanksgiving," Hatch said sarcastically.

"Funny man," said Lewis. "I told you to get out of town."

"I ignored you," replied Hatch.

"Well, I'm not making the same mistake again. You are coming with us. We'll take you a little ways out of town."

"Didn't think you could do it yourself, so you brought some help?" Hatch knew he was taunting Lewis. That wouldn't get him where he wanted to be, so he tried to talk. "Why do you want me to leave?" he asked.

Lewis walked over to the back door of the car, opened it, and ordered, "Get in."

"Nice car," said Hatch.

"If I have to tell you again, we're going to take you apart and put you in piece by piece."

"Sounds to me like you've been drinking," Hatch said without moving. "Are you sure you want to try taking me apart when you're not at the top of your game?"

"I could be a lot drunker than this and still handle you." Lewis walked toward Hatch.

"Why don't you tell your buddy to step aside, and you show me how you would do that."

"Nope, we're going to put you in the car. We're doing this my way."

"Don't think so," replied Hatch.

As Lewis and his partner advanced toward Hatch, all three men were surprised by a voice from the other end of the sedan, outside the circle of light. "Steady boys. No fights in this town on Thanksgiving night." Deputy Paul Spanos stepped out into the light. He was in uniform, his hand on the gun at his belt.

Hatch hadn't heard the deputy's Ford Explorer drive up, but Spanos lived just around the corner to the south by the elementary school. He could have walked. The question was, how did he know that a fight was imminent?

Lewis laughed. "It's Depidy Dog. Haven't seen you for a while, Spanos. Where you been hiding?"

"Chad, take your friend and git."

"We're not breaking the law here, Depidy. We were just about to give your neighbor a ride. I don't think he's got a car of his own, or anything else for that matter. Have you checked this guy out, Depidy? He comes blowing in here, sweeping all these country bumpkins off their feet. At the least, he's a vagrant. At the worst, he could be a criminal."

"He's none of your business." Spanos had not moved. His hand still rested on his weapon. Lewis' companion stepped back a pace, still not speaking.

"He's my business because he has been turning my own daughter against me." Lewis was shouting as he advanced on Hatch. He was several inches taller and had fifty pounds on Hatch, who now weighed maybe 175 pounds. "He's told her to stay away from me, and he's putting the moves on her mom."

Hatch remained silent.

"You're just going to get yourself in trouble, Chad." Spanos hadn't budged, but he also was doing nothing to deter Lewis.

Suddenly Lewis swung on Hatch. He was not as fast as Trevor had been, and Hatch had seen hundreds of punches coming at him since then, during his sparring sessions in Nampa. He ducked the punch and stepped back. Lewis advanced on him again. At the same time, he called to his companion, "Come on, Charlie. Depidy Dog doesn't want to explain this to the judge. He's not going to do anything."

Spanos roared, "Stand fast, Charlie. If I have to draw my weapon, I'm gonna use it."

Lewis looked around. Realizing that Charlie was going to be no help, he charged Hatch. The street was slick with snow. Hatch dodged Lewis, who went down on one knee.

Hatch now knew that Deputy Spanos was going to do nothing to stop a fight. He could also tell from Lewis's two moves that he was drunk enough to impair his reactions. Hatch knew that he could hurt Lewis if he wanted to. He became angry. His whipping at the hands of Trevor Martin was thoroughly humiliating. He despised himself for his weakness. For months he reflected on his cowardice in begging Sylvia to come to his aid when Tattoo and Assistant had threatened him in their Escalade. For eight months he endured beating after beating at the gym in Nampa until he learned to fight.

Now he could fight. Right now, right here, he could take this blowhard bully apart. Doing so might change the course of Lewis's life for the better. In many ways, Hatch saw his old self when he looked at Lewis. Pampered, everything he needed handed to him on a silver platter, good looks, and gradual decline. Maybe Lewis needed a Trevor in his life.

But Hatch also knew that he couldn't be the one to do it. That realization made him ache all over. He wanted to do it. He wanted to cut Lewis down to size. His hands itched inside his new gloves to go into action. He could feel the adrenaline in his system. This was his moment.

The trap he had stumbled into angered him. He was angry at Lewis, who was a jerk. He was annoyed at little Rachel for loving her father so desperately. He was angry at fate for robbing him of this opportunity that he had prepared himself for ardently. He hurt that this chance to redeem himself in combat was not to be his.

As Hatch reflected on the fate that brought him to this moment, he felt suddenly ashamed. How could he complain against a fate that had spared him, lifted him, and prospered him repeatedly? How could he feel angry over a fate that had put so many wonderful people in his path? Who was he, a beggar, to rail against a fate that bestowed grace evenhandedly on victim and aggressor alike?

Hatch knew that his bloodlust was just thinly disguised selfishness. He could not risk hurting Rachel or hurting Molly further. He loved them. He could not indulge his own appetite at their expense.

Lewis began to pummel Hatch with blows. Hatch would not fight back, so he ducked and weaved. Most of the blows were way off target. They glanced off his head, arms, and shoulders. The two men struggled in the street for several minutes. Hatch could hear Lewis beginning to breathe hard. His punches were losing their velocity and impact. So far, Lewis hadn't hurt Hatch. As Hatch kept moving, he could tell that the fight would soon be over. Even in the heat of battle, he began to pity Lewis. The big man cut a pathetic figure, half drunk, out of shape, consumed by rage, doubtlessly sensing that his glory days were over, fearful that life would pass him by. Hatch had been there. He had been spared, rescued. Who was going to rescue Lewis?

Lewis backed off to catch his breath. As he did so, Hatch said to him, "Lewis, you can't hurt me unless I let you. You are a bully and a coward. You hide behind your daughter's skirts. No one in this town will stand up to you, not because they're afraid of you, but because they don't want to hurt her. Even the deputy there, who prides himself on being the law in this town, is breaking the law right now for her sake."

Hatch knew what he must do. He couldn't pour out his anger on Lewis. But he could absorb the anger, swallow it up for his own sake, for Lewis's, for Rachel's, for Molly's, for the sake of all who were being touched by Lewis's tragic decline. Soberly, but not in anger, he said to Lewis, "Go ahead, Lewis, hit me. Get it out. I'll take your punches for Rachel's sake, because I love her the way she wants you to love her."

Lewis was enraged. He swung on Hatch again and again. Hatch dropped his guard and let the blows come. One blow landed directly on the end of his nose. He felt a blinding pain and heard the bones snap in his nose. Another punch stuck him on the left eyebrow that had so often been cut at the gym in Nampa. Another hard punch hit him midsection and doubled him over. But Hatch did not go down.

Shortly, Lewis's rage was spent. He gasped for air. His hands were on his knees. His chest heaved.

Hatch wiped his bloody nose with the back of his hand. "Okay," he said to Lewis, "you did your thing. That one was free. It was on me. But you see, Lewis, I am still here. And I will stay here until I decide to leave. There is nothing you can do about that."

Lewis stood, turned, and signaled to Charlie to get in the car. Hatch walked over beside Charlie and said to him. "Charlie, you got off easy tonight. Lewis gets away with this stuff because of his daughter. But you don't. Spread the word in Tremonton that Lewis had better come alone in the future. Anybody who comes with him goes down."

Charlie looked shaken by what he had watched. He nodded soberly and got into the car. Lewis gunned the Lexus and fishtailed his way to the corner.

Hatch and Spanos watched them go. "Why do you think he stopped when you were taking punches?" Spanos asked.

"Have you ever been drunk?" Hatch asked in return.

"Nope. Don't drink," Spanos answered.

"The exertion made him sick to his stomach. Any more and he would have lost all of his Thanksgiving dinner."

"Nice way to spend a Thanksgiving," Spanos commented.

"I'm glad you showed up to keep Charlie entertained."

"I got a call," replied Spanos.

"You just don't like me, do you?" asked Hatch. "Seemed to me that you'd have been happy if Lewis and I beat each other senseless."

Spanos sighed. "I just don't want to see Molly or Rachel get hurt. Or David. But, after watching your little performance this evening, I don't suppose we have any reason to worry about you. Have a good one."

Deputy Spanos walked away, leaving Hatch in a lonely circle of light on a snowy road.

forty-seven

HATCH STOOD IN FRONT OF HIS LITTLE mirror, wiping the blood from his face and inspecting the damage done by Chad Lewis. He was no longer angry at Lewis or Spanos. But the combination of his growing homesickness and the futility of dealing with people's troubles left him feeling a little discouraged. He reflected on his walk with Molly the evening of his first run-in with Lewis. He was certain now that she joined him on the walk just to bring him solace. What a great gift that was to people in distress.

Hatch heard a gentle rap on the door. He quickly put his shirt back on and opened the door to find Molly standing there in the dark. He felt sudden alarm. It was only thirty yards to the Fields house, but it was a cold night, the path was slick, and the wind was picking up. He could feel it through the cracks around the windows.

"Molly, what are you doing out here? You should have just yelled from the house."

"I'm okay, Hatch. Really, it's easier to walk over here than to yell. Can I come in?"

Hatch didn't know how to answer. He had never expected to have a visitor in the tack shed. He was almost embarrassed for her to see how he lived, though she knew the building far better than he did.

"Of course. You own the place," he said, pushing the door open wide.

"That may be true," she said quietly, "but a man's home is his castle. That can never be taken for granted."

"Or, in this case, his home is his tack shed." Hatch pulled the sole chair in the shed over near the stove, offering it to Molly. She sat and looked around.

"This shed brings back so many memories," she said softly. "As children, we usually played in the barn. But when we wanted to be alone, this is where we came. Other than us kids and the animals, Dad's most prized possessions were here."

She picked up an old spur and spun the wheel with her fingers.

"I understand you had a visit this evening," she said, looking at Hatch who continued to dab at his nose as he sat down on the cot. "I'm sorry that my troubles have come to roost on your doorstep."

"That's an interesting figure of speech," Hatch said. "But believe me, you have brought me no grief—only happiness."

"My ex-husband is not a happy person," Molly seemed to want to talk, not to discuss. Hatch did not respond, choosing instead to listen. "Please don't resent him for my sake. I don't resent him. I feel badly that his life is moving in the direction it is. But I hope that it's just temporary, and that it will turn around—for his sake and for Rachel's.

"Some people have wondered how I ever married Chad. He wasn't always as unhappy as he is now. But he was beginning to move in that direction, and I guess I thought I could help." She paused and then added, "But, I couldn't. I think maybe you were standing up for me and for Rachel this evening. That was very kind of you. Very strong. Very noble. Thank you."

Hatch nodded his acknowledgement but said nothing.

"Hatch, you may be aware that I am ill. It seems fairly serious, and I'm not sure how long it will take until I get better. It's possible that I won't recover. That's all right. No one ever had a happier, more wonderful life than I've had. If something goes terribly wrong, the only real regret I'll have is that I won't get to see Rachel grow to adulthood. I would love to be a grandmother."

Molly's eyes were wet. Hatch reached for a clean washcloth near his washbowl and handed it to her.

"Thank you." She dabbed at her eyes.

"But I really didn't come to talk about me, Hatch. I came to talk about you or rather about us. I want to tell you a story. Do you have a few minutes?"

Hatch nodded.

"Two years ago this coming spring, I learned from my doctor that my heart condition was advancing. He thought I might have no more than a year to live. I was devastated—not that I mind missing out on a long life, but that I had a daughter who had just turned five. Dave and I were trying to steady the business after Dad's death, but Dave wasn't ready to run it by himself. It was a very wearisome period.

"I prayed a lot. I cried a lot. The summer neared its end and Labor Day came. That was just a year before you came to Snowville. David and I went to the park for the Labor Day picnic. Rachel was with Chad. It was his turn to spend the holiday with her. When he brought her home that evening, we had hard words. Rachel cried to see the two people she loved most being unkind to each other. I was very sad.

"That evening I couldn't sleep. I had two needs that loomed mountainously before me. First, I needed help. I needed someone strong to stand beside me at the end, to help me help Rachel across the chasm. To help me help Dave shoulder the full weight of his responsibility. And I needed someone to protect me against any more unpleasant moments with Chad.

"Second, I needed to find someone who would be willing to receive a gift. This may sound strange to you. It may seem like a conceit on my part. I hope it won't. Since my earliest childhood memories, I've been happy. When things went wrong, I was happy. When others were disappointed, I was happy. My dad raised a few sheep, and I fell in love with the lambs. During a freezing spring storm, two of my lambs froze to death. Even my father shed tears over the sight of my poor dear lambs taken by cruel circumstance. 'Don't cry, Daddy,' I said to him, 'they are happy where they are now.'

"That native happiness made it easy for me to love people, and in turn, people loved me. I didn't do anything to deserve this gift. It just came to me. It seemed to me to be the most precious gift a person could receive. When I pass away, I want that gift to go to someone. I can't bear that it should be lost. I think Rachel has a similar gift of her own.

"That night on Labor Day, when I was so saddened by the hard words between me and Chad, and I realized that I couldn't do anything about it, I started to think about all the people in this world who are sad and can't seem to do much about it.

"All that night I prayed. I believe in God. I asked him to help me with my two big needs. 'Please,' I prayed, 'send me someone strong to help me. And take this gift of mine and give it to someone who really needs it—who will really appreciate it.'

"As I prayed, there came to my mind a phrase from the Gospel of Matthew, 'Inasmuch as ye have done it unto one of the least of these my brethren, ye have done it unto me.'

"I know it sounds silly, but I prayed that when I leave, my gift might be given to one of the least of His brethren, not somebody famous, fabulously wealthy, and surrounded by abundance, but somebody poor, and simple, who had almost nothing else to live for.

"Near morning the following day, after praying all night, I seemed to hear a voice, probably just in my mind—or in my heart—and it said simply, 'It is done.'

"Suddenly, my heart was lifted. I was weak from the lack of sleep, but I knew my prayers had been heard and answered."

Molly looked steadily at Hatch to see what kind of impact her story might have on him. Hatch had gone pale. He looked at her unblinkingly. Tears were forming in his eyes, rolling down his cheeks, and falling into his lap. He remained silent.

"I waited a long year, trusting that the Giver of Good Gifts would be true to his word. When you came into the store looking for a job and told me, even in barest detail, the story of your journey, I felt I was seeing the answer to my prayers in front of me. Since then, I have become even more certain."

Molly waited a bit longer and then continued, "If I have misjudged, please forgive me. Maybe these are the ramblings of a silly girl, and there is nothing in all that I've said." She lowered her gaze and was silent.

"You have answered a million questions that I have asked a million times," he whispered. "The only mistake you have made is that I am not strong, I am weak. And I am not worthy of your gift and would be afraid to accept it. I have squandered every gift ever given me."

Hatch buried his face in his hands and wept.

In time, he felt Molly's cool hands on his. She lifted his face toward her. "That is not for you to say," she said, smiling down at him. Molly's face was always luminous. Now it shown brightly as though lit from within. The power of her presence was amplified in her voice, which was uncharacteristically full and resonant. "*I'm* the boss here," she said.

"Soon I will be beyond the reach of any mortal arguments. I tell you now, and don't you dare challenge me, you *are* strong and you *are* worthy. You may never doubt that again. Because I said so."

She kissed Hatch on the forehead. She rose and turned to the door. Hatch sprang to his feet to assist her to the house, but she held him back. "Stay here. Think about what I just said."

forty-eight

THE MORNING OF THE FUNERAL DAWNED GRAY and cold. If there was ever a day that deserved a gloomy spirit, it was January 11. Dave announced that the store would be closed all day. Most of the other businesses in town, except the truck stop and the forest service office, were also closed. The principal of the elementary school sent notes home with the children the day before announcing that there would be no school.

But, from the moment he arose, Hatch noticed a hint of cheer in the air. Part of it was within him, and part, he thought, was the result of the mutual consent of all the townspeople that it just would not do to be sad or gloomy on the day Molly Lewis was to be buried. For twenty-seven years she had been the heart and soul of the town. Its smile was an extension of her smile.

Hatch had asked Paul Spanos to buy him a white shirt and tie in Tremonton. Knocking on the tack shed door, the deputy delivered it to Hatch. Hatch had never been to Tremonton and had no desire to go. In fact, Hatch had not been out of Snowville since the day he arrived.

"Here are your new duds," Spanos announced, "along with best regards from Judge Lewis. He'll be at the funeral this morning."

Hatch thanked him for the favor. He noticed that the deputy was hanging back, slow to leave. Hatch offered him a seat.

"Hatch, before we go to the funeral and lay Molly to rest, I want to apologize to you. I gave you a hard time when you came to town. You have taught me different. I just want to say that I'm glad you are here. I hope you'll forgive me. I'd be glad if we could become friends."

"Paul," replied Hatch, "you are a good soul. I already consider you my friend. Don't give it another thought."

"I guess," said Paul, turning his hat in his hands and looking at the floor, "I've always been a little jealous of the men in Molly's life. I never did like Chad. They married while I was in Belgium. Their divorce sort of kept my hopes alive. So, when you came along, you just fell into the spot that Chad left vacant.

"Since I was little, Molly was the only girl I could ever see. The house I live in belonged to my parents. We only lived a block from Art Fields and his kids. My dad died when I was a boy, and when I came home from Belgium, Mom went to live with my big sister, leaving me the house. Seems like I was destined to live where I could always see Molly, but she could never see me. Sometimes I wanted to hate her, but I could never stop loving her long enough to do it."

Hatch nodded his understanding, and the two men parted with a handshake.

Hatch had been invited to speak at the funeral. He respectfully declined. Since Molly's entire family consisted of Rachel, Dave, and Sarah, Hatch sat with them on the front row of the chapel. Rachel sat beside him through the whole service. She was very quiet and laid her head against his chest much of the time. Hatch didn't notice whether her father was present.

The funeral was uplifting and focused both on Molly's exemplary life and on the tenets of her faith. A string of brief speakers paid tribute to her.

When the service ended, Molly's coffin was loaded into the back of Dave's pickup. Dave and Sarah drove slowly to the cemetery with Rachel between them. Hatch joined the townspeople in the slow walking procession that followed the truck. Near as Hatch could tell, every citizen of Snowville was present. As they walked along, the mourners spontaneously began singing snatches of favorite hymns. The atmosphere was far from despairing. It seemed to Hatch that Molly would feel right at home with what was happening in her honor.

Partway to the cemetery, snow began to fall. It continued unabated until the procession returned to town but did not detract in the least from the comfortable spirit of the occasion. Hatch stayed behind to watch the town's appointed cemetery sexton fill Molly's grave with his backhoe. The headstone would be placed when the weather improved. The sexton offered Hatch a ride on the running step of the tractor. Hatch decided to walk.

Hatch looked long at the spot where Molly now lay interred. He couldn't escape the feeling that he had been singled out by a benevolent fate, or by Molly's God, to receive this singular good fortune. He had grown accustomed to thanking people. Standing alone in the wind-blown snow, Hatcher Alvin Stephens III bowed his head and thanked God for Molly, for Rachel, for Dave and Sarah, for Paul Spanos, for Madge, for friends of the past, and for his family.

Each time he had faced a change in the past, Hatch had been driven to go east. Now he knew there was no place farther to go. He had already come to the place where the sun rises, and he had embraced the sun. Next time he moved, he would travel with the sun as it moved west.

forty-nine

W INTER SEEMED LONG BEFORE IT GAVE WAY to spring. Days and
nights in the tack shed were brutally cold, and Hatch could
feel the wear and tear on him. He had no desire to walk around
town much, so he missed many meals. His clothes hung loosely on
his frame. He continued with his healthy habits but now longed for
spring.

Dave and Sarah moved into the Fields home. Rachel was taken
away to Tremonton to live with her grandparents while custody
was decided. Since her grandfather Lewis was a county judge, custody was awarded to the grandparents. Hatch didn't see her again
after the day of the funeral. The loss so saddened him that he visited
Molly's grave often, seeking solace. Each visit brought him comfort. Molly was assured that Rachel would be okay. Hatch should
be as well.

Business was good. Dave had settled into the harness with relative
ease. Hatch began to feel a little unneeded. He was respected, even
honored, throughout the town. When he sat in his booth at Madge's,
a group of people gathered. From time to time, townspeople would
knock on the door of the tack shed if they knew he was in. He borrowed two additional chairs from Dave and Sarah so visitors could
sit while he generally sat on the cot, his legs out straight before him.
Sometimes the light in the shed burned well into the evening, talk and
laughter audible out on the street.

Maybe the highlight of Hatch's winter following the funeral was a chance encounter with the woman who had been Rachel's teacher at the elementary school. Her name was Hannah.

"You know, Hatch, the people in this town held onto Molly so tightly because they were afraid her gift would vanish when she passed away. But it hasn't happened. It's like she is still with us. A part of her is in all of us. And of all I can see, you are the most like her. You came just in time."

"Hannah," he replied, "you are a jewel. But the truth is that when I came I didn't bring anything with me. I was empty. She, and you good people, filled me up."

Standing behind the service desk one afternoon in early March, the door opened with a jingle. Hatch had been thinking about the joy of having Rachel working alongside him. He hoped she was doing well wherever she was. He knew she would be happy, because that's the way she was.

He looked up to greet the newly arrived customer. Standing before him was his friend, Mark Lester. "Mark!" Hatch yelled. Half vaulting across the service desk he reached Mark in a bound. The two men embraced, slapping each other on the back.

"Mark, you look great." Hatch pushed him away, looked him over, and then hugged him again.

It was Mark's turn. He pushed Hatch back to arm's length to look him over. A worried look crossed his face. "Hatcher, you don't look too well. Man, you are skin and bones." Then he added, "Though I can tell that you are still working out. You feel like iron."

Mark looked at him again. "Did you get hit in the nose? Things are a little crooked there."

"I did," replied Hatch with a smile. "The nose is crooked, but the character is straight." He could tell that Mark didn't quite know what to do with his comment.

"The gal who runs the diner told me you were working here. She says you are the grand marshal of the town. How're you doing?"

When the two friends had spent fifteen minutes getting reacquainted, Mark said, "Hatcher, I have come to take you home."

"Home?" asked Hatch.

"Partway," said Mark, smiling.

"Are you on your way back to Nampa now?"

"I am. Are you ready to go?"

"Wow, I haven't quite come to grips with that." Hatch could feel anxiety welling up within him. He hated that feeling. He shook himself to be rid of it.

"Are you okay?" asked Mark.

"I'm okay. In fact . . ." Hatch paused as if he'd changed his mind about what he wanted to say. ". . . yeah, I'm okay."

Mark laughed. "How about it? Come with me."

"Mark, I'm ready to go." Hatch walked over to Dave who had been watching the old friends. Putting an arm around Dave's shoulder Hatch told him that he would be leaving without notice but with apologies and handed him the key to the tack shed.

"What about your stuff?" Dave asked.

"I don't have any stuff," Hatch replied. As always, he carried his money with him wherever he went.

"Do me a favor, Dave. Give my love to the townspeople. I'm sorry to leave without saying good-bye, but my ride has come. And give my love especially to Rachel."

Dave nodded, shuffling his feet awkwardly. "You'll be missed here, Hatch," he said with some difficulty.

"I'm leaving you in charge," Hatch said.

As Hatch and Mark walked out the door, Hatch expected to see Mark's truck and trailer. What he saw instead was a mid-nineties burgundy Porsche Carrera. Hatch laughed, giddy as a schoolboy. "You've got to be kidding!"

Mark tossed him the keys. "You drive. I need a little shut-eye."

fifty

A STOP AND A KISS AT MADGE'S DINER was all that stood between Hatch and Mark and the freeway to Nampa. The Carrera was like a dream. Hatch drove all the way. They arrived four hours later to dinner at Mark's house. The kids had already eaten, and Patricia served them pork chops and a green salad loaded with complementary vegetables. The apartment was rented, so Hatch slept on the couch.

Back at the garage the next morning, Hatch could see that many of his suggested refinements had taken hold. He met the new marketing man and got a hug from Karynn, who also commented on his nose and the knot on his eyebrow. "The nose is crooked, but the character is straight," Hatch replied. Karynn looked to Mark for an interpretation. He shrugged. Hatch could tell that the quip wasn't working for him.

"Karynn, take Hatcher downtown, and do some clothes shopping."

Hatch laughed. "I know I need them," he said. "But I don't want to be wearing new clothes while I hitchhike back home. Better wait until I get there."

"No hitchhiking this time," said Mark. "The Carrera is on loan until you get home. Just ship it back to me."

"No," said Hatch with a laugh. "What if I wreck it?"

"You break it, you buy it. Isn't that the rule?"

"That's the rule," replied Hatch.

The next afternoon, Hatch motored into North Bend, Washington. Butterflies tumbled in his stomach. He pulled into a parking spot on North Bend Way as close to Sylvia's as he could get because it was raining hard. He dressed as he had in his glory days. He reasoned that he needed just one quality outfit, but now found it difficult to spend hard-earned cash on clothes. He had also stopped to have his hair styled. He wasn't dressing for Sylvia, but he wanted to look nice when he saw her.

Waves of nostalgia engulfed him as he pushed through the door into the shop. Two women were browsing the inventory. Sylvia was waiting on a third. Hatch said to the woman nearest him, "That would look good on you."

Sylvia heard his voice and whirled to face him. Hatch was struck again with her beauty and natural appeal.

"Hatch," she cried, crossing the sales floor with long rapid strides and throwing herself into his arms. He was almost thrown off his feet but returned her embrace with the same vigor. It was so wonderful to see her, this woman who helped to drag him out of the gutter.

"Hello, Sylvia," he said smoothly.

Sylvia studied him. The customers in the store were watching with unabashed enjoyment.

"Hatch, you look great, but I think you need a few good meals. What happened to your nose? Did you break it?"

"No," he replied, "somebody else did."

"What a shame," she said, touching his cheek with her hand, still unable to take her eyes off him.

"I guess the prince has turned into a frog," he said with a smile.

"You're joking," Sylvia replied with tears filling her eyes. "I'd say the prince has become the king."

She hugged him again.

Sylvia's sales help returned from her lunch break and took over the duties in the store. Hatch and Sylvia stepped into her office to visit. They caught up with each other a little, Hatch as always telling almost nothing about what had transpired in more than a year's time. But he did let her know he was still sober, still on his way up. He asked her about Trevor. Trevor's house was his next stop.

"Hatch, I have some very sad news," Sylvia said. "Trevor's gone."

"He moved?"

Sylvia shook her head and lifted her hand to wave off his questions. "No," she reported quietly, "Trevor suffered a brain aneurism last fall. He died the same day."

Hatch sat stunned. "No." He shook his head. "Tell me it's not true." His head went down onto his chest. "Oh," he moaned, "what a terrible blow. I needed to see him. I needed to thank him. There are so many things I have wanted to say to him."

"I know," said Sylvia, taking him by the hand. "I'm sorry, Hatch. You can imagine what a mess I was for weeks on end after he died. He was my friend, too."

"Yes, you were his friend," said Hatch. "Sorry to be thinking about my own grief. I'm sure you've missed him."

Sylvia nodded.

"I wish I'd known," Hatch continued.

"Trevor forbade me to tell you," Sylvia said. "He wanted you to run your full course without interference from him."

"I'd hardly call his help interference."

Hatch looked at Sylvia, remembering the many times he had found strength in her eyes when he needed it so badly. "I'm sorry I wasn't here. I only lived with Trevor for a few months, but those months made all the difference in the world. I have thought endlessly about what you and Trevor did for me."

Sylvia smiled her acknowledgment. "Can you stay for a few days?" she asked.

"No," Hatch said and smiled warmly. "I have a date with destiny. I can't put it off another day."

"I understand," Sylvia said with another nod.

"I had to stop because I've missed you so badly," Hatch told her. "And I owe you this."

He took from his jacket pocket an envelope that he now handed to her. She opened it hesitantly. The envelope contained twelve thousand dollars.

"It was only ten thousand," she said firmly.

"It is still not enough. Take it."

Sylvia put the envelope in her desk drawer. "Thanks for paying your debt, Hatch. Now I can get something important off my mind."

"What's that?" he asked.

She drew from the desk drawer a large manila envelope, handing it to

Hatch. "This is from Trevor. He gave it to me about a month after you left. He told me to give it to you when, and if, you paid your debt to me."

"I guess he wasn't too sure that I would come through," said Hatch as he opened one end of the envelope.

"I think he was sure. But Trevor always liked to live with realities, not hopes."

Hatch extracted a packet of legal documents. He began to read the cover document aloud. It was Trevor's last will and testament, bequeathing to Hatcher A. Stephens III, his entire estate. Hatch stopped reading and sorted through the other documents to get a feel for what was happening in this legal action. Then he rubbed his eyes and face, mystified by this unexpected development. He fingered the bump on his nose as he often did since it appeared following his Thanksgiving battle with Lewis.

"I wanted to show Trevor my nose," Hatch said when he noticed that Sylvia was watching him touch the nose. "I've been practicing the line that goes with it, 'The nose is crooked, but the character is straight.' That's the lesson Trevor taught me. I owe him everything for that."

"I'm guessing you owe him more than you can imagine. Trevor didn't ever advertise it, but he had a significant estate. It was one of the mysteries about him."

Hatch shrugged, "His house. The car. His weight set." He smiled as he continued, "Trevor lived simply. I plan to do the same."

"I'm sure you do," said Sylvia in a more businesslike tone. "I think you should stop by Riser and Marshall, the attorneys," she said, pointing to the letterhead Hatch was holding. "All the details aren't in that envelope. I think they will tell you that Trevor's estate is worth between three and four million dollars. It's mostly in land, so the real value will depend on how well you can develop or sell it. But that's not shabby."

Hatch was speechless. "Impossible," he said flatly.

"Very possible," Sylvia replied.

"Where would Trevor get that kind of money?"

Sylvia returned Hatch's gaze. "You know as well as I do that Trevor wasn't one for making his private life public. In a lot of ways he was a mysterious man. Your guesses are as good as mine. I do know that you are not the only person Trevor helped to lift up. He did the same for me and for others."

"I wondered how you knew Trevor," Hatch said with a question in his voice.

Sylvia simply shook her head, signaling that there was a door to her past that could not be reopened.

"I think there is a good chance that someone did the same for Trevor. He never told me for sure, but my guess is that someone lifted him out of the gutter. That someone could have bequeathed him the resources to do good wherever he saw a need. I do know that he provided a helping hand to a goodly number of people in this town. When he realized he was going to die, he may have felt the need to put those resources into the hands of a reliable successor."

"That couldn't have been me," Hatch murmured.

"Trevor was very perceptive," Sylvia replied. "Maybe he saw more in you than you could see in yourself."

Hatch's reunion in North Bend was as sweet as his reunion in Nampa.

"I'm sure you realize that your creditors have been looking for you," Sylvia told him. "Are you going to need some upfront cash to get in the clear?"

"I'm not sure exactly how much I'll owe," Hatch said. "But I have fifty-some thousand to apply to it. I think I'll be okay."

Now it was Sylvia's turn to be speechless.

Hatch cut the visit short, wanting to spend more time with Sylvia but feeling the urgency of getting to Seattle by the day's end. Sylvia walked him to the door. As they parted, she took his face in her hands. "Hatch, I hope everything will work out for you. I trust that it will. I want that for you and your family. But," she paused, "if she has already moved on or is afraid to take a chance on you, please come back to me. I'm not afraid."

Sylvia watched Hatch run through the rain to a classy Porsche and jump in it. He waved as he drove past the store. She shook her head in amazement. "The frog became a prince. The prince became a king," she said out loud. She turned back into the shop with a sigh.

fifty-one

PATTY STEPHENS WORKED IN THE GARDEN DESPITE a light but steady
drizzle. She was pulling the deadfall away from her shrubs and
putting it on the rubbish pile at the back of the yard. She was in her
mid-thirties, the divorced mother of two elementary school children.
Patty had taken impeccable care of herself through the years. She was
fit, healthy, and happy. Not everything had gone perfectly for her, but
well enough that she thanked God daily for her life, her family, her
home, and her circumstances.

Patty had grown up in a favored situation. Her father was a dentist
who practiced and then taught at the University of Washington dental
school. He was now on the State Board of Regents. Her mother sprang
from a family of Seattle socialites.

As a young girl going to a private high school, Patty had fallen
in love with one of her kind. Hatcher Stephens was the son of a
prominent attorney and a mother much like her own. To say that
Patty had fallen in love with Hatcher was an understatement. She
was that kind of person who only truly falls in love once, and does
it completely.

Hatcher was stunningly handsome, smart, and athletic, lettering in
tennis in high school and again at the university. He had his choice out
of an endless array of girls. But he had chosen Patty.

Graduating from the university, he went on to law school, following in his father's footsteps. He was a brilliant student, becoming editor
of the school's law review.

They married when he graduated from law school, and she finished a master's degree in English literature.

After a few years of marriage, their fabled union was blessed with two children, a daughter whom they named Jenna, and later a son, Ryan.

Cracks began to show in the façade of their larger-than-life existence soon after marriage. Hatcher was hired into his father's firm and had wonderful career prospects, but he was never satisfied. While he put up a good front in social settings, Hatcher was also fearful and uncertain about his own abilities. He was apologetic when he should have been strong. He was preoccupied with his image instead of the substance of his work. His deficiencies were recognized by the partners in the firm, and especially by his father who knew only how to badger the son, but not how to guide him to better performance.

Hatcher was constantly under tremendous pressure. He began fleeing from the conflict, missing work, and sometimes staying away from home. Eventually, it became obvious that he was slipping into alcoholism.

Patty was sympathetic toward Hatcher and his increasing addiction. She helped him check into a rehab program. The help he received there seemed to revive his prospects until he settled back into work. He fell off the wagon, this time into a far worse condition.

Hatcher was never abusive, but he became deceitful and irresponsible with their money. Gradually, he lost the ability to work and was dragging her and the children down into debt and eventual poverty.

She pled for him to try harder. She was supportive wherever she could be. But in the end, all was lost. She divorced Hatcher and set him free to find his own way. Her parents bought her a modest home north of the university district where she still lived. They also supported her, but expected her to work. She found a job as editor for a small publishing company. It paid well for the time she spent, and it allowed her to work from home when the children weren't in school.

Hatcher finally disappeared, nearly two years earlier. She had received only two notes from him in that time. No return address was provided, apparently because he was hiding from creditors. One note was mailed from Spokane, Washington, the other from Grand Junction, Colorado. As far as Patty knew, Hatcher was still in Grand Junction.

She never tried to locate Hatcher. He had too many problems to solve. All of her effort and energy were needed to keep afloat as a mother and provider.

Had Patty loved Hatcher? *Yes*, she answered over and over. When they married he was everything she wanted.

Did she still love him? *How can I love a person I don't know?* she would ask.

Did the children love their father? *Absolutely.* When he was sober he had been a wonderful father in spite of his agonies.

Did the children miss their father? They asked about him all the time. But as they aged, other interests were coming to the forefront. They could no longer really remember him.

Where would all of this lead? Patty had no idea. So she mothered her children, worked in her garden, and tried to keep peace with her world.

"Mama," called nine year-old Jenna from the back door. "You're wanted on the phone."

Patty pulled off the rubber fingered garden gloves, being careful to avoid a few rose thorns clinging to the outside. She dropped the gloves on a carpenter's bench under the roof on the back porch and stepped just inside the door.

"Sweetie, will you hand me the phone. I don't want to take my shoes off."

Jenna was tall for her age and erect in posture. She had clear blue eyes, blond hair like her mother's, and a slender nose that turned up slightly on the end. Very pert. Very cute. She bounced across the kitchen carrying a cordless phone to her mother.

Patty tossed her head to the side to sweep the wet stands of hair out of her face and away from her ear. "This is Patty," she answered.

The voice on the other end made her heart stop.

"Patty, this is Hatcher."

Patty could say nothing.

fifty-two

W HEN HE LEFT SYLVIA'S SHOP, HATCH HAD visited the offices of
Riser and Marshall, attorneys, just long enough to introduce
himself and make a return appointment to discuss Trevor's estate and
the settling of his own long-overdue financial obligations. Then he
drove the thirty miles to Seattle and found a motel where he could stay
for a few nights while he tried to settle back in. From the moment he
arrived in Seattle, he remained constantly alert to avoid any contact
with places or things from his alcoholic past. He consciously began
establishing patterns that would lead to the sober, happy life he envi-
sioned.

Sitting in his motel room, he was aware that the afternoon was
flying by. He wanted to ask Patty to see him and wanted to allow
enough time so that she could make arrangements for the children. He
picked up the phone and dialed her familiar number.

Patty was clearly shocked to hear his voice. Hatch was not surprised. When he told her that it was Hatcher calling, he felt awkward. He no longer thought of himself as Hatcher. He had repeatedly
rehearsed what he wanted to say to Patty in his mind.

"I know this must be a shock," he said. "I'm sorry for that as I am
for so many things. Please listen and don't hang up. I won't keep you
long.

"I'm sober. I've been sober for nearly eighteen months. I have
worked the entire time. I've put my financial life in order. I feel like
I'm ready to help build a better future for us all.

"I don't know if anything has changed in your circumstances, but I would like to see you and the children. I think I'm ready to do that without bringing any more hurt into your lives."

Patty was silent while Hatch spoke. When she finally spoke, she asked, "Hatcher, where have you been?"

Her voice was soft but filled with intensity. Hatch could almost hear an ocean of anger lapping at the pilings, ready to spill in upon him. He steeled himself and reasoned that Patty's anger was well justified. He wanted to hear her speak, whatever she might say.

"We," she began, but changed course, "the children have missed you so much."

"And I've missed them," Hatch said. "I want to see them. But I didn't want them to see me the way I was. I couldn't bear the shame of it."

He paused, struggling with the emotions those memories resurrected. "I think I can see them now without doing them any harm. I don't want to be melodramatic, Patty, but I feel like a man who has come back from the dead."

"I'm glad for you," Patty said. Her words were nearly buried under the weight of sadness they bore.

Hatch waited, but Patty said no more.

Reaching out to her, Hatch continued, "I have to see you before I talk to the children, Patty. I have missed you dreadfully. I want to know how you are. I want to know where you are. I want to know what I can do to make up for the hurt I have caused you. I am so sorry, Patty. Please believe me."

After a pause, Hatch asked her softly, "Can we meet? Will you have dinner with me? Do you think you could get away for a couple of hours this evening?"

When Patty spoke, her voice quivered. "Hatcher, you know how much I've loved you. I hope you know how deeply I care and how hard I have tried, but those years wore me down so terribly. I'm afraid to hope again. I don't know if I can take another disappointment."

Hatch could hear the tears in her voice.

"I know you've loved me," he said. "I promise above all else that I won't do anything to hurt you. I believe I can keep that promise now."

"Can you even afford to take us out to dinner?" Patty asked, her voice brightening a bit. "We live very close to the line, and I can't afford to pay."

This practical challenge posed by Patty stung Hatch. He admitted that she was right to ask. The last time they spoke, he was borrowing money that he never paid back.

"We can afford it," he replied.

"I want to see you, Hatcher. Of course, I do." Patty's voice betrayed her nervousness. "But I'm so afraid."

Hatch scratched his head. This was not going the way he hoped. Clearly, Patty was afraid to commit to anything. She was doubtlessly remembering the countless times past when Hatcher pled for her understanding, made promises, and then proved he couldn't be trusted. Hatch straightened himself in the chair of his motel room.

He could almost hear the voice of his internal coach. *Come on, bud. This girl is doing everything she can here. She should have hung up on you but hasn't. Try to remember what you were like when she saw you last. Your job is to convince her that the old guy is gone. Good riddance! You're the new guy. All I'm hearing from you is, "I think I can," and "I feel this or that." You're not convincing me. How can you expect her to fall into your arms when you can't do any better than, "Gee, I think I can."*

Hatch took a deep breath. For a couple of seconds he thought about where he had been. He remembered the Christmas beating at Trevor's hands, his days in the Nampa gym, the showdown with Chad Lewis, paying his debt to Sylvia, and especially Molly's edict in the tack shed, "I tell you now, and you dare not challenge me. You are strong, and you are worthy. You may never doubt that again."

"Patty, I understand your fear," Hatch said evenly. "But hear me now. I will never hurt you again."

His words rang in the silence that followed.

"Please meet me."

"I'm not sure what you expect to happen." Patty's voice was stronger.

"I don't expect anything," Hatch answered. He felt better, assuring himself that he didn't have to crawl back to Patty. That was not Patty's way. His best bet was to be himself.

"I want to see you because I care about you," he continued. "I won't try to push you. If you're afraid or uncertain, I'll give you whatever space you need. Patty, if you refuse to see me, I'll understand. If you say that you have tried too hard and been hurt too much, I will be the first to agree. Please believe me when I say that if things had not really changed, I wouldn't even ask to see you. But they have. I have."

"I could certainly use your financial support," Patty said bluntly.

"I know you can. I'm ready."

A long silence ensued. Hatch waited.

"Where do you want to meet?" Patty asked.

"You choose."

"Someplace that has no memories attached to it."

"Sure. Tell me where and when."

Patty Stephens trembled as she hung up the phone. She wiped her tears on the wet cuff of her gardening jacket. Her insides were in turmoil. For just a second during their conversation she felt she was talking to the man she thought she had married. But the thrill that passed through her was quickly swamped by images and feelings too painful to endure. She didn't know whether to hope or to hide.

"Who was it, Mom?" asked Jenna.

"An old friend," said Patty, realizing that Jenna hadn't even recognized her father's voice.

fifty-three

H ATCH WANTED TO WATCH PATTY ARRIVE AT the fish house. He had thought of this moment in practically every waking hour for many months. He had also dreamed of her often in his dark nights.

The evening seemed unreal. He was back in Seattle. Places looked familiar. Old feelings floated around, waiting to be embraced. But Hatch was seeing everything through new eyes. After all, he was only eighteen months old.

He wanted to start all over with Patty. She was the girl of his dreams. But he was not the man she had married. He realized that she might no longer want him. If she didn't, he would surely understand.

His stomach was rolling, but he was not afraid. He could not afford to be afraid of the future. He just hoped desperately that the evening would go well, or at least not go poorly. He hoped to open a door that would never close again, even if he and Patty, as a couple, needed time to reach the same space.

He stood across a small side street from the entrance, sheltering himself from the rain that continued to fall. The hour they had agreed on for their meeting approached and passed. Hatch counseled himself not to panic. *You knew this wouldn't be easy for either of you. Fear and suspicion are not easily vanquished, even when the best intentions exist. Besides, parking is difficult to find near the waterfront. The weather is bad. Patty has kids to arrange for. She can't just walk out of the house. It's understandable that she would be delayed.*

Another half hour passed.

Hatch began thinking that Patty had changed her mind. Still, he wasn't ready to give up hope. He wasn't tired of waiting. He would wait here all evening, if necessary. Nothing could pull him away from this opportunity.

Fifteen more minutes passed. Hatch kept looking at his watch. He had started making plans for his next step just in case this meeting didn't happen. He couldn't blame Patty. She had been hurt. He knew that her disappointment was immense. She had given all and had received little.

He could imagine how it would feel to be in her shoes. If she didn't make it this evening, he would understand. He would try again. In fact, he would continue trying until she told him to stop.

Darkness was falling and the incessant rain and cutting breeze chilled him through. He turned his collar up against his neck. He had shed all his insulating fat and now had little protection against the weather. His fingers went automatically to his crooked nose and knotted eyebrow. Would Patty find him attractive as she once had? Or had the wear and tear taken the shine off? Hatch had to hope for the best. He was eager to face the music and was frankly wishing to get in out of the cold.

Just before it became too dark to see clearly, Hatch thought he spied Patty at the end of the block coming in his direction. She was wearing high heels and walking slowly, trying to keep her balance on wet concrete. Her umbrella hid her face. But he recognized the grace with which she moved. He felt he knew her as surely as he knew his own reflection in a mirror. His heart began to throb in his chest.

Holding his breath as she approached, Hatch watched her move toward the restaurant, confirming his hopes. She stopped in the doorway to close her umbrella. Hatch saw her there, framed in the light from the doorway, the woman he had always loved, though he had not always been worthy of her. Time had nearly erased her image from his mind. He had forgotten how truly lovely she was. He was amazed all over again that Patty had fallen in love with him. And once in love, she never gave him reason to doubt her love.

How fortunate he had been to love the sort of woman whose head was not turned by male attention. When her unpretentious beauty attracted catcalls or flirting advances, she paid them no heed. She steered her life by an internal compass from which she never veered to accept flattery or satisfy a need for praise.

To Hatch, Patty was goodness clothed in grace and poise. Suddenly all the striving of his pilgrimage made perfect sense. He had to blink back the moisture from his eyes as he recalled that somewhere in the universe a deal had been struck to drag a failed and drunken bum back onto his feet and make him man enough to protect and care for this woman of his dreams.

❧

Hatch gave Patty a few minutes to get seated. With gathering confidence, he walked briskly across the street and entered the restaurant. For better or for worse, he was ready to meet the future.

The dinner rush was now past, and the crowd in the popular seafood restaurant was thinning. Hatch looked around as he stepped to the hostess desk, but could not see Patty's trademark blond hair.

"How many?" asked the young hostess with pen poised over her seating list. Her nametag read, "Kim."

"I'm expected by a woman whom you just seated two or three minutes ago. Tall, blond, very striking. A few years younger than I am."

"Yes," replied Kim, a light of instant recognition in her eyes. "Follow me."

She led Hatch to a section of seating set off partially from the main room by a long, low planter of greenery raised a couple of steps above the main floor. Behind were three round booths, each large enough to seat about six people. As they approached, Hatch could see Patty facing him, sitting alone in the center booth. The booths on either side were empty at the moment. Patty had either asked for or been led to the most secluded spot in the busy restaurant.

Hatch felt an additional flutter inside and swallowed deeply. He was counting so much on doing and saying the right things, even though the real test would stretch out into the months ahead.

Patty looked glorious. She was dressed up for the occasion. Her face and hair, as always, radiated unmistakable elegance. Hatch hoped that bode well for his endeavor.

He smiled at her as the hostess gestured toward the empty side of the booth with her outstretched hand.

"Thanks." Hatch nodded to Kim.

Patty's gaze was fixed, as if she could not take her eyes off him.

"Hatcher?" she asked in a near whisper.

"Hi, friend," said Hatch, using the endearing term from their early married years that he had abandoned later on when his behavior robbed him of his confidence.

Patty's lips parted. She was clearly astounded. She sat back in her seat, folding her hands in her lap. Regaining full composure, she shook her head. Only her smile gave her away. Hatch could guess what was going on inside her. She had just been reintroduced to someone she knew intimately for many years who had recently undergone an extreme makeover.

"Well," Patty said, catching her breath. "If I passed you on the street, I would hardly recognize you."

"Do I look that bad?" Hatch asked.

Patty flushed slightly. "No, of course not. You know that's not true."

Tears began to well in her eyes, and she reached for her purse.

Hatch didn't feel a need to speak. Like a man athirst, he was drinking in his first impressions of their reunion.

Patty dabbed at her eyes for a second with a hanky she had extracted. "Sorry! I promised myself I would keep all emotion out of our visit."

Hatch smiled at her. "You can't know how much I have missed you."

Her gaze dropped. "You don't think so?" she asked.

Hatch nodded. "Maybe it's me who doesn't know."

A waiter interrupted to take their drink order. When they were alone again, Hatch said, "Patty, you look wonderful."

Patty smiled sadly. "Thank you, Hatcher. But to be honest, I'm not feeling that wonderful."

Hatch nodded.

"Since you called this afternoon, I've felt that old knife in my heart. It's not a new feeling. One of the nice things about you being away was that I was freed from that feeling. Your hand is on the handle. You placed the knife, and it seems that only you can remove it. The question is always whether I will survive the wound."

Hatch continued to nod his understanding.

There was no hostility in Patty's voice, none of the bitterness she could have heaped upon him, just a plea to let their first order of business be a safe removal of the knife.

Hatch wanted to say to Patty, *Please call me Hatch. The old guy is dead. I'm the new guy. You can trust me. I trust me. Those past problems, they are all gone.*

But that was his agenda. It was time to attend to Patty's agenda.

"You're right," he said. "Let's take care of that knife."

Hatch and Patty Stephens talked until she felt she absolutely had to get home to the kids. Patty seemed to relax. She watched him closely as if she could hardly believe she was talking to the same man. Before they rose to leave, Hatch held her hand for a moment and asked, "How's the knife?"

Patty smiled, though she was tentative, as she had been throughout their visit. "I'll never get over you, Hatcher. My problem is that whenever the pain begins to subside, hope tries to crowd its way back in. I don't know which to fear most, the pain or the hope."

"I'm pulling for the hope," Hatch said. He wanted to ask her if there was any hope for him, for them. He didn't ask. He would leave her all the time she needed. He would trust himself to the light. Hatch Stephens no longer feared the future. Just beginning to reconnect to Patty brought him a sense of wholeness. *This will all work out*, he reasoned.

He knew what Molly Lewis would say to him at this moment, *Hatch, you and I both know that the Giver of all Good Gifts would not bring you this far and then abandon you. You have a gift. Use it. There is no reason to fear. After all, no matter how dark the night, the sun rises.*

epilogue

THE LATE-MORNING SUN DUCKED IN AND OUT of view behind a blue- and white-checkered sky on the longest day of summer. Not more than a dozen people were gathered in front of the Solstice Rose Arbor in Seattle's East Montlake Park. The arbor looks out toward a finger of Union Bay. Despite an early morning rain, the grass was dry enough to be walked on in dress shoes. The moisture had tweaked the ambient floral aroma to its zenith.

"Such a gorgeous day," muttered Doris Stephens as she surveyed the waters of the bay below and the mighty Cascades in the distance. Doris wore a light peach-colored chiffon dress that rippled slightly in the warming breeze. "This is a day we have longed for."

"Thank you, Mother," replied Hatch. "No one more than I."

Standing next to her father and hanging upon his arm as though she had grown there was nine-year-old Jenna, apple of her father's eye. Blond, thin, and precociously elegant, Jenna was the miniature of her mother in more ways than mere appearance. Allowed to choose her own dress, Jenna had chosen a cream-colored party dress with complementary accessories including dress gloves and a smart beret. She was watching her little brother, who at the moment was chasing butterflies.

Hatch felt a familiar hand in the small of his back and turned to face his sweetheart, Patty, accompanied by Reverend and Mrs. Peter Downey. The Downeys were friends of both Hatch and Patty, but Patty had become especially close to them during the years of her ordeal with an alcoholic husband. When Hatch and Patty decided to remarry, Patty pled to have Reverend Downey perform the ceremony. Hatch happily acquiesced. Reverend Downey was in his early sixties, nearing retirement. Known to have been a firebrand in his younger years, the reverend had seen so many of life's ups and downs that his association was now treasured for his wisdom and compassion. His wife, Lois, gently rotund, wore a perpetual smile. Her homeliness complemented his more formal demeanor.

"We can start any time you're ready, Hatch." Patty stood close to Hatch and smoothed the lapels of his suit coat with her gloved hands. She looked exquisite. The sun, playing on the highlights in her hair, illuminated her upturned face. Though Hatch had known her since they were sixteen, he was stunned once again by her unintentional elegance. He leaned down and kissed her on the lips, lingering there while his senses absorbed the touch of her, the smell of her, the taste of her. She did not try to pull away. Both Hatch and Patty were old enough to let their affection have its time without becoming self-conscious in the presence of these others whom they knew so well.

"Patty, will you marry me?" Hatch whispered.

Patty reached her arms around his neck and buried her face in his chest. "Please don't make me cry," she said. "I'm doing all I can to keep it together."

Hatch laughed. "Is that a yes or a no?"

Patty took his hand and whirled around, tugging him forward to their spot in front of the arbor. "Reverend Downey, let's do it now. I think he's ready. Let's not give him a chance to change his mind."

"Not going to happen," replied Hatch as the reverend straightened himself to begin the ceremony. Doris, Patty's parents, and a few extended relatives gathered around. Hatch and Patty had sent cards to Sylvia Rencher, to Mark, Patricia, and Karynn Lester, to Dave and Sarah Fielding, and to Madge, announcing the happy occasion and promising to visit them soon, as a family.

Ryan was on Patty's side, holding her hand and looking up at both of his parents. Hatch winked at him. Ryan smiled back and then turned his gaze up at Reverend Downey, seemingly intent on catching each bit of action in this much-talked-about wedding. Hatch felt Jenna step to his side, grasping his arm at the elbow with both her hands. He took a deep breath. This was it. Pay day. The moment he had wished for, waited for, worked for. What more could a man hope for than this? To be married to the woman he practically worships and to live with the greatest kids alive—that is all Hatch really wanted. There were still many questions to be answered about their future, but the question that mattered most was being answered at this very moment.

Hatch put his arm around Patty's waist. She leaned into him, her elbow bumping the ribs he had bruised during his early-morning sparring session at the gym. He winced and couldn't help vowing to wreck revenge on the young sparring partner who had pummeled him viciously despite knowing that it was the *old man's* wedding day. Hatch would get even. At least his face had been spared for the day.

Perhaps it was the coincidence of Patty's bump on his ribs as Reverend Downey began the ceremony that caused Hatch to glance up to his right and see two men approaching down the gravel path at a distance. They looked vaguely familiar. Certainly the one with the tattooed sleeve was Hatch's old nemesis from North Bend, James Quan's goon. Hatch felt an instant flash of anger. Of all the times for these unwanted guests to appear, now was the worst. *But this is how their kind works*, Hatch reasoned.

For months after their first visit to Sylvia's shop, Hatch had dreaded their reappearing. He felt no dread now. The next encounter, if it was to be today, would be far different than the first.

The two men stopped at a distance and watched. No one else in the wedding party seemed to notice them. Tattoo's smirk showed around his dark glasses. Assistant looked up and down the path, possibly watching for any source of interference.

Hatch straightened himself and turned his attention to Reverend Downey. *First things first.* Nobody would rob him of this sweet moment. Life would go on. Troubles would come and go. His fortunes would rise and fall. But this moment, this sacred moment, belonged to Patty, to Jenna, to Ryan, and to those who had trusted in him. He would not let them down. After all, he was Hatch Stephens. How many other men could say they had paid the price to go to the place where the sun rises? In a perverse way, he was thrilled to see Tattoo and Assistant here at this crucial moment. Seeing them standing there made him so glad to be Hatch Stephens. And glad *not* to be Hatcher. Of all the people missing from the gathering, the one Hatch most gladly bid good riddance to was Hatcher Stephens III. *Thank you, Trevor. Thank you.*

When Reverend Downey asked Hatch if he would take Patty Stephens as his lawfully wedded wife, to embrace, to nurture, to cherish, in poverty and wealth, in sickness and health, until death, Hatch felt a sudden surge of emotion. His voice caught in his throat and tears formed in the corners of his eyes.

After a few seconds, with Patty, Jenna, and Ryan looking up at him in anticipation, Hatch turned to meet Patty's gaze. "Patty," he said, "I do. I do. I do. Forever."

The couple embraced. Hatch kissed her on the brow, on the lips, on the cheek, on the temple. "Thank you, Patty. Thank you. I love you."

Patty took his face in her hands. He could feel her breath and see through her eyes into her soul. "I am yours, Hatch," she whispered. "I have always been yours. I will always be yours. Please don't ever leave me again."

"Never," replied Hatch Stephens.

Reverend Downey cleared his throat. With a smile, he urged, "Please, children, at this rate we'll never get you married."

A ripple of happy laughter surrounded Hatch and Patty.

As Hatch looked up toward Reverend Downey, an errant ray of sunlight threaded its way through the speeding clouds and momentarily struck a tear at the inside corner of his eye. At the instant the ray touched the liquid orb, it refracted into a brilliant prismatic array. Hatch felt a tremendous jolt of electricity course through his being. He knew that feeling. He had felt it before. He felt an inexpressible thrill.

"I do," said Patty.

"I now pronounce you man and wife," said Reverend Downey.

I know you, said Hatch Stephens. *You are there when the blessed and fortunate celebrate, surrounded by their loved ones and admirers. You are also there when a miserable wretch lies forsaken in his own filth. Thank you. Thank you. Thank you.*

about the author

F RANK RICHARDSON HOLDS DEGREES FROM THE UNIVERSITY of Utah and the University of Washington. He served as a military chaplain during the Vietnam era, then earned his living as a trainer and administrator for a private worldwide humanitarian organization. He presently teaches at Weber State University. Frank and his wife, Diane, live in Fruit Heights, Utah.

0 26575 53153 4